Bright Star of Heaven

Marie Leonard

WestBow
PRESS
A DIVISION OF THOMAS NELSON

WestBow Press books may be ordered through booksellers or by contacting:

WestBow Press
A Division of Thomas Nelson
1663 Liberty Drive
Bloomington, IN 47403
www.westbowpress.com
1-(866) 928-1240

Because of the dynamic nature of the Internet, any Web addresses or links contained in this book may have changed since publication and may no longer be valid. The views expressed in this work are solely those of the author and do not necessarily reflect the views of the publisher, and the publisher hereby disclaims any responsibility for them.

ISBN: 978-1-4497-0548-0 (sc)
ISBN: 978-1-4497-0549-7 (e)

Library of Congress Control Number: 2010935780

Printed in the United States of America

WestBow Press rev. date: 12/3/2010

Chapter 1

Night was falling. 19-year-old Rod, slender, youthful, and slightly long-haired, found himself outdoors with few marks of civilization and no immediate future other than a lengthening trek across the countryside. For the first few days of his journey he was in luck: he was able to hitch several rides across the Southwest, and the scenery was wonderful to his young schoolboy vision. The highways were almost all two-lane, and Rod could look to his left, and then to his right, and see the majesty and panorama of America, the country his teachers talked about with such fervent patriotism. Sometimes he rode with a truck driver, but even in a seat set high above the ground, he could make out the mountains, the occasional rivers, and sometimes the barren, cacti-dotted deserts that passed by. He was past all the mountains, now; he was now in an area characterized by "rolling plains" and filled with trees and odd vegetation. There were miles and miles of road between towns, and rides were scarce: he hardly met anyone other than farmers on tractor equipment.

He decided to stick to the highway. It was two-lane, and rather flat, and the shoulder was half dirt and half pebbles, which seemed to poke through his worn tennis shoes. To his right was a grassy, shallow, continuous ditch, and beyond that was a railroad track. The track ran nearly parallel to the highway. It was atop the usual grade of white stones and packed dirt, and as Rod continued on his journey, he saw it occasionally split into two tracks, with markers

1

here and there. Of course he passed tall signal blocks, although during the day he could not tell if the color was red, yellow or green. The old semaphores were positioned to show stop, wait or go, but these modern signals had a single light atop a silver platform. The signals were more modern than the grade crossings, which by and large, had only a white crossbucks to warn motorists of a rail crossing.

Rod sometimes walked on the railroad tracks. He noticed some of the rails were rusty, and the creosote wood of the rail ties had different, uneven shapes, although the colors ranged from dark brown to gray. The gravel stone between them was usually white. Without fail, the railroad tracks were lined with telegraph wires. The poles held up scores of wires, which hummed and vibrated in the wind, and other poles, which had only one or two wires at the most, were probably power conductors, rather than telephone lines. Rod knew to follow the tracks *and* the power lines. Even though he was probably "a thousand miles from anywhere" he knew eventually he would reach some kind of civilization.

As night fell, he jumped off the highway shoulder, crossed the ditch, and crawled onto the railroad tracks. The sky was clear, and like a tremendous dark blue dome, and millions upon millions of stars dotted the sky, as there were no city lights to dim their vastness. Up ahead Rod could see a block signal: it was green, and its beam showed sharply in the darkness. Way beyond, in the fields, a starlike radial wave streetlamp came on: a farmhouse was situated somewhere in the fields. Rod walked on: miles and miles of railroad track; and night was completely upon him. The pale blue line in the west, that was left of the sunset, was completely gone. The highway was deserted, too.

Somewhere in the vast night, a coyote howled, and Rod was beginning to feel tired. He had not eaten since noon, and because he had not reached a town, he decided it was time to find a place to bunk in. It was, thankfully, a warm night.

He hoped his mom and dad weren't worried. After all, he was perfectly all right.

He remembered when he told his folks he wanted to make the trip. He wanted to "see America." He had saved some money working at the local gas station, and he could do odd jobs, "on the way." His mother immediately raised a wail, as mothers will do, but his father, perhaps recalling some far-off adventures in boxcars during the Depression years, gave him some support, saying he needed to get to know the world. Finally, his mother gave in. "Please be careful," she said tearfully, and he promised. He sometimes wondered what he was doing, but his father seemed to understand. He left home partly because he wanted to clear his head.

And here he was. His tennis shoes made a crunch—crunch—crunch in the grade gravel, and as it was dark, he occasionally stubbed his toe against a railroad tie. Earlier in the day several trains had gone by; he wondered when the next would come. So far the night was still. The black, starlit sky was undisturbed, and a slight breeze whispered in the tall grasses below the railroad grade. The telegraph wires hummed, and Rod plodded doggedly on. He had reached the tall signal block, and ahead both the railroad and the highway seemed to curve—and dip—toward a phalanx of trees.

He made up his mind to go toward the trees. And he thought of Junie.

Junie was one reason why he wanted to "clear his head." She was the girl next door, and he had known her most of his life. They went to school together, helping each other with science projects and homework; they rode bicycles together and climbed trees, and generally had a good time in each other's company—until a few years ago. Then Junie had changed. She went from being a good companion to—well, a girl. She began plastering her face with makeup, torturing her hair into sweeps and curls, and—Rod knew this was a probability because of having three sisters—she began encasing her body in girdles and nylons and crinoline petticoats. With all this her personality changed, too—she became self-conscious, especially around men, and her talk became falsely sweet, especially about her girl friends. She was critical and conscious in a way she had not been before, and she seemed to be watching people for flaws—and Rod couldn't stand it any longer. If this was "growing up," he would rather seek companionship elsewhere. He missed Junie as she was before, and he wanted to think about something else. This adventure across America gave him a chance to think about something else, and he had never felt so free in his young life—or so worried.

He came close to the trees, which spread black branches and leaves against a bluer night sky. Beneath them, he found that the highway intersected with another highway. There were even road signs, giving the numbers of the highways, but the numbers did not clue him in as to where he was. Beneath the trees, the railroad crossed the other highway, and here there was not only a crossbucks, but an old-fashioned wigwag signal, its white, black-crossed banner hanging quietly from a short cantilever. Good. He shouldn't be too far from at least some small town. He was so tired, though….

He got back on the railroad track, and noticed ahead, still under the trees, a small, trestled railroad bridge. As best as he could make out in the dark, there was some sort of gully, or creek, maybe. He couldn't tell. But it was not very deep. Perhaps he could bunk out under the trestles.

As he stepped onto the trestled bridge, the wigwag came to life, breaking into the stillness with almost obscene insistence.

Rod jumped, and nearly fell off the bridge. First, a clanging, rhythmic bell, and he turned and saw the banner light come on. Then the banner began to swing, the red light flashing on and off, and as if to confirm the bad news, a far-off, low foghorn sounding train whistle rent the darkness, and Rod stared down the track—into a powerful, white searchlight beam. It was time to get off the track. He swung down into a copse near the main highway, hoping mightily he would not find a snake or rabid raccoon; it was too dark to tell what would be down there, but it was safer that staying up on the bridge.

The wigwag was still noisily clanging and swinging and flashing, and soon a bright light flooded the entire area, followed by the measured rumbling of the train engine. For good measure, a loud blast of the train horn, and Rod was nearly deafened by the sound. If the train had been a slow one, he might have taken his chances trying to jump it, but it was going at quite a clip, so that the bridge rattled and some of the trees branches were blown back. Finally the train passed, the red light on the caboose fading away, and the wigwag's swaying banner came to a halt. The bell was silenced, and only the breeze pushing on the dark branches could be heard. Rod sighed, and settled on a sloping ground near the trestles. He was terribly tired.

The night remained still, and Rod drifted off to sleep, the large, gnarled trees forming a canopy of sorts over his inert, damp head. Now and then a coyote howled, but Rod was dead to the world and did not hear the howls. The wind whispered through the leaves and gently tapped the tree branches, but Rod slept on. He did not wake until the sun had fully risen the next morning......

Rod awoke and looked about him, rather dazed, and not sure where he was. He was extremely thirsty, and because of the position he took while asleep on the ground, his neck began to cramp. He noticed the railroad bridge, and the trees spreading a natural cathedral over his head, and it all came back to him. As if to confirm his memory, he heard the clanging bell of the wigwag signal. Another train was on its way to the bridge, and he decided to stay where he was until it passed. He didn't have to wait long, and the train was an extended one. Idly he counted the boxcars until the caboose finally showed; then he leaned back into a pile of dead leaves. From there he studied the gully in which he had taken refuge.

As such things went, it was not a large gully. There was barely any creek at all; just jagged rocks here and there at the lowest point, with a sliver of water winding through. All around was grass, vegetation and trees; he didn't know much about trees but he was sure he was sitting beneath a silver-leaf maple. Toward the other end of the trestled railroad bridge some of the trees seemed to be growing sideways out of the gully bank. Then his head jerked up—something odd was over by those trees—a car, if he was not mistaken. It had blue paint, whatever it was, and it was partially hid by the trees.

Of course he had not noticed it last night; it was too dark. But now—he decided to go take a look.

Groaning, he rubbed his aching neck, and sipped some water from the small canteen he was carrying. It was lukewarm and old-tasting, but it took the edge off his thirst. Then he walked across the gully, his shoes crunching the dead leaves, and he easily stepped over the tiny creek. As he got closer, he saw he was not mistaken—the blue object *was* a car. Somebody had slid off the highway, and crashed. He wondered when it had happened. It was not last night, for sure—he would have heard the commotion. Besides, from the dirt on the windshield and on the paint, he judged this was no recent accident. He wondered why no one had come and towed the car away.

He was finally up with the shielding trees. The car was nose down, barely dented, and Rod could make out the silver plate that read "Henry J." It was a small car, painted blue, and very simply made. It was what was known as, rather snickeringly, an "economy car." Was it a Kaiser or a Frazier? Rod couldn't remember. This model was probably built in 1951; it was about ten years old, anyway. Where had he heard about Henry J's—Oh, yes, Sears advertised them at one time. His father had joked to his mother that mail-order catalogs had a booming business going; they could even sell a nice, cheap car! And long ago, he saw an advertisement in a magazine, that had a United States map with dots on it, bragging, "All over the country, you can find expert Kaiser service---" or something like that. He couldn't really remember, but it seemed glamorous at the time.

Rod pressed his luck and got closer to the car. The windshield was shattered and dirty, but both cardoors were shut and the side windows were uncracked. That didn't seem right to Rod—one of the doors should have been opened, unless—he nudged even closer, and began wiping the dust off the passenger door window. He peered in—and that was enough. He jumped back, screaming all the obscenities he had ever heard in his short teen-aged life—and some that he didn't know, for good measure—the shock was that horrible. There was a body in the car. As soon as he stopped swearing he began to shake, and he fell against the dead leaves and dirt beneath the car. He thought for a moment he was going to be sick.

He sat on the ground, gasping, and attempted to calm himself. Then he willed himself to look again into the car window, to be sure he saw what he *thought* he saw.

Gingerly he peeped into the now-smeared window, and looked carefully. There was the simple bench seat, the 3-speed clutch, and…. the woman. Her head was smashed against the steering wheel, so he could not see her face, but she was wearing a simple blue teachery looking dress, and her head was clustered with short brown curls all over, that had a few small streaks of gray. She appeared to be very slim and tall. As he gazed more closely, it was evident her arm, sticking out of her dress sleeve, was not an arm—it was a couple of bones covered with a slight bit of flesh. Rod jumped back—he couldn't look anymore; he was almost dizzy. He needed to report this right away. He was going to catch the very first motorist he could and get to town—he could tell the police, and call his parents to let them know he was all right, although he wasn't sure that he *was* all right.

He dragged himself out of the copse and jumped onto the highway shoulder, and began to walk hurriedly, looking back every once in a while to see if a car was coming so he could hitch a ride. The belt of trees continued to conceal the railroad tracks to his right, and ahead was the inevitable Stuckey's billboard, advertising food and gas and pecans. It was true that he had had nothing to eat for some time, but the urgency of the situation gave him an extra surge of energy. As he turned and looked behind him, he saw a battered old green Ford moving up the highway, and he stood and jerked his thumb frantically. The Ford pulled up beside him, and he gratefully got into the passenger's side. The driver was a grizzled old man, probably in his late fifties.

"Where to, son?" he asked. "You look like you've been rolling in the dirt."

"To the very next town," Rod gasped out, "and to the police station!"

"Why, son, what happened?"

Rod turned on the worn bench seat and pointed out the window. "Those trees back there. Somebody had a wreck. And she's real dead!"

"Are you kidding me?" The man was incredulous. But after looking at Rod's pasty, horror-filled face, he said, "I guess you're not. Okay. To the police station we go. Town's just three miles up ahead. You can get some food, and a bath. You look like you need both. You're too young to be running around alone, anyway. You're about my boy's age, and I'd be worried about him, if he was hitching rides. You know, you can't be too careful nowadays."

The man meant well, and Rod knew it. He said, "I know" and sank against the rusty old cloth. He could not tell what color it was, it was so old. To his left, the man guided the huge steering wheel and glanced from time to time at the perfectly round, plain speedometer. Rod looked at the clock placed at the very middle of the dashboard; the time was 9:35 am. They had reached the outskirts of town: there were billboards, more trees, a gas station, and then bricked streets. They were soon downtown, for they passed an intersection with a single-flashing light overhead, and there were rows of old-fashioned stores with false fronts and metered parking spaces. Rod's host pulled up to the police station, and Rod got out, his heart thumping hard.

"Lose your way, sonny?" a uniformed officer asked as Rod stepped into the small, musty building, with its all-business furniture and phones, and fluorescent lights and aluminum blinds. Rod shook his head. "N-no," he stammered, "I want to report an accident. It's just out of town. Over by that railroad bridge near the wigwag signal."

The deputy officer rose from his desk. Turning to his colleague, he said, "He must mean that intersection at—" he named the two highways. "That's funny. I've been by that area and never noticed anything unusual. What did you see, sonny? Were you involved in the wreck?"

At this time the rattling entrance door burst open, shaking the blinds over the glass. Rod's driver had come in, and the deputy said, "Mornin', Bill. Have you taken to picking up hitchhikers? That ain't the best thing to do, you know. Sometimes these guys have pockets full of grass. And I don't mean the kind you find out on the lawn."

Rod flushed, and Bill said, "Nonsense, he's just a kid. And he was as pale as a ghost when I found him. We probably better see what's up. Can you show him?" Bill turned to Rod, and Rod nodded.

"Well, let's all pile into the patrol car," said the deputy. As they got into the black and white car, complete with red and blue lights and a mounted bullhorn, the deputy took it upon himself to scold Rod for hitchhiking. "I've seen a lot, young man," he said, "and none of it pretty. You best call your folks, if you've got'em, or take the bus back home. I've peeled more guys like you off the pavement than I ever want to remember. Well, here we are. You said it was near the railroad bridge?" He pulled the cruiser onto the highway shoulder, and Rod got out, making toward the gully. Bill and the deputy followed him, and the three of them jumped into the area close to the creek. The blue Henry J was in plain sight, bashed forward against a misshapen tree; and the deputy began, "Holy...." blessing something he usually found in the barnyard or on a horse trail. Rod looked nervous; he knew what was in that blue car and he really didn't know if he was up to seeing it again.

The deputy had no such qualms. He swung himself into the upper branches, and peered into the car window. "Yep, dead body," he diagnosed. "I wonder how long she's been there. More than a month, probably. Trees hid her pretty good. I wonder if anyone filed a missing person's report—" he continued talking to himself. "Well, there's her purse. She'll have identification, anyway. Good, because I've never seen her before, or that car, neither."

"Watch yourself," called Bill. "Don't get snagged in those trees!"

"Oh, I'm coming down," replied the deputy. "I'm not going to mess with the car with it sitting that way. I'm gonna have Jed tow it out, if he can. That's funny; I wonder what happened. It doesn't look like anyone ran her off the road or anything. The car doesn't have any marks, except what the trees did. She must've fainted at the wheel and come off the road. That would explain why she's pitched forward like that."

"May I see her?" asked Bill.

"Okay, but be careful. You don't know anyone who drives a blue Henry J, do you?" Bill shook his head.

Bill was on the heavy side, and when he climbed the branches, everything trembled, even the car. He looked into the window, and then he screamed, "Oh,_____!" Both Rod and the deputy looked up. "I jiggled the car, I'm afraid," explained Bill. "She moved. Oh, no---!" He jumped away, terrified. The officer climbed up and looked in, and even he blanched. Rod felt sick, but he had to know. After the deputy came down, he went up to take a look. What he saw stuck in his mind literally for the rest of his life. He wished he had never looked, but he couldn't help himself—he was too curious.

The woman's head had fallen back, so that her face could be seen. Only there was no face. Above her schoolteacher's dress, and framed by the brown, slightly grayed short curls, was a grinning skull. Rod never forgot it. And his life was never the same again.

Chapter 2

"WHY DID YOU CALL ME? WHY? I don't know how I could have possibly helped you." The woman faced the deputy with tired anger, toying with her purse. Her plain brown hair, tortured into a style that made her look years old than she actually was, was bound by a pale red scarf. Her flowered crinoline dress scraped against the deputy's wood desk, and her heels clacked against the tired gray-and-black linoleum below the officers' furniture. She obviously resented being called from whatever town she lived in. No, she couldn't help. Rachel was only a cousin. She really didn't know her. Rachel taught elementary school in _____ton. That's all she knew. Why did they call *her*?

"We needed positive identification for the body, and your phone number was in her purse, ma'am. She didn't have any closer relatives, possibly?"

"None that I can name," said the woman. "She lived by herself. She was an old maid school teacher. The town's full of them."

"I—my colleagues—would like to do an autopsy. And we need to know what funeral arrangements to make. Is there someone we can contact?"

The woman shrugged. "Cut her up; I don't care. She isn't my concern. Then dump her in the trash bin. I don't have any money to bury her." She turned and stalked toward the entrance door, and three of the presiding officers stared at one another. "I guess that is consent," said one. Finally, the deputy yelled to the woman's retreating back, "at least give me the phone number to her church. She went to church, didn't she? I can call her minister." The woman turned, wrote down a name and number on a shred of paper, and handed it to the deputy. "Now, that's the last I want to hear about it!" she announced. "Goodbye!" The entrance door slammed, rattling the venetian blind and stirring a bit of dust from the window.

"Pheeeeewwwww," one of the officers exhaled slowly. "Sounds like one happy family. Well, I guess we can call the coroner. Steve will be tickled pink to see what we have for *him*. I never saw such a mess. That poor hitchhiker kid won't ever get over it, that's for sure. I hope he's back home with Mama and Daddy by now. Deputy Niles, you did well to insist Bill drive him to the bus station. I heard he made darn sure the kid got a ticket back to California. He wanted to buy him a meal, but the kid couldn't eat it."

"*That* doesn't surprise me," said another officer. "Anyway, what have we got? She was not from around here, I take it."

Deputy Niles set the recovered purse onto his desk, and faced his colleagues. "According to her identification, her name is Rachel Evanson. She was born in 1915—that would make her about 47 years old—and her driver's license said her eyes were brown. She was rather tall for a woman, and slim—no shape, I don't think, judging from her dress. A beanpole. Anyway, we'll get Steve on it, and I'll contact her minister, to see what—what we should do with her afterward. Her nice cousin seems to think she was a schoolteacher; I imagine that's true. One thing I don't understand was what she was doing around *here*. _____ton is nearly fifty miles away."

"Might have been just passing through," said his colleague, "but where was she going?"

Deputy Niles snorted. "I don't know. Old maid schoolteacher, huh? Meet a boyfriend? I don't think so. Doesn't seem like the type, and I didn't find any lover-stuff in her purse or in her car. I guess we can rule that out. Nobody filed a missing person's report in _____ton—I checked—she's a teacher, and wouldn't be missed until school was in session. Besides, she went on a trip. Everyone there would have known that. I talked with the chief of police at ___ton this morning. He says he'll go with whatever we find. I don't think there's much to find—she conked out at the wheel, and her car ran off the road and into a gully. Ladies pick the durndest times to go into a faint. This one did it at the wrong time."

"Did she have a suitcase?"

"Yes, in her trunk. But nothing revealing. Just the usual travelling stuff. Books. A Bible."

"A Bible." One of the officers snickered.

"Hey," said Deputy Niles, with displeasure, "I happen to own one myself."

"Yeah, but do you carry it around with you?"

"Considering the kind of stuff I have to deal with every day, I should," said Deputy Niles with finality. He sat down at his desk, and gave the purse another puzzled fumble, as if he were trying to solve a mathematical problem and the answer might be found in the purse. At that time a middle-aged man appeared, knocking the much-abused entrance door open with a bang. Deputy Niles looked up, then stood up quickly. "Steve!" he exclaimed. "I was just thinking about you!" "I know," was Steve's reply, "word gets around fast in this town. I heard you have a stiff for me to look at."

Deputy Niles frowned and stared at the city map on the wall ahead of him, covered with pins and writing in colored markers. Then he looked back at the coroner and said, "Well, there's not much left of her, really. Mostly bones and hair. Her out-of-town cousin, genteel Mrs. Anne Milner, graciously gave us permission to—what did she say—'cut her up, and toss her in the trash bin.' Your lab is ready now, isn't it? I've got her stashed in a bag, so we can send her over your way. We found her in a wrecked car; that's all I'll tell you. You can take it from there."

"Hmmmm," said Steve. He appeared intrigued.

"George will show you where she is," Niles pointed to one of the officers, "he's doing nothing of real importance at this moment. George, take Steve to meet his new client. I have a phone call to make." He fished into his uniform pocket and took out the slip of paper Anne Milner gave him. It was hastily written down, but Deputy Niles could read both the name and the phone number. It read, "Rev Roger Mayfield." It was a long distance call, to be sure, but the area code was probably the same. He dialed the operator, and had the call put though to the written number. It was like walking around in the dark—he had no idea who would be at the other end of the line, and he didn't know how this somebody would react to the news of Rachel's death. He just hoped it wouldn't be a cold reaction like the one displayed by the cousin Anne Milner.

After a couple of clicks and rings, a deep, rather gentle voice came on the line, "This is Reverend Roger Mayfield speaking." Now came the worst part of the business.

"This is Deputy Kenneth Niles of the ___shire Police Department. Hello, Reverend Mayfield. I wish to know if you are acquainted with a Rachel Evanson?"

He could already detect concern in the reverend gentleman's voice. "Yes, yes, I do," he said. "Is she all right? Is she in some kind of trouble? She would never do anything—"

It was best to get it over with. "She's been in an accident," said Deputy Niles. "She's dead."

A gasp on the other end of the line, and then a moment of silence. Then—"How may I help?"

"We are doing an autopsy now, to see if we can determine the cause of death, but I believe it to be accidental. What we need to know is, what funeral arrangements need to be made. We can bury her here, but her cousin gave me your phone number and I thought I might consult with you. Does she have any close relatives I might contact?"

"No, but—we want her back here," replied the pastor. "I would like to give the funeral service. Oh, this is terrible! The children are not going to take it well at all!"

"Children?"

"Her students. They really love her. A lot of the kids asked me if they could get into her class. There was something about her.... She always understood another's pain and grief and trials. She was troubled—I knew that, but I never knew why. She wouldn't tell me or anyone else. But she was a fantastic teacher. The kids learned easily from her, and they enjoyed being with her."

"I see," Deputy Niles felt his heart sinking. A closed casket service was a downright necessity in a case like this. "I need to tell you this, Reverend Mayfield. We found her just a few days ago—in fact, a hitchhiker found her." Realizing how faintly shady that sounded, he tried to amend his words. "It was a very young boy hitchhiker, probably not much older than Rachel's students, and he was shaken up. We sent him home to his parents. Anyway, she had been dead for well over a month, and---"

"All right, I understand." Deputy Niles could hear the wince in the minister's voice. "Let me know when the autopsy is complete. Meanwhile, I'll make the arrangements here. I have to make a few phone calls now." Deputy Niles knew he wanted to break the connection, and so he said, "Thank you, Reverend Mayfield, we will be in touch." He then rang off.

Having replaced the heavy black receiver in its cradle, he turned in his ancient swivel chair and stared out the window. The paint on the sills was a very dull light green, cracked and peeling, and he looked past the open venetian blinds, day in and day out. Nothing ever changed in the police headquarters: the building seemed to have been ancient and worn out forever. The window air conditioning unit was nearly as old as everything else, but it still worked, as did the metal heating unit mounted on the ceiling, near the entrance door. But though the office never changed, peoples' lives did, and a lot of the changes and tragedies ended up on pieces of paper that sat in the office file cabinets. Not before the damage was done, though. Deputy Niles would be glad when the Chief of Police, Jack Cameron, came back from his vacation at Yosemite Park. Jack had perfect faith in Deputy Niles and his abilities, and had no qualms about leaving him in charge of the office. Deputy Niles did his duty and did it well, but the very thought of young children seeing their beloved teacher still and faceless, made him want to turn in his badge.

He shook off the troubling thoughts, pulled out a ledger, and began writing his report. All he needed to do was to record an account of the discovery, get the autopsy report, and forward everything along with the body to ___ton. He would perhaps meet with Reverend Mayfield, but otherwise, it was out of his hands. He never met the woman; all he knew was apparently her pastor and her students liked her but her closest relative did not. She was troubled, the reverend said. That covered a lot of ground. That possibly pointed to suicide, but Deputy Niles really didn't think that was the case. The accident had too much of an element of surprise. Besides, why would she drive fifty miles out of town to do it, with a full suitcase and a Bible on hand?

He wrote a terse, lucid account, stating the facts—where her found her, in what condition, and the subsequent contact with her cousin and then her minister. He stuck to the objective facts. He couldn't mention what he saw just before he zipped up the body bag—her blue dress was torn at the side, and her white, bare ribs were sticking through—no flesh on them at all. Her short curls were still intact. The skull was grinning at him, and he didn't look any more than he had to. The odor made him gag, too; although he was unfortunately used to dealing with dead and decaying bodies. It came with the job—but somehow, this case bothered him more that he liked to admit.

The headquarters entrance door burst open, and Jed, the town's main mechanic, stepped in. "Just to let you know, Ken," he said, "I combed that blue Henry J down. It hasn't been tampered with, or anything like that. In fact, it was in great condition—better than most cars I've seen. She must've really took care of it. It's a simply made car, but you still have to change the oils and fluids and everything—she seemed to have done that pretty regularly. Too bad it's totaled. Should I junk it?"

"Yeah," Deputy Niles sighed. "Unless her preacher wants it. But I wouldn't know why."

"Durn shame," said Jed, and he turned to go out. The door slammed noisily behind him, and Deputy Niles finished the report.

When the report was done, Deputy Niles glanced at the corner of the office where he had placed Rachel Evanson's personal effects. There was a suitcase, which contained the normal clothing a woman would wear, some toilet articles, a few paperbacks, and the Bible. He thought a minute, and then went over to the stack and picked up the Bible. Bibles often contained personal information such as birth records and death records, and marriages as well. He should have thought of this before. He opened the Bible, and searched the front pages. But there was nothing really helpful. Rachel had written her name, "Regina Rachel Evanson" on the corner of the flyleaf, and a date nearly twenty-five years ago, but there were no other names recorded, not even in the registry in the front of the Bible. He held the Bible in the palm of his left hand, and flipped the pages with his right. A bookmark with Psalm 23 printed on it fell out, and a Christmas card, and that was all. He opened the Christmas card. It said "To Rachel 1939. Love, Nancy." That was a long time ago—before the awful World War II. There wasn't much chance of finding Nancy now.

He sighed, and slipped his written paper into a manila folder. He needed the autopsy report, and then he was done....

"Inconclusive," Steve announced. "I really can't put anything on the death certificate. You know I didn't have much to go by, but the wreck didn't do it. She died before she went off the road, or she was dying, at least. They'll have to check her medical records in ___ton. My guess: a heart attack. But I can't be sure, you know."

"It's okay, Steve, you did what you could. Sign it 'unknown cause' and I'll forward it. I'll add a note saying to check her medical history. If they want to do anything further they can. You did make a report of your findings."

"Of course. Here you are," Steve handed over a folder full of typed pages. "She was too dead to be tested for anything, really, but nothing suggests drugs or alcohol. I looked at the car, too. Typical old maid, I think. Her cousin was right about that. The car was really, really clean and orderly, like she cared for it real well. It had a bit of a scent—like lilacs. Anyway, she wasn't a girl-around-town. Everything looked neat and goody-goody—except for her, heaven help her."

Deputy Niles remembered Jed's earlier comment about the car being in great condition—except for the wreck. Maybe she was a typical old maid—her dress suggested that she was. But according to her pastor, her students loved her—even begged to be in her class.

She must have had something attractive about her—but what? And why was she single?

Steve left, and Deputy Niles took all the files, and bound them together with a rubber band. These, along with both Rachel's body and her personal effects, would go back to ____ton. The Henry J would remain, but Deputy Niles would personally see to it that the blue car was placed as far away in the junk yard as was possible. He didn't want to look at it again. Every time he saw it he thought of that grinning skull—and then of a troubled teacher whose students loved her.

Somehow, he didn't believe that was the only thing that was bothering him.

Chapter 3

It was late August. The small town of ___ton was quiet, elderly, and shaded by many trees of various types, but still the sunlight glinting overhead was almost too bright, golden with a hint of chill, although the temperatures were as warm as ever. The sky was brilliantly blue—indigo, in fact; and the very blueness suggested the autumn weather to come, and the beginning of the school year. In ____ton it was always the same—the kids walked together to the neighborhood supermarket to buy their school supplies; that being done, they gathered together for bike rides, impromptu softball games in the well-fenced schoolyard, and other adventurous activities. They knew who their teachers would be and what they would be studying: nothing much ever changed, and the monotony was familiar and even comforting.

There were three school buildings, and they were all old. The elementary school was situated in the newest neighborhood, which wasn't saying much. The houses were already dwarfed by oak trees and silver leaf maples and even fruit trees, and some of the tree roots were already upending the concrete sidewalk blocks. Most of the houses in ___ton were very small anyway: four or five rooms at the most. Two-story homes were practically unheard of, and even though the high school and junior high school boasted two story buildings, the elementary school had one story. Only the auditorium showed any sort of height: the rest of the school was three one-story wings connected by a lunchroom and gymnasium.

All of the schools were within walking distance of the students, and some students had bicycles. Since nearly everyone knew everyone else, the children walked in groups, and they talked about what classes they would be in, and whether the teacher they would have would be a "tough one." The lucky ones whose parents owned black-and-white televisions discussed the latest Perry Mason episode or described what they saw on "The Ed Sullivan Show." They visited each others' homes, and most mothers set out milk and cookies on checked tablecloths in the kitchen. The children usually stayed outdoors, though; the houses were very warm, even though some had A/C window units or hallway attic fans. Most of the families raised all of their windows; the breeze would gently waft in the homemade curtains, but did little toward actually cooling the house.

It was the usual back-to-school atmosphere in the town. But this year had a disturbing note that didn't exist in the previous years.

The elementary school was bothered the most. It was now known to the teachers and students that Miss Evanson would not be teaching this year. Miss Evanson was dead. In fact, she was now in the cemetery in the outskirts of town: there was a place under an oak tree where there was a rectangular mound of fresh earth. The students never actually heard the details surrounding Miss Evanson's death, except that she had been in a car wreck, but they sensed that their parents and the other teachers were not comfortable with the subject. They knew not to ask questions. But they huddled together and thought up their own versions of what happened, and the students who knew Miss Evanson well, and had her for a teacher, were distinctly unhappy. The principals of the elementary school knew this, but they did not know what to do about it.

The head principal, Dr. Hinton, had assisted Roger Mayfield in bringing Rachel's body back and arranging her funeral service. He was told everything, and he had read the reports sent by the deputy from ___shire. He was of course upset by losing such a good teacher, and he had to make quick arrangements to replace her in the classroom. But personally, he never knew what to make of Rachel Evanson. She taught well—nearly all her students passed; she rarely sent anyone to the principal's office, and the children seemed to like her. Also, she had taught at the same school for twenty years, and he had no complaints about her. Still—something was strange—*she* was a little strange. It was his experience that most maiden ladies were a little odd and off kilter, but she was in a class by herself. She was not really old, but she was not young, either, and an air of almost sweet correctness seemed to follow her wherever she went. She was quite an enigma.

She was as familiar as the classroom furnishings. She drove up regularly in her pristine blue economy Henry J, parked it in the same spot near a silver leaf maple at the edge of the teachers' parking lot, and she carried her books and lessons right away to the classroom. She was rather tall and as completely slim as a woman could be: her face was pretty and sweet, and she had large brown eyes. Her most telling feature was her short brown curls clustered all around her head; even Dr. Hinton could tell they were natural curls. She always wore straight dresses with large collars and cuffs—she never seemed to care for the crinoline stuff. Wherever she went there seemed to be a scent of lilacs, and an air of goodness as well. As much as Dr. Hinton didn't even want to think such thoughts, he admitted to himself that he did not find her in the least sexy; she embarrassed him too much. He didn't know why; after all, she was really rather attractive.

Also, she did not interact with the other teachers that often. She didn't go to the lounge to drink coffee and discuss scandals about her neighbors, and she didn't talk about her students, either. Usually there was a "bad kid" in every classroom, and most of the teachers were not shy in pointing out who their least favorite students were. Rachel never did this. She hardly talked with the other teachers at all, although she seemed to have nothing against them, and she worked side-by-side for years with many of them. Still, she did not make any one of the teachers her special friend.

Rachel did help her students, though. If a child needed extra tutoring to pass a certain test, she stayed after school and did it. She found out when her students had birthdays, and made sure the other students sang "Happy Birthday." When class was in session she expected complete attention and concentration, and she usually got it; but during recess and after school, she was patient with students who wanted to talk her ear off. She was a good teacher. Most importantly, her students learned the material; many upper grade teachers who received Rachel's students into their classes commented on how well the students were prepared. Even if Rachel was a little odd, she did what she was hired to do. That was more than Dr. Hinton could say for some of his staff, and he was sorry he would have Rachel no longer.

He even admitted to himself the school would not be the same without her. She was too much a part of it—for too long.

The first day of school finally came and there was the usual hustle and bustle: kids getting lost and not finding the right classrooms; fights in the lunchroom and at recess, and the inevitable noise. September had just begun, and the leaves were turning; the students were still rowdy from summer vacation and were not ready to settle down yet. Dr. Hinton spent very little time in his office; he was patrolling the halls while the classes were in session to see how things were progressing. He was experienced enough to know just by listening outside the door to the sounds inside. He knew every inch of the school building: the lockers in the hall, the dull linoleum and the peeling green paint; the long windows with the painted, dirty sills, the tilted windows that were placed above the regulation metal classroom doors. The long, hanging fluorescent lights covered by metal egg-crate grills, the dusty black chalkboards, and the forever grinding pencil sharpeners. The sound system still worked well, but the speakers were old: the wooden boxes with rough brown cloth showing through the front carvings, tacked on every wall. It was all routine, even to the United States flags in every room and the front schoolyard as well. He would have the same visitors to the principal's office, most likely, and it was time to be ready for another school year.

He made his rounds and came back to the office, which had one window that overlooked the school playground. Just beyond the hedge that grew beneath his window was the asphalt hardtop, that had hopscotch lines marked in yellow, and tetherball poles installed. Dr. Hinton raised the window, pulling back the flowered linen curtains; he had an oscillating fan in his office but it was still hot. The recess bell rang, and hundreds of voices whooped and hollered as the children banged out of the building. Soon the playground was filled, and several girls gathered around in a spot near Dr. Hinton's window, producing a jump rope. That was all fine and healthy; two girls began turning the rope, and the other girls began clapping in rhythm; then one girl jumped into the swinging rope. At that time, a pack of treble voices lifted up to the tune of "Hot Time in the Old Town"---

"One-two-three, Dr. Hinton's in the tree!

"Four-five-six, he's breaking off some sticks!

"Seven-eight-nine, he's gonna bust off my behind!

"There'll be a hot time, in the office, tonight! Wham! Wham! Wham!"

From many years as an educator, Dr. Hinton learned to choose his battles. He learned by experience what was important and what was not, and he chose to ignore this. Besides, the words did imply a certain amount of respect for his authority. He turned away from the window, just as one of his fifth grade teachers, Mrs. Anderson, came in. She lived two doors down from Rachel Evanson and was probably more affected by her death than the rest of the faculty. He looked at her questioningly, and she glanced out the window at the students, then sat down on one of the office "hot seat" chairs. She appeared rather nervous.

"What's up, Teresa? Is something wrong?" he asked.

"Uh—well—sort of," she replied. "Reverend Mayfield over at the Lutheran church called me yesterday. They want to go through Rachel's house and sort out her things, and he asked if I would be there. I don't know. I liked her well enough, and she didn't seem to want close friends, but---"

"They probably want a lady there, to, you know, make it nice...."

"I know," Mrs. Anderson looked pained, "but didn't she have any friends at her church?"

"I wouldn't know," sighed Dr. Hinton.

"I—I suppose I should go—I guess," said Mrs. Anderson. "I mean, what could I possibly find? Like you say, it would be better for a woman to be there. I—well—she *was* nice, but I never got to know her, you know what I mean? She seemed like she was hiding some—some pain. She didn't want people close to her. That's the impression I got, anyway. But then again, she seemed to—I don't know. She was hard to figure out."

"I know what you mean, I assure you," said Dr. Hinton. "I couldn't figure her out, and I have a PHD in child psychology. She was a good teacher and I had no complaints about her, so I let well enough alone. Anyway, Teresa, if I were asked to pick a woman to go through her things, I would choose you. The Lutheran Reverend was right about that, so don't worry about it. It's better a woman should be touching her personal things, and you have the compassion necessary for such a job."

Mrs. Anderson was nearly in tears, but the end-of-recess bell rang and put a close to the conversation. She nodded to Dr. Hinton, wiped her face with a tissue, and set off for her fifth grade classroom. Dr. Hinton looked out of his open window; the playground was quiet now and he could hear very little but the whirring of his oscillating electric fan. It was all so strange. Outdoors it was a beautiful day, so fair and bright, and songbirds sang outside his window as they prepared for their autumn migration to the south. Everything was familiar and supposively happy, and yet death came and took one of his best teachers—suddenly and unexpectedly. It was really hard for him to accept. He had assisted with bringing her home, proving her insurance policy, and making the funeral arrangements, together with Reverend Mayfield, and he attended the funeral, but he was warned not to look at her. The out-of-town deputy was emphatic about that, and Dr. Hinton took that to heart. The funeral was a closed-casket ceremony, and a surprising number of people attended the service. Of course, the students like her, and wanted to be there. But what had she taken with her to the grave, that she was such an unfathomable creature?

Reverend Mayfield gave a good sermon. "She was a lovely human being," he said, "one beloved by her students, who grieve her loss.

She loved God, she loved teaching, and she never harmed any other person in her lifetime. There was a time I truly understood how beautiful she was. She was in the choir, and she sang a solo 'Beautiful Savior.' I have heard that song many times in my life; in fact, I've sung it myself many times. But to hear the words sung in that pure soprano voice—she meant every one of them. 'Fair are the meadows, fair are the woodlands, robed in flowers of blooming Spring. Jesus is fairer, Jesus is purer—He makes our sorrowing spirit sing.' And I believe she meant that. She had some deep sorrow in her heart. But she trusted Jesus to be her Savior and her Friend, to help her with whatever pain she did have. It came out in her voice, the love she had for her Savior."

Dr. Hinton was a Baptist, not a Lutheran, and he never heard Rachel sing, but some of his Lutheran cohorts did attest to her beautiful soprano voice. In a way, he was sorry he missed out. Now that she was dead, he would never, ever know what that voice sounded like, although he was not really curious before. She was just another teacher, one who did a satisfactory job, and she was strange, besides. And after all, the school would continue as it always had even without her—other teachers would take her place and some were more typical than others. She was unique. But her chapter was now closed.

The school day was drawing to a close, and Dr. Hinton knew he could look forward to many more like it. The kids would be noisy; the teachers would gossip in the lounge; the school programs would take place in the auditorium; there would be fights and bad grades and kids sent to the principal's office. The students would think up more chants like the one he heard the girls sing at recess—kids were pretty inventive, really—and he would in fact have to wield the paddle a few times before the year was out. The weather would turn cold, there would be Thanksgiving and Christmas, and then the restless, chilly, months of January and February. It was like that every year. Students would come and go. All these things would happen.

But there would be no more Rachel Evanson.

Chapter 4

THE LANDLORD MET THE MAYFIELDS AND Teresa Anderson at exactly one p.m. on Saturday, as he promised to do, at the small house Rachel had rented for over twenty years. The landlord was of the opinion that maiden ladies who paid the rent regularly made the best tenants—they had no noisy, wild children, nor did they indulge in sometimes destructive cocktail parties. Rachel Evanson was a particularly satisfactory tenant from his point of view. She kept both the house and the surrounding areas almost rigidly clean, and she did some of the necessary repairs to the house herself. He certainly wouldn't have wanted to *live* with such a woman, as her orderliness was this side of obsessive, but it was a lucky blessing in a tenant. She paid her rent on time, too. In fact, in June she mentioned she was going on a vacation for possibly a month, and she would pay ahead through July, if he would keep an eye on the house. He readily agreed, and spread word that she was going out of town.

The property was small, but beautifully kept. A small red-brick home with concrete trimmings sat directly in the center, and to the left was a graveled driveway and a single-car garage. The house was almost engulfed in huge shade trees. A metal chain-link hurricane fence lined the back yard, and a lengthy clothesline took up part of it. A large telephone pole at the alley behind the fence sent down a large, thick cable to the back of the house. Here was the electric meter and power feed; everything was in good order. Several hedges surrounded most of the house, but there were flowerbeds as well, and a large bird bath was planted on the fresh St. Augustine lawn.

The landlord opened the screen and unlocked the front door, and the entire group filed quietly in.

The inside was nearly like a museum. Even Mrs. Anderson, who had visited in many of her students' homes and had seen many households, was somewhat chilled and wondered if she had stepped back into the past. The house itself had hardwood floors, except for black tile in the kitchen, and the walls and ceilings were beige textured plaster. A brass leaf light fixture graced the living room ceiling, and the furniture was slightly Edwardian, with a large oval braided rug on the floor. The windows had venetian blinds covered by soft embroidered curtains, and a fireplace covered the west wall. It was very, very peaceful, but a little chilling. A faint scent of lilac permeated the air, and the one picture in the room was a still life painting of flowers.

"Not much in here," said the landlord. "I talked to some of her relatives. They don't want any of the stuff. Nice lot they are. They could sell it at least, but not they! I guess it's mine now, but you can tell me what to do with it, Preacher. Does the church need some furniture? This all looks well kept."

"I know what you could do," said Reverend Mayfield. "I don't think Rachel would mind. You could rent this home as furnished, to maybe a young couple just starting out. We can collect her clothes and books and such, and leave the rest. It's all as well-kept as it can be." He ran his hand across the back of the couch. "Maybe a dusting. But that's all it needs."

"Hmmmmm," said the landlord. He looked a little doubtful. "I guess I could rent it, furnished, to a little old lady. I can't see anyone young in *here*."

The Reverend went back out the front door, to get something from his car, and Mrs. Mayfield and Mrs. Anderson looked at each other helplessly. Then Mrs. Anderson said, "When Mr. Mayfield brings in the boxes, I'll do the bedroom."

"Thank you," whispered Mrs. Mayfield.

Reverend Mayfield came back with the boxes, and Mrs. Anderson retreated to the bedroom, taking some of them with her. Reverend and Mrs. Mayfield went into the kitchen, and began to carefully remove and pack the kitchenware. There wasn't a lot, and there was nothing in the pantry or icebox. Mrs. Mayfield stopped for a moment, then raised the window over the cast iron kitchen sink. The wind blew the short flowered curtains inward, and Mrs. Mayfield could see the fluttering leaves and huge trees in the back yard. Between the branches, she could see patches of the bright blue autumn sky.

The black tile beneath her feet—decorated with streaks of white and some gold specks—was carefully waxed and very clean. The cabinets were lined with shelf paper, and the paper had been put in recently. The stove was clean and well-tended, and the cabinets had no smudges. The Reverend and Mrs. Mayfield soon had everything packed away, and Mrs. Mayfield closed the window over the sink.

"Leave the curtains," she said. "They look just right. Anyone would be glad to see them."

In the bedroom, Mrs. Anderson was opening the bureau drawers, carefully laying the already folded garments in the boxes, reserving two boxes for the many books she found. The room was small, but as neat as the rest of the house. One wall had three long windows, which were blinded and curtained; a gas jet protruded from the wall near the door, and the light fixture in the center of the ceiling was an old-fashioned bowl-shape. The bed was a rigid brass bed, and the bureau and bookcases were mahogany. The hardwood floor was bare, and one corner had a desk of sorts. This was where Rachel must have graded her papers and made out her lesson plans. Several textbooks lined the back of the desk toward the wall, and Mrs. Anderson had already made up her mind to give these to Dr. Hinton.

They had been handled gently, and another teacher could use them. The other books could go to the public library—and—and—she would keep the Bible herself, if the Mayfields didn't want it. She heard rumors about how nasty Rachel's relatives seemed to be, and she wanted respect shown to the Holy Scriptures. After all, she could read and study that Bible, in memory of her shy neighbor.

Once the books were sorted and labeled for their intended destination, Mrs. Anderson began to open the drawers at the bottom of the desk. At first it was rather innocuous: she found extra school supplies such as notebook paper, pencils, a ruler, crayons, and a few small binders. Mrs. Anderson reached for her smallest cardboard box, and piled the supplies in, for the school could use them, and—well, they would help the students, which was Rachel's motivation more than anything. She wouldn't mind her supplies going into the students' hands. That done, Mrs. Anderson opened the leftmost drawer. It was then that she had her unexpected surprise. In that drawer was a metal box—some kind of safe, it appeared to be. Mrs. Anderson could nearly guess what was in here—her teacher's certificate, perhaps, or her car title or a birth registry. What she did find—the box opened right away—shocked her beyond measure. It was a very thick stack of papers, all in Rachel's handwriting, and it seemed to be almost years and years of writing. What on earth was she doing—writing a book?

Outside the bedroom door, she could hear the landlord conversing with the Mayfields. "Yes, she told me she was going on that trip back in June," he was saying. "Something about a womens' missionary meeting taking place in a big city somewhere, but I wasn't really paying attention. I don't bother with that kind of stuff. Missionary meetings, pah! Oh, sorry, Preacher. I know you have to do that kind of thing. But, begging your pardon, Mrs. Mayfield, all the missionary meetings *I've* seen were gossip and gabble and talking about each other and who collected the most money. I know Rachel went to church, but she didn't much take part in that sort of thing, I don't think. You know, she did say she wanted to see a bit of the country. She had been living in the same town year after year, day after day, and she finally saved up enough money to travel for a bit. I think that's why she really went."

Yes, thought Mrs. Anderson to herself, and she would also have something to share with her students when she got back. Mrs. Anderson knew about that—the year she went to Carlsbad Cavern, she took pictures and purchased some souvenirs, and taught the children about caves and how they were formed. The textbooks issued by the school had pictures of faraway places, and some of them were photographed quite well, but it was another thing to be able to say, "I was there" and produce tangible objects relating to the faraway place studied. Mrs. Anderson could describe what she saw when she was in the cave, and give some idea of the majesty and the awe she felt, that could not be detailed in any geography textbook. The children were very interested, too; they plied Mrs. Anderson with all sorts of questions about the cavern, and more than one student hoped that some day his parents would take him *there*.

Nothing taught the way experience did, thought Mrs. Anderson, as she lifted the handwritten pages from the gray box. The stack was very thick. Rachel must have written them over a number of years—since she was a young woman. Mrs. Anderson glanced at the top page—the handwriting was very legible. Rachel was neat in that as everything else. A faint whiff of lilac seemed to exude from the pages, and Mrs. Anderson was very uncomfortable—it was as if, in touching Rachel's written pages, she was touching Rachel herself—something she had never done. She had never seen Rachel physically touch anyone—not even one of her students. She listened to the children patiently and looked after their intellectual needs, but she never touched any one of them—not even a hurt child. She always directed hurt or sick children to the proper authorities—to the school nurse, for example, or to the parents. She seemed to shy away from emotional contact.

So why did the children like her? Mrs. Anderson wondered. It was evident she cared about them, and of course they knew it. But adults, like Mrs. Anderson herself, could not know it. Rachel would not let anyone near her—at least not adults. She was friendly, and kind, and very helpful—but she didn't let anyone get close to her. Mrs. Anderson had never seen Rachel laugh aloud, nor had she seen her cry—although she was certain that Rachel had cried sometime in her life. Now Mrs. Anderson did have the impression Rachel was more comfortable with *her* than anyone else; after all, she was a next door neighbor as well as a fellow teacher, although they did not attend the same church. But still, Rachel never confided in her, or said anything about her past. Mrs. Anderson clasped the yellowing pages in her hands, and called for the Mayfields.

They both came. "Did you finish?" the Reverend smiled.

"Yes—but—" Mrs. Anderson looked at the pages in her hands— "I don't know what to do with this."

The expression on Reverend Mayfield's face changed to consternation. "What is it?" he asked. "Letters from her family?"

"No, I don't think so," replied Mrs. Anderson. "It looks like all of it was written by herself. There's quite a lot here..... I honestly don't know what she'd write about, but it's all her handwriting.... Here, Reverend, do you want it? She was part of your flock."

Reverend Mayfield appeared to be trying to come to a decision about something. Then he finally spoke. "Teresa, I have already imposed upon you a great deal. I have asked you to be at the funeral, and I have asked you to help us today. You've done all that and more, and we thank you so much. I would like to take this burden from you, and if I were a woman, I would. But there are things only a woman can—and should—do. I'm not going to take those papers, nor am I going to read them. I am going to burden you—again, and I apologize deeply—and tell you to keep them. You may read them, or dispose of them without reading them. But one thing I can tell you—if you read them, you will be opening a window to her soul, to be looking in. If anyone were to do that, it would best be you, Teresa. I know you have plenty to do as it is—you're a wife and mother, and you teach—but if anyone has a right to look upon her soul, it is you."

Mrs. Anderson looked instinctively toward Mrs. Mayfield, and the Reverend's wife nodded gently. Mrs. Anderson sighed and held the papers to her chest, as if holding Rachel there. She glanced again at Reverend Mayfield. "Teresa, I would like to add one more thing," he said. "As a pastor I have run into many terrible situations, things that would be truly shocking and incomprehensible to the general laity. I have learned one thing about it all: keep a Godly perspective and remember His teachings and rules, but do not judge or condemn the person. I did not know Rachel Evanson, really, and I do not know what was troubling her. If you read the papers you will probably find out, and I hope you are prepared to be shocked. But please, never condemn or think less of her, Teresa. She was a true Christian woman, no matter what happened to her. Can you understand?" Mrs. Anderson nodded—she did understand, completely.

Off in the living room, waiting near the front door, the landlord was looking unusually pensive. The others caught sight of him, and the air of silent meeting was broken into.

"We'll load up my car," said the Reverend, and the group began to move the boxes. Reverend Mayfield owned a large 1958 DeSoto, sparkling with chrome and with twin antennae rising from the gaudy fins, and he had plenty of room for boxes in both the passenger area and in the trunk space. The landlord got into the spirit of things and assisted with the loading, and soon the job was done. The large DeSoto trunk had to remain open to accommodate the boxes, but the lid was secured with ropes. The Reverend and Mrs. Mayfield took their places and the DeSoto's metallic-sounding ignition fired up, and they were soon moving up the constantly repaired neighborhood street, the twin antennae waving in the wind. The landlord locked up the front door and shut the screen, and Mrs. Anderson got into her own car, a red 1957 Plymouth Belvedere. She placed Rachel's written papers carefully on the floorboard under the passenger's seat. Then she adjusted her crinoline petticoats onto the front bench seat and started the ignition.

Why did she drive? She lived only two doors down. But she wanted to be prepared: She might have been asked to haul something downtown, or take boxes back with her. Actually, the latter part was true: She did load the books and supplies for Dr. Hinton in the Plymouth, and planned on leaving them there until she went to the school on Monday. She had Rachel's Bible, too. But the most important thing of all she could carry in her hands. Somehow she knew she was going to learn more about Rachel than she had in her actual life.

Chapter 5

It was weeks before Teresa Anderson could bring herself to even *look* at the papers.

She told herself she was busy. In truth, she was: her husband was a police officer and she needed to make sure he had hot meals when he could get them, as well as clean laundry, and she had children, too. It was true that her two older daughters were grown and married, one having moved out of town, but her two younger children—a boy and a girl—were teenagers in high school and still needed some watching over. Then she had her students: they were fifth-graders and not quite as rowdy as the junior high school bunch, but they were lively enough. Dr. Hinton ran a tight elementary school and there were not many discipline issues, but still twenty-five to thirty students in a classroom would keep any teacher awake and on her toes.

Still, she knew these were not the real reasons she kept the papers packed away unread. She did read Rachel's Bible many evenings before she retired to bed, after grading papers. It was a King James Version, as most English Bibles were at this time, and she read the archaic language carefully, to make sure she understood the meaning of certain verses and passages.

It was when November began, and she was making her plans for Thanksgiving, both at home and in her class as well, that she began to wonder if she might have the strength to look. The weather outside was turning to chilliness, and the leaves turned yellow, red, and then brown, falling wildly in the whipping wind. The skies were usually overcast now, sullen and bluish-gray and white, and sometimes it rained. Teresa often lit the floor furnace near the living room, and turned on the space heaters in the rooms. Even though the overhead light fixtures sent out very bright light, the house seemed to be in the grip of the coming winter. Teresa graded her papers, decided what she would have her class do for Thanksgiving, and then she went into her bedroom closet, and brought down a hatbox in which she had placed Rachel's manuscript.

She removed the lid, her heart beating faster. Here were the papers—they hadn't changed. Would she read them?

She looked at the first page. It began---

"Dear Friend—

I have so much to say, but to whom can I say it? I call you friend, because it is to a friend that I can reveal my thoughts, and yes—my feelings, without fear of condemnation or loss of opinion. I know of no one but the greatest Friend—My Savior—because I know that too many people here on earth would be shocked by the things I know about life. They are all good men and women, but they have lived good, ordinary lives, and cannot understand. Can I tell you—Friend? I know that many people go to psychologists nowadays, to tell their deepest secrets, but I would not do that, even if I could afford it. A psychologist may be trained in certain things, but a psychologist usually has not experienced things, and therefore cannot understand, either. This is why I write to you—you will not act shocked; nor will you probe my 'unconscious' to tell me what I am thinking 'wrong.' You will just listen, and without judgment.

Do not think I am more than ordinarily bad: I am not, but do not think I am trying to escape judgment, for I am not trying to do that. But God will judge, and He alone, for only He can judge fairly and without partiality. What I am going to tell you is what I have seen and heard and experienced. I know you will not tell me that I am wrong; that I am out of my mind. I do not believe that I am; my powers of observation are as good as the next person's, and 'reality' is experienced in different ways by different people. I think a lot of those who angrily say, 'You are wrong!' are really uncomfortable, and they do not want to face the truth about themselves, especially if it exposes an unpleasant truth about them."

Teresa read that far, and was already feeling uneasy. She tried to remember that Rachel was dead and she probably never intended for anyone to see these words. It was likely a relief to her to write them, for she never confided in anyone, and apparently she was in pain. Teresa read on---

"It is hard for me to write this. But it is the truth, and I must tell it.

As far back as I can remember, I had decided to be a teacher. I did become one, and taught for a long time. It earned my living, and allowed me to live a peaceable life in a small town, without interference from any of the people I grew up with. I am very thankful for that. God was good to me, in giving me the opportunity to do so; He protected me. I must remember that. God is good, and He loves those who turn to him and ask for His care. I believe this, although I've seen things happen, where I even began to wonder if He was asleep at the switch.

This world is not perfect. I know that. Terrible things happen, and they always will, until the Last Day shall come. My earliest memories were of war. The dreadful Great War—the war that was supposed to end all wars. That didn't happen, as we all know. The war broke out again, even worse—for now man has invented weapons that can blast away entire cities—and truly, he is looking for a weapon that will blow the earth apart. But the first World War was terrible enough. I was a very young child, and I heard the neighbor women mourning and crying as the news came—they no longer had a husband, a son, or a brother. I lived in a dreary, small apartment with two brothers and my mother; it was one of those places with gas lighting, no windows, and tired-looking, brown walls. My father had gone away, even before the war. My mother was tired all the time, angry, and she always yelled at the boys and sometimes me as well. We were not really looked after: I was usually locked in the small bedroom and told to be quiet.

One day I sat in the corner of the bedroom, when I heard a woman screaming. I tried the bedroom door, and found it was not locked, and I tiptoed into the kitchen. My mother wasn't there. But I heard the screams. "He's dead! He's dead! My precious boy is dead! They killed him!" Her sobs filled the hallway, and a drunken voice yelled, "Shutup! You're not the only one who's lost a kid, you know! Put a sock in it! There's a war on!" The woman did not stop screaming, and then I heard a very loud smack. The screaming stopped then, and I crept back into the bedroom. I did not know if I would be fed that night, or when my mother would come home. I didn't remember anything at that time other than the noise, the darkness, and the dirt; someone outside was always yelling or screaming, and my mother dumped food on the table for me and my brothers. That was the extent of her care, except when she took us to church.

Church attendance was simply something we did; just like eating or sleeping. On Sunday morning my mother put me into the huge iron sink in the area that served as our kitchen, and she rinsed me down with cold water and dried me off with a rough towel. She did the same with each of my brothers, and then she dressed us in our best clothes, which were slightly threadbare but still usable. Then we walked to the local sanctuary, which was a profusion of stone and stained glass windows. Inside was a studied neatness I had never known at home—and a brightness as well. Candles lit up the red, gold and glazed wood interior, and the altar rails shown with neatness. This was God's home, I was told. He would want it to be neat. He liked neatness, and cleanliness.

I learned about sin in that neat, quiet, beautiful place. I learned that God hated sin. I learned that His Son was crucified because of sin in the world—because the world was sinful and wicked. I learned that *I* was sinful and wicked. Soon I would have to atone for my sins; I would go to a priest and confess them, and he would tell me what I must do to expiate them. I went to Mass and saw The Presence lifted high; I saw the censor shaking the aroma over the altar. God was there, I was told. And I was unworthy to be in His presence, because I was very sinful.

I was glad to go to His beautiful house, though, with the candles and the red carpets, and the shining gold patens. The stained glass windows were so high and so glorious! When the sun shone through them, the colors reflected on the wooden pews and on the carpets, and I had never before saw such brilliant colors all in one place. My home was so drab and dirty. The wooden floor was almost colorless and the planks were nearly rotten, and the walls were colorless, too. But I could barely see anything in my apartment, anyway—the lights were gas jets covered by tulip-shaped glass, and they were dim, even when the gas was turned all the way up. The smell of the gas was all-pervasive, and the odor sent forth by the censor at Mass smelled heavenly by comparison. I didn't grudge God His beautiful home, or all the shining colors, but couldn't He have sent a little bit of His beauty home with me?

I was too young to go to school at that time, so I stayed in the bedroom and lay on the dirty blanket, wishing that I at least had a doll to play with—but I didn't. I had nothing to do except sit and listen to the discordant sounds outside, and wonder if the entire world was like this dreadful place. I knew that some places looked beautiful, like the inside of the church, but all the people I met were either solemn, tired, or angry. The word 'love' was said sometimes when the priest talked of God, but I didn't really know what the word meant, for I had not experienced it. My brothers were older than I was, and they were already wild. They made fun of me and pushed me against the wall when they noticed me; but usually they were out roaming the streets. My mother never touched me or said, 'I love you' or 'you are precious to me.' I knew later that she was tired from trying to make a living after my father left us: she worked in a sweatshop and she never had a lot of energy to begin with.

I learned early never to ask about my father. My mother never explained anything to me anyway—she hardly spoke to me—and she certainly wasn't going to give any information on a subject that was undoubtedly painful for her. Once or twice when I was walking to church, I heard in the street some snickering reference to 'that drunk Sam Evanson' and I heard another word applied to him that I later innocently used in the presence of my mother. She was instantly furious, and throwing me across the worn bed, she smacked me hard many times, telling me I had a filthy mouth for so young a child, and

I was going to grow up to be a _____--a word I also didn't understand the meaning of. Then she locked me into the bedroom, telling me to pray for my wicked soul, or else I would be damned forever because of my evil nature. Once she was gone, it was quiet; but I felt sore, and nearly as evil as I was accused of being. I was told to pray and in fact I knew how—I was taught that at church. But if God was so angry with me, how dare I approach Him? He was called God the Father at church, but I knew about fathers: they got drunk and ran away, leaving their children destitute and hungry and trapped in a dirty apartment.

I don't know how I survived those years, but I do know the Great War was devastating to many people—and I was born into it. It was a dreadful time because of the fighting, but then another catastrophe happened toward the end—I remember that, too. One night I heard the usual screaming from another apartment, and then—'Take him away! Take him away—now!' It was almost like the bubonic plague scares of the Middle Ages—only, this time, it was the influenza. It was very nasty and contagious, and it especially went after the young. Signs containing public health warnings were put everywhere, although I was too young to be able to read them. But when I went outdoors I saw people everywhere wearing face masks, and many funeral processions went past, while the neighbors worried and spoke quietly, wondering if the entire world was coming to an end. It seemed to be.

In fact, my older brother became ill, but he somehow recovered, although Mother didn't want to go near him, knowing he was contagious. The flu sometimes killed very quickly—within hours— but my brother had the fever for two days and was delirious most of that time. I had to take his food to him, and my other brother was told to clean his messes. Truthfully, my mother couldn't mention she had a sick son at the shop where she worked; she surely would have been sent home and we needed every penny she could possibly make.

He did get well, and was soon out on the streets again, although he was not as strong as he used to be. And the end of the Great War finally came. There was cheering in the streets, confetti everywhere, and bands playing. The soldiers were welcomed home. But my life hadn't changed a bit—I was still in the dirty room, with poverty and anger and despair all around—and I didn't know anything different."

Teresa set the pages down at this point. She couldn't bring herself to read any farther—not yet, anyway. She knew everything that was recorded to be true—in fact, it was textbook history, but not a history she would ever share with fifth graders. College students, maybe—but never young children. The world was a dreadful place, and everyone found that out sooner or later, but Teresa was a firm believer in preserving innocence for as long as was possible. But to Rachel, innocence seemed to be an unknown quantity. Teresa herself had been born around the time World War I took place, but she had come into a loving family who supported one another and the troops as well. Her mother had worked with the local Red Cross Chapter, and her father had been an Army chaplain. Her earliest memory had been welcoming home the young men from town who had survived the war—and her father and mother stood with her, their faces rapt with pride as they waved to the soldiers. What a difference a loving family and community made! It was little wonder Rachel felt peace in the humdrum job as schoolteacher in a small town. At least that life was not punctuated by screams and slaps and filth, even though Rachel had not availed herself of the care she might have received, had she been more willing to open up.

Teresa did not know it, but worse was yet to come. She placed the papers back into the hatbox, to await another evening when she could devote some time for reading. She put the hatbox away, and then heard her husband opening the front door. Relieved, she went out of the room, to welcome him home.

Chapter 6

THE HOLIDAY SPIRIT DEFINITELY ENVELOPED THE small town of ____ton, and winter did as well. While it rarely snowed in this particular area, it was still bone-chillingly cold, and the townspeople bundled up as they continued their outdoor activities. Thanksgiving had just gone by, and now the Christmas decorations were put out. Main Street had several tinsel-and-electric light banners stretched between telephone poles and streetlamps, each with a gaudy silver Star of Bethlehem placed in the middle. Stores and shops were swathed in holly, twinkling Christmas lights and shimmering tinsel, and most had a small Christmas tree placed near a window for employee gifts. Advertising, too, was stepped up, and there was a noticeable hustle and bustle in the air, as well as well-known and well-loved Christmas carols.

It was a busy season: arguably the busiest time of the year. Teresa Anderson, along with everyone else, was going through the rush: teaching restless students and grading many near-to-end-of-term papers, while keeping up with things at home. Thanksgiving had just taken place, and all four of her children were home for it, plus two sons-in-law and four grandchildren. Even given the fact that everyone got along reasonably well and her daughters helped her with the immense cooking, Thanksgiving Day was still hardly a Norman Rockwell tableau. Teresa was truly exhausted at the end of it, though she took comfort in the fact that all the food was abundant and delicious, and everyone seemed happy: her eldest daughter saw how tired she was and told her to take a nap: *she'd* see to the cleaning up. Teresa didn't even argue—she went straight to bed.

That gave her a little respite, but when Thanksgiving was over, the Christmas rush came on, and Teresa hardly had time to think, let alone breathe. Dr. Hinton was crankier than usual because of the pre-holiday exams and the upcoming Christmas pageant, not to mention the restless, unruly students who were eagerly awaiting the Christmas holidays with no school. The drab school building had been decorated and seemed to come alive; and the students were noisier than usual. At recess time they shrieked and ran across both the hardtop and the schoolyard itself: the cold, fresh wind was invigorating and they ran around to keep warm. And of course, being the winter season, more kids than usual became ill and had to be sent home. The school nurse was very busy indeed, and it was not unusual for her to have four or five students in the nurse's station at a time, because of some of the colds and viruses that were going around.

Teresa and the other teachers usually never got sick: they had been exposed to nearly every germ known to man over the years of teaching, and they developed a certain amount of immunity. Still, the Christmas decorations oddly seemed to become synonymous with illnesses like the flu, although, thank heaven, nothing like the virulent influenza described by Rachel in her papers. *That* flu had been very, very dangerous. Nowadays the flu was just a three-day annoyance that accompanied the holidays. It was rare for anyone *not* to have it, and it was far rarer still, for anyone to die. Every family knew about the colds and the flu, and they all had their personal remedies, which were about equally effective.

Needless to say, Teresa hadn't had time to look at Rachel's papers. But she often thought of Rachel. It was hard not to, since Rachel had been part of the school.

It was strange to walk past Rachel's old third grade classroom and not see her in there. A new, very young teacher was there instead, who had just graduated from college, and Teresa had trouble even remembering her name. She hoped she would never embarrass herself by accidently addressing the new teacher as "Rachel." It hadn't happened yet, but she came close sometimes. The new teacher didn't look like Rachel at all; she seemed the average young woman: her reddish hair was shaped into a 'mature' hairstyle by curlers at night; she wore crinoline dresses and uncomfortable high-heeled shoes, and she showed every sign that she would become the typical "schoolteacher"—when the newness wore off, she would be just like any other member of the faculty. She had none of Rachel's wistfulness. She taught the children the way most of the teachers did: she drilled them through the textbook material during class time and gave them homework to be turned in the next day. She answered questions during class and gave pop quizzes on Monday. Teresa noticed she didn't interact with the students very much, but that could be due mainly to her inexperience. Once she had been teaching for several years, that would probably change; she would by then be comfortable with having the students near her.

Teresa herself had plenty of students coming up to her after class, to seek assistance for various reasons. She was one of the teachers in charge of the Christmas pageant, and she spent many afternoons after school helping with the rehearsals. Every day she brought home papers to be graded, and then her daughter and son come home from school, and she checked *their* work, too. Eveningtime came early, for the days were now short, and Bill would pull up to the house in his patrol car, to have dinner with his family. Sometimes he had the night off, and when he did, he helped Teresa with the dishes and cleanup, and then spent time with his two younger children. In fact, he often played games with them, took them on errands, and helped them with their homework problems. It was tacitly understood that Teresa was to use these quiet times to rest and relax, while he oversaw the house. Teresa did thankfully rest during these times, but she could barely make herself sit down. There was so much to be done during a holiday season....

Bill had just brought home a Christmas tree, and the festive aroma of evergreen pine needles now filled the house, along with the baked pies and cookies. Teresa helped set the tree in its water stand, and she placed the sparkling embroidered felt tree skirt around the stand. Her part was over, then: Bill put the strings of colored lights on the branches, and then the children put the glass ornaments on. It was the family tradition—they did it that way every year. Teresa had already bought and wrapped some presents, and as soon as the tree was up, she went to her bedroom closet to take them down. It was then that she noticed the hatbox. Tentatively, she brought it down, too; she set it on her great double bed, and took the presents into the living room.

Bill and the children were gone; they were probably out shopping, and the living room was dark, except for the tree, which vividly showed lights of blue, yellow, red, green and white, and the iridescence lit up the metallic ornaments. The blinds of the front windows were open so the neighbors could see the tree, and it was very dark outside—and cold. A frosty wind rattled the panes, and the floor furnace, while heated at full blast, did not seem very effective. Teresa turned on one of the living room lamps; then went into the bedroom. The hatbox was still on the bed, where she had placed it.

She sat down on the bed, and listened to the heavy wind rattle against the bedroom windows, the tree branches scraping on the eaves. After a moment, she flicked on a bedside lamp and opened the hatbox. She pulled out the pages, and looked for the place she left off. Rachel, what are you going to tell me now? she wondered.….

She found the next paragraph:

"The end of the war had come, and our country won. But for me—nothing had been won.

My mother was working harder than ever, and for longer hours. She could not afford to lose her job. The men had all come home from war, and they were finding it hard to adjust. They were desperate for work, and many of them began to drink. I heard more fights outside and more yelling, and sometimes I heard the drunken soldiers singing loudly, off-key, words I had never heard before. On occasion during these impromptu concerts, someone would throw a bottle or a brick at the performers, screaming, 'Shutup, you drunken ____!'—I didn't understand the epithet; however, I knew it was not complementary. But even a brick seemed to have no effect on the singers, for they continued on, stopping only to knock on a door or a window, or to get sick in the streets. I heard one neighbor say the coming Prohibition was going to put a stop to it all, thank heaven, but I didn't know what she was talking about—I was too young to understand a big word like Prohibition.

The crowds of men around the neighborhood became thicker and more menacing, as they could not find employment; they loitered near the streetlamps in torn, wornout army uniforms, holding onto whiskey bottles. Some of them emptied firearms into the air, and that truly scared me. For the first time, I was glad we had no windows. We did have a door, and that was a bad thing—the men hammered on it and kicked it, and threw beer bottles at it. They whooped and hollered as they did so, and I spent most of the time hiding in the bedroom. It was as dirty and filthy as ever, but seemed to be the only safe place—I even hid under the bed, because the noise seemed to be so near.

I did not know what I was afraid of. But soon I was to find out—and how!

Friend, I have talked with You honestly. I have told You how it was. You know it is the truth. I will continue to tell You. But—Friend—how can I write these words? How can I tell You? My hand shakes, and I still recoil, as I think of what I must tell You next. Please don't turn away from me—my Friend! I don't know how to put this down on paper, or what words to use to describe it. I could never say anything about it aloud. My neighbors would turn from me, as though I had a loathsome disease, and I might not ever be able to teach again, or anything. But I must tell You—and be as truthful as I can.

I was young, about five years old, I think. Mother was at work, as she almost always was, and my two brothers were out goodness knows where. I was alone in the cramped, filthy apartment, and frightened to death. I was used to the noise outside, but this day I heard footsteps outside the door that were totally unfamiliar, and suddenly true, unreasoning dread took hold of me. Something was wrong. The footsteps were heavy mens' footsteps, and they began hammering on the door. 'Let us in! Let us in!' they yelled, and with a smash, the door came open. The apartment seemed full of men;

I don't remember how many of them there were. They were large and strong and brutal-looking, and they began traipsing around the apartment, looking for something—whiskey or beer, probably, as both were increasingly hard to find, and they kicked over furniture in their search. They looked through cubbyholes and then swore, and then grouped up in their way to the bedroom.

At first they didn't find me. I was hiding under the bed, and they were tearing through the closet and through the bureau drawers. But finally, they stopped going through the drawers and decided to look under the bed instead. They probably heard that alcohol—or money—was sometimes hidden under the mattress, and reasoned that, since the booze wasn't in the closet or in the drawers, it must be under the bed. There were so many men, and they were strong—they yanked up the entire bed, and there I was!

'Oh, look at the curly-headed little moppet!' shouted one of them. 'Ain't she sweet? I didn't know we would find such a cute piece---'

'Come on, idiot,' broke in one of his cohorts, 'She's just a teeny kid. You don't want that, do you? There's plenty of good sixteen-year-olds down the street, that are just fancy girls—let's go find them.' Three of the men dropped the bed, and one of them said, 'I'm game. Where are they?' The first one seemed to know, and he left, the other men following him, except for the one who called me a curly-headed moppet. He watched and made sure they went out, and then he turned to me. 'Okay,' he laughed. 'We're alone now. Let me touch your cute, shiny curls.' He laughed again, and it sounded really obscene. Not knowing why, I screamed, and he jerked me off my feet, clapping his hand over my mouth. 'Shutup, you little ____!' he said angrily, 'I'll teach you something!'

He threw me across the bed, and stripped off my ragged clothes. He held me down by the neck with one hand, and with the other, made some adjustments, and he was on top of me. I couldn't understand what was happening to me, but it hurt, and I felt his rough clothes scraping my back. I could barely breathe, and both pain and shame overwhelmed me. I was pinned so that I could not move or cry out, and he touched me again and again, whispering and laughing. I was in pain—and in such a way that was unspeakable and embarrassing, and I could no longer stay conscious. Sparks seemed to fly up before my eyes, and then I floated away into the darkness, not knowing where I was going, but in a way, I hoped I would never return...."

"Oh, God!" Teresa screamed aloud, not knowing that she had made a sound. She listened to the wind blowing in the dark outside, and heard the distant clicks of the floor furnace, trying to warm the hallway.

She forced herself to turn back to the papers, but she was beginning to shake as she read---

"When I came to, the man was gone. I was lying in a pool of blood, and I hurt dreadfully. I knew I could not tell my mother about this at all—she would have given me such a whipping as I had probably never had in all my short life, and she would have asked me why I let the men into the apartment in the first place. Even though I could barely walk, I dragged the sheet over to the iron sink, and rinsed it out the best I could. Hopefully it would dry before my mother came home, and then I wouldn't have to think of some story to tell her. After I put the sheet back, I got into the iron sink, and washed myself off, even though the water was nearly freezing. I wanted to wash that feeling off, but I couldn't do it. My mind seemed violated as much as my body, and I was not the same ever again. I still bled, so I searched until I found a small, forgotten washrag in a cubbyhole; I stuffed it between my legs, and shaking, I put my clothes on—which I found thrown in the corner of the bedroom.

At the time, after the first shock, my mind seemed to bury the episode. When my mother finally came home, I had forgotten it—or rather, I had blotted it totally out of my conscious. Truly, I could not process it, as they say nowadays. They say many things nowadays, as it is. They—especially male psychoanalysts—say women like me make things up, to get attention. But Friend, I never made this up. I couldn't have made up anything so horrible. And where—where— *where* were You, my Friend, my Lord and Savior, when this happened to me? You are God; You could have prevented it. Couldn't You have saved a young child from such devastating violence—didn't You *care!?*

Such thoughts I had later on, when some of it came back to me. But just after it happened, I blotted it away, and I threw away the bloody towel as soon as I healed. I didn't want my mother to know.

I didn't want her to know, but at the same time I must have felt—why wasn't she there and why didn't she protect me?

Those were my thoughts. That was also what happened. Now You understand why I cannot speak of it—the shame, the disgrace of it all! Were I to say anything, I would have been pointed out as an unclean thing; I would have been talked about, and I probably would have lost my teaching job. Who would want someone like me around their children—tainted and soiled as I was? Only those with the best of character have a right to be around children, to teach them, and I fully agree with that. I'm sorry that I deceived Dr. Hinton and the school board into thinking I was a good, pure woman—but after all, I taught the children their lessons, and never did them any harm. They knew nothing about my past, or what kind of person I was. They only knew me as someone who taught them how to write, to enjoy reading books, and to solve math problems. They did want to talk with me sometimes, and I listened. How happy were the lives of most of them! But it was right; children *should* have happy lives, and I was glad most of my students did….."

Spoken like a true teacher, thought Teresa helplessly. In spite of herself, she reread the last paragraph, and she thought—Oh, Rachel! You *were* a good, pure woman. You did not deceive Dr. Hinton or the school board in any way. What happened to you was not your fault, and it did not lessen your moral goodness at all. Didn't you know that? However, Teresa was not surprised at her silence. She probably *would* have been talked about, had anyone known what was written in the pages she held. She now knew for certain why Reverend Mayfield had warned her as he did that day in Rachel's home. Now that she read so far, he was proven right—she *was* carrying a great emotional burden. Teresa could read no longer—at least not tonight. She put the papers gently into the hatbox, and put the hatbox into the closet.

"Goodnight, Rachel, sleep well," she said aloud. "It's too late to pray for you, or I would. But I know you are at home with God, and you are happy there. I'm sorry you suffered so."

She heard the front door opening, and the voices of her husband and children as they conversed and carried in their purchases; and she was thankful as never before to hear them. She was thankful for her life, as busy as it was, as she had never been before. Rachel, now dead, was still teaching. She was teaching Teresa gratitude.

Chapter 7

CHRISTMAS SEASON WAS FINALLY OVER. SANTA had visited most of the boys and girls of ____ton, bringing many brightly wrapped gifts, candy canes, and oranges and shelled nuts to fill the stockings. It probably happened that many a child got a special wish on Christmas morning, but few children were as happy as Teresa Anderson was that morning. It turned out Bill had a very special present for her. They had a relatively new, stereophonic hi-fi which they purchased two years ago—a large, walnut paneled monstrosity with cloth-covered speakers and a diamond-tipped stylus. Bill and the children usually played loud rock-and-roll records or some other such noisy musical concoctions on the hi-fi, and though Teresa tolerated it with good humor, it was not her style. She actually liked classical music, which was not quite the thing, but her family respected her tastes. For Christmas they had a 1962 Firestone collection of Christmas carols sung by Rise Stevens and other noted voices of the time. But the surprise wasn't over yet.

Bill had special-ordered a beautiful, expensive set of records for Teresa—Bach's Passion According to St. Matthew—a brand new version just put out in London that year, and directed by Otto Klemperer. Teresa was astounded. Her husband didn't even *like* classical music, and she certainly didn't know he was aware she liked Bach. The set had ten records, and it was complete with a booklet that had the entire libretto printed in both English and in German. There was a short history about Bach, and the musicians and orchestra selected to make this album were among the best that could be had in that day. Teresa was never more surprised and happy as she was that Christmas Day.

Her older daughters had come with their families, and she dished up the traditional but very tasty Christmas dinner—turkey and dressing, glazed ham, wild rice, cranberry and asparagus, and her daughters brought assorted vegetables and pies. Bill and the children had purchased Coca-Cola and Lay's potato chips on one of their errands out, and those were served up with the evening meal of turkey sandwiches and hot soup. The grandchildren watched the boxy, cloth-speaker dominated black-and-white television in one of the bedrooms, and Bill talked sports and other "guy stuff" with his sons-in-law, who respected him since he was a police officer. It was a happy enough gathering, and one of the happiest Christmases Teresa had known. She was also glad it was over—as soon as New Year's passed by, things would go back to routine.

New Years came and went, and all the Christmas decorations were taken down. School was back in session, and the January days were mostly gray and depressing. The routine in the classroom was firmly established by this time: Teresa knew all of her students' names, what they would do in any given situation, and how well they would perform their work. Now that the holiday rush was over and the Christmas pageant played, she could concentrate more on the classwork. The children were fortunately mostly well-disposed: they were fifth-graders, after all, and had not reached the teen years.

It was the typical school year, like most others. But Teresa knew in her heart that things were not the same.

Since it was now quieter, and January passed by in sodden temperatures and gray skies, Teresa cooked, cleaned, and graded papers—and studied Rachel's Bible. Teresa and her family went to church nearly every Sunday, and she and Bill were active members of the church, but she was still surprised how much she learned studying on her own. As a schoolteacher she was trained to grasp both overt and hidden meanings from any given text, and because she was familiar with Shakespeare's classics and Bacon's Essays, the King James English didn't throw her the way it might have discouraged a newer Christian, who didn't have the training. "They need to have newer English translations of the Bible," Teresa thought to herself. "Some that can be easily read." The King James Version was the "language of the streets" in 1611, but that was well over three hundred years ago. The English language, idioms and all, had changed since then. Of course, there was a time that an English-language Bible was a novelty and at times it was illegal to read one. Fortunately, that had all undergone a revolution—printing presses and all.

One January night Teresa glanced over the Bible, and thought of the previous owner. She had not taken down the hatbox since she read of Rachel's assault, but she knew it was now time. She understood Rachel a little better now, but the picture was not complete. Even though Teresa led a conventional life in a small town with mainstream values, she was not unaware of the rough side of life. This was partly because her husband was a patrol officer, and some of the situations he had to deal with had a profound effect on him; but also because she had worked in slum clinics during her college years, when she earned her master's degree. She had not become cynical or insensitive, but she wasn't easily shocked by life, either. Because of her training and experience she was thoughtful and understanding, which was probably why Reverend Mayfield insisted *she* take the manuscript.

Still, knowing what happened to Rachel brought the rough side of life rather close to home. Teresa forced herself to bring down the hatbox, when she had graded her papers and updated her lesson plans. Bill was on patrol that night, and her two children were occupied with school events. In the cold silence, Teresa drew out the manuscript and read:

"Like I said, I am glad my students were mainly happy. A child should be a child, and not have the burden of the sorrows of this world placed upon him too soon. When a child is thus burdened, he grows up unnaturally, and parts of his soul do not develop at all, because something has been burnt out in them. To some degree the child psychologists are right: the way a child is raised, and the experiences he has when he is very young, *will* have an effect on him, although as an adult he can make a conscious effort to correct any earlier mistake. Children should be children. They should not be exposed prematurely to gratuitous violence or seamy sexuality—that should be no part of their world. They should learn about reading, writing and how the world is made—and the plants and animals God created to beautify it. They would—and will—learn of the ugliness soon enough…."

If anyone had a right to write such a paragraph, thought Teresa, Rachel certainly did.

"I did have a major change in my life, finally, when I was seven or eight. At that time, my mother died. They gave the cause as 'consumption' which was sort of a catch-all term in those days, mostly applying to diseases of the lungs. I think she was just worn out. In any case, some people I did not know took me and my brothers to the lofty cathedral near my home, and there she was, lying still in a cheap coffin, while the priest said a short mass. Hardly anyone was there, but a middle-aged man and his wife turned to me after the mass, and asked where my clothes were.

'In the apartment,' I said, and led them to it. Both of them where shocked when I brought them there—they decided they didn't want any of my clothes. 'Throw them out!' cried the woman. 'We can buy a few new ones, but that is all--I *told* you nothing ever good came of Cindy! Look at how she kept her place—she didn't even keep it! I bet that child is crawling with worms. Now we'll have to take her to a doctor, and the expense! Really, Charles, we should leave her at a home somewhere!'

'Anne,' said the man reprovingly, 'she's just a child. We would have to spend the same money on our own.'

'Yes, on our own! But she isn't ours! We have barely enough to take care of our own as it is!'

They bickered for a long time like that, and they didn't even tell me who they were. The woman, even though she was undoubtedly fussy and shrewish, was clean and neat, and her clothes were the finest looking I had seen in some time. Styles had changed quite a bit since the war, and dress lines were much simpler and a slight bit shorter. Hats were smaller, too: a tub-like simplicity hugging the head. The woman wore one of those kinds of hats, and peeking under her skirts were the shoes known as 'Mary Janes.' She wore silk stockings, too; what was visible of them glinted through her shoes, and I wondered a little at her daring, especially since she seemed to be such a proper woman.

After the argument between the man and the woman, I was taken to an inexpensive 'ready-made' shop, and fitted out in fresh, clean clothes. New shoes were added, and then I was taken to a health clinic at the hospital. That was a truly frightening experience for me. I know it shouldn't have been, but, Friend, You must understand I had never seen a doctor or a health professional before in my entire life, and I did not know what their procedures were. As the large man in the white coat began to undress me, I began to scream, and the woman named Anne was clearly irritated. 'Rachel, stop it this minute!' she scolded. 'What is the matter with you?' I definitely couldn't say—I may have even forgotten. I forced myself to stop screaming, but I was tense and terrified as the doctor examined my entire body—he looked grim when the examination was done, and he took the man and the woman aside.

'Definitely malnourished, but no diseases or worms. No, no consumption. But—' he whispered a few words to them, and the woman called Anne gasped. 'Soldiers, I think,' said the doctor, 'they were crowding around this area, up to no good. But don't ever talk about it, if you are going to raise this child. She's probably too young to remember it, and it wouldn't be good for your reputation, if such a thing came out, and there's no real need to discuss it.'

'Is there a disease we need to be concerned about?' asked the man named Charles.

'I don't think there is, from the look of things. Just injury. So don't give it another thought. Put some food into her and make sure she has daily baths and clean clothing. I do believe getting her out of the city will do wonders for her.'

The man and the woman nodded, and the next thing I knew, I found myself on a train, moving away from that dirty city apartment forever. Riding on the train was a new experience for me, too, and I learned to be silent about things that frightened or surprised me.

The man and the woman took me onto a day coach, which was rather warm even though there were electric fans on the ceiling, and the velvet seats were hot. I was placed next to the window, and I spent most of the time quietly looking out, because the scenery was truly new to me. At first we went though my home city, and we passed by buildings I never knew existed, and through places that had many trees and fancy homes, and even fountains. Then we were out of the city, and I saw stretches and yet more stretches of land, which I had never seen before. Telephone and telegraph wires swooped past the window, and the loud train horn blasted from time to time, as we whisked through the country. We passed small towns during our journey, and I couldn't believe I could see an entire town from the window—I was so used to the big city and its continuous concrete and iron construction. These towns had very small, white houses—with trees around them and picket fences, brick streets, and one-story shops and stores. I could guess how peaceful these towns were.

All the while, Charles and Anne, as I knew their names to be, sat quietly beside me, and both of them seemed tired. That was one things I sensed would never change: I would always be around people who were tired and irritable, like my mother had been. I didn't dare say a word to either of them. In a way, I wanted to ask what had happened to my two brothers, even though I hadn't been close to either of them and they probably were not concerned about me, judging from the fact that they never stayed home with me. But I refrained from asking. I didn't know what Charles and Anne planned to do with me, but I didn't ask that, either. So far they had put clothes on me and bought my meals, and they were taking me with them. Where, I did not know.

The trip lasted quite a while. But finally, we pulled into a station, and Charles and Anne indicated that we were to get off at that place. So I followed them, and found that this station was neither as noisy or as crowded as the one back home. It was a single building, in fact, with small enclosed waiting rooms, a ticket window, and a chalked schedule board. A long metal roof shaded the loading area, and beneath the roof were incandescent light bulbs, hanging from radial

waves fixtures. Charles carried the luggage away from the loading
area, and he signaled for a taxi. A black sedan with a flat roof, spoked
wheels and a snide-looking driver appeared at the curb, and we all
got in. It was my first ride in an automobile. Such things were not
so common in those days.

The taxi rumbled and shook, and finally got us to a heavily
shaded, quiet neighborhood with small, neat houses. Most had
picket fences and gardens of some sort, and nearly all had trees. The
houses were nearly all wood sided, with shutters and large porches,
and some of the houses were resting on large blocks, with a great
crawl space underneath. The yards, both front and back, seemed
unusually large, and I saw makeshift swings hanging from some of
the trees. It was safe to say I had never seen such a neighborhood
before.

The taxi stopped, and the man called Charles said, 'Okay, Rachel,
here we are.' I got out, and followed Charles and Anne into their
home. It was a white house, with green shutters and a screened-in
porch. The windows were all open , and I could see a young woman,
with several children about her. Charles and Anne went through the
door, and I followed. The young woman looked up, and seeing me,
said in a grating voice, 'That her?' Charles nodded and disappeared
with the luggage. 'Humph,' she said, this time addressing Anne.
'Curly-headed. Not too bad looking. But ignorant, I bet!'

'Tish!' replied Anne. 'Cindy never sent her to school, I can tell
you that right now. We'll have to put her in first grade even though
she's bigger than that. Well, it can't be helped. I'll tell you right
now, though, I do not like having to put up with such a mess! I told
Charles I'll care for the girl, but I will not have the boys!'

'There were two of 'em, huh?'

'Yes, and I said, absolutely not! Rachel's young, anyway, and a
girl. I can keep some sort of rein on her. But those boys are already
wild, and I told Charles I was not having any of that in my house.
It's an imposition enough as it is, with Rachel.'

'Well, I'm sorry, Anne. I know its hard for you. But I best be
getting back home. Good luck.'

The young woman left, and Anne turned to me. 'There is a cot in the back bedroom, next to Anne's bed. That's where you'll sleep. And I'll show you where to put your clothes, and where you will sit at the table. You will have your chores. I will explain them to you later, when you are settled in. I expect you to behave yourself. Do you understand, Rachel?'

Later on I learned that Charles was my uncle—he was my mother's brother. His name was Charles Dunn. He and Anne had three children, but when my mother died, Uncle Charles didn't want me to be sent to an orphans' home. I know now that my uncle and aunt tried to do the best that they could by me—they honestly wanted to, and they couldn't be faulted for lacking imagination and a sense of compassion. Unfortunately, it was hard on them, and they let me know it in various ways.

Anyway, I had a place to stay, such as it was. It *was* clean. And soon I started school…."

Teresa put the papers down. She was tired, and decided not to read any more that night, but her mind would not be quieted. She thought of the beautiful music her husband had ordered for her and presented to her for Christmas. Oftentimes during the cold evenings, especially when she was alone in the house, she played the records on the large hi-fi system, and she was amazed by the full sound of Bach's masterpiece. She was blessed to hear such true beauty, and she knew she was also blessed in having the wonderful family she had. Her parents loved her—and each other; they raised and cared for her in such a way that she was ready to meet life and its challenges. Her husband, Bill, was a good man, who watched over her and their children, and her adult children were loving and thoughtful as well. She could not even imagine a life like Rachel's, who did not seem to be wanted anywhere, and in fact was treated very much as a liability. No wonder she was so shy! Even though she had been a very capable teacher, she apparently had never felt truly worthy.

Teresa placed the papers in the hatbox, and put it away. She would continue to read, but she was suddenly overwhelmed with a wistful sadness, which rarely ever came into her life. She got into the large double bed, pulling the quilt up to her neck, and she listened to the wind moaning and whipping the bare tree branches near the eaves. The night was overcast, and neither moon nor stars were visible, to give hopeful light. Teresa lay staring at the shadowy ceiling, and then she got up, and knelt beside the bed. There she said a very thankful prayer to the Lord, telling Him of her gladness that He had blessed her so much and so often. Afterward she got back into bed, but it was long before her eyes finally closed in sleep.

When she got up the next morning, to go through her usual workday routine, she found that she saw it all in a new light....

Chapter 8

FEBRUARY HAD ARRIVED. THE WEATHER WAS still cold and dreary, although every now and then, a sunny day brightened an otherwise drab season, to remind the townspeople that spring would come at last. But it was usually overcast outdoors, and always cold, and the bundled-up students were restless and hard to teach, and the school hours seemed never ending. It was nearly always windy: one side of the classroom was all windows, and the panes rattled with the frozen gales. The painted radiator beneath the windows hissed and sputtered, but did not seem to put out much warmth. The students often wore their coats and sweaters in the classroom, and even when they did not, they kept them close by, draped over the back of the desks.

Valentine's Day was coming up, and Teresa Anderson knew she was in for a rowdy afternoon on February 14th. She usually had two "class mothers" come in on Valentine's Day afternoon; the mothers would bring cupcakes with alternate red and white frosting, and heart-shaped cookies to go with cherry-flavored Cool-Aid. The classroom would be decorated with red and white streamers and balloons, and the class bulletin board would be devoted to drawings of Valentine cards, done by the students. Teresa allowed a few hours of one February afternoon to be used by the students for their artwork. Most of the time this worked out well, although Teresa kept close supervision over the proceedings. Since the fifth graders were so young, she usually didn't have to deal with any vulgarity or boy-girl squabbles, but occasionally she had student who wanted to show off, and that had to be nipped on the bud.

Since Valentine's Day would fall on Friday, Teresa planned the "coloring day" for Wednesday afternoon, and she instructed the class accordingly. She had already conferred with the "class mothers" the week before, and the details concerning the party refreshments were worked out. So now the children would make their Valentine creations, and Friday morning, before class, Teresa would tack up the streamers and balloons. Everything was going smoothly: the blessed result of years and years of routine experience.

Wednesday afternoon was cold and gray: the clouds hung sullenly from the sky, and all things outdoors were frozen to the touch. It was not particularly windy, but it was dark because of the thick cloud cover, and the overhead fluorescent lights in the classroom seemed extremely bright in comparison. Teresa gave the orders for the students to begin the work, and she made sure each child had his or her supplies—crayons, construction paper, scissors, glue, tape. The students were already noisy, creating something of a holiday mood in the classroom, but after an initial shushing Teresa let them talk, provided they didn't shout. The conversation was then a steady hum, and scissors clunked against desktops and paper crumpled and fell to the floor, all around the desks. Teresa sat down at her "teacher's desk" in the front of the classroom, and allowed them to get on with their work. Of course they compared work and criticized, or praised, as the occasion called for, and now and then there were snickers and a few minor arguments. But nothing truly alarming happened, and Teresa began looking over her lesson plans for the next day, while the children worked.

As she went over her plans, she became aware that a student had tip-toed to her desk. It was one of her shyer students, a small girl named Lila. Teresa looked up and saw her intent gaze. She held her half-finished work in her hands, and Teresa smiled. "I am sure you are doing a good job. Go to your desk and finish it, and I will look at it."

Lila usually would have turned back, as she was so shy, but this time she didn't. "N-no, Mrs. Anderson," she said, "I gotta ask you something."

"Okay, Lila. What is it?"

"I-I want to make this Valentine for Miss Evanson," replied Lila, a look of pain in her face. "I-I was in her class when I was in third grade. Now that she's dead, if I make it for her and it gets put up on the bulletin board, do you think she'll be able to see it from Heaven? She still knows where the school is, doesn't she? Won't God let her look?"

Teresa had heard many things over the years of her teaching, but this time she was completely taken aback. Not stopping to consider her theology or what she believed about the afterlife, or even stopping to think about her answer at all, she said—

"I'm sure God will allow Rachel to see how much you cared about her. Go ahead and finish the Valentine, and we'll put it up so Rachel can see."

Lila seemed satisfied, and went back to her desk. Teresa continued the review of her lesson plans, but the question, as innocent as it was, bothered her, and helped her to realize that, as silent as it was, there was a pervading, and possibly overwhelming, grief for Miss Evanson among the students, that had not abated. It was never discussed, at least not with the faculty. Teresa knew that. School was a very busy time and many things had to be done; the lessons had to be taught by a certain deadline, and most of the time spent with individual students had to be utilized toward helping them grasp the concepts so they could pass the tests. Rachel's death had never been formally or openly discussed. Teresa was sure her name had been mentioned during recess or lunch among the students who grouped together for their activities, but no one ever mentioned her in Teresa's classroom. Until now.

Teresa was glad her students were at the moment thoroughly occupied: she did not think she could give her whole mind to teaching, as she usually did. She realized that she, too, was still grieving for Rachel. Probably even more so, as she was getting to know Rachel better through the latter's written words, and in a sense

Rachel was still alive when Teresa read about her. Teresa did not know if this was helpful to her or not, but even so, the manuscript was already in her hatbox, and she was reading it. She could stop any time—she knew that; however, curiosity—and very possibly grief—drove her on. Rachel's death was so sudden, that perhaps reading the manuscript eased the shock. Teresa did not know.

The final bell was about to ring, and Teresa ordered her students to turn in the Valentines and put away the supplies. The class became correspondingly noisier and more active, but when the bell actually rang most of Teresa's instructions had been effectively carried out, and the students rushed out of the door, shouting and swinging books, while locker doors slammed out in the hallway. Teresa waited a few minutes for the bustle to clear out, then inspected the classroom as she usually did. The students were fairly faithful in carrying out her orders: the scissors, paper and glue were in their proper places; most of the trash had been thrown in the garbage pail, with only a few bits of bright construction paper here and there on the floor. The custodian would sweep that up. Teresa turned her attention to the double-stack of newly made Valentines on her desk, and smiled a little as she checked the names on the back and began to put them in alphabetical order. That's the way she placed the students' work on the bulletin board—alphabetical order. Sometimes she reversed the order, but the students knew their work was placed on the bulletin board by reason of their last name initial, and no other reason. That way there was no preference intended.

As she sorted, still smiling with amusement, she came upon Lila's Valentine. She stopped smiling. The artwork was sticky and a little clumsy, as any fifth-graders artwork is apt to be, and the red heart, cut out on a doubled-over piece of red construction paper as Teresa had taught the students, was stuck haphazardly on the white background paper. But around the heart was many well-drawn and colored-in flowers, and the words were written on with blue crayon, "Dear Miss Evanson: I love you. I hope you are happy in Heaven. Maybe God will give you some nice angel-children to teach. Love, Lila." For some reason that brought back memories of Rachel that nothing else did, and Teresa, for a moment, saw Rachel standing before her, tall and slim and dressed in a severe-looking blue dress, her brown curls hugging her sweet face, and her large brown eyes focused on something far beyond anything Teresa knew. Teresa gave herself a shake and ran her hand gently over the Valentine; she had always felt a sense of loss, but never so deeply as she did now.

"I must put these Valentines up and go on home," she told herself sternly, and mechanically, she finished the sorting and began to do so. The day outside was dark and dank, and it would be short, too. Teresa hurriedly tacked up her students' work, Lila's included, and when that was done, she gathered up her lessons and went down the familiar hallway to the teachers' parking lot, not far from the double doors at the end of the upper class wing. It was very cold outside, and she walked quickly to her Plymouth, unlocking it and tossing her lesson books onto the floorboards.

Once she was inside of the car she was out of the "wind chill" but nonetheless, it was still cold. The ignition did not turn over right away, and as she cranked the engine and tapped the accelerator, the Plymouth's engine railed in protest, almost, Teresa thought, like a weeping lady. Teresa turned the key to "off" and waited for a bit, then tried again. This time the ignition caught, and Teresa reached to the left of the steering wheel, where the "push button" transmission selections were set in an anodized gold strip. She was finally out of the parking lot and on her way, and she ran the heater in the car, which she did not usually do. The clouds hung very low and sullen, and some of the streetlights had already come on. The leafless tree branches hung over the town streets like brownish-black skeletons, and Teresa pulled into the bare concrete-and-shelled driveway of her home. Bill had not arrived, and she ran, shivering, to her back door, and once in, turned the porch light on.

For a moment, she thought of Rachel. Rachel was not here this day—did not feel the cold air or see the grayish clouds hang down. Rachel was—she knew not where.

But part of Rachel was *there*, in Teresa's own home, up in a hatbox. Teresa knew she would have to look again, and find out what happened next, when Rachel was still in this life. She was taken by an uncle and aunt—Teresa read that far. What happened next? She would have to look—maybe even this night.

But there were things to do. She lit the floor furnace, and then went into the kitchen to began laying out the ingredients for dinner, when both of her teenagers burst through the front door. "Man, it's freezing out there!" exclaimed her son. "Mom, I got to go to the store tonight. I got to get some stuff for school—you know, Valentine stuff. Can I borrow the Plymouth?"

"Can't it wait until tonight?" asked Teresa. "The Plymouth's acting up a little."

"Well, you've been driving it, Mom, haven't you?" her son protested. "It should be warmed up by now. It was probably acting up because the engine was cold."

Teresa's teenaged daughter grinned. "Oh, he's in a big hurry because he wants to get this big Valentine for Mary Lou," she smirked, enjoying her older brother's scowls. "He thinks Dean Wilton will see it and buy it first, and then Mary Lou won't pay attention to him anymore. Now, Billy, you know it's true. You're sweet on Mary Lou, aren't you--?"

"Cut it out or I won't take you with me," fussed Billy. "Then you won't get that candy you want over at the drugstore."

Teresa interposed. "Okay, Billy, but be careful," she said, giving him the keys. "You two buy what you need to buy and come straight home. I don't want you hanging around the drugstore tonight. It's too dark and cold. Supper will be ready, anyway." Billy nodded assent, and he and his sister dashed out again. Soon Teresa heard the metallic sound of the Plymouth's ignition, but it caught right away, and Teresa, looking out the front living room window, saw the red flash of finned taillights. She sighed, and went back into the kitchen. It was chilly in there, but the overhead light fixture put out a very bright light, and Teresa lit the oven for good measure.

As she prepared the food she glanced out of the kitchen window from time to time, watching the sparse daylight fade. It seemed a little lonely now, but Bill would soon be home, and so would her teenagers Billy and Mandy. She could not imagine living alone all the time, though. Not like Rachel. Somehow she could not picture

Rachel as a wife—or a mother. Had the damage been that great? Teresa could understand the shyness, but Rachel had virtually cut herself off from any kind of close relationships. She didn't even dare to have friends. It wasn't that she wasn't capable—Teresa ascertained from what little she read, that Rachel was able to feel love and did want closeness. But her fear was too great. She had been hurt early on, and—Teresa tried not to think any more—she wanted to concentrate on her cooking.

"But I will be with you tonight, Rachel," Teresa promised in her mind. "I wish you could have heard what your student Lila said today. Did you see the Valentine? She made it especially for you."

She frowned, and turned away from the kitchen window. The Plymouth was pulling in, the headlights cutting a beam through the darkness in the driveway. The kids were safely home, and dinner would soon be ready. She knew *she* was far from being alone.

Chapter 9

THAT EVENING, AFTER BILL WENT BACK to work and her teenagers to their various diversions, Teresa took down the hatbox. She turned on the bedroom reading lamp, and turned the papers to the spot where she left off.

"I began school very late—I was over eight years old when I went into first grade. That fact alone set me apart from the rest of the class, but the fact I was a 'poor relation' put a mark on me forever. As small as this town was, it was prosperous to a degree, and one must remember this was during the 'roaring 20's' when wealth and good family background mattered quite a bit. I realize the same is true now, but the nation had not experienced the Great Depression as of yet, and the general feeling was that nobody worthwhile had any business being poor. Already several families in the town owned roadsters or sedans, and the women dressed in new, fancy creations that draped rather than outlined their figures, with long, heavy beads. Even my first grade teacher looked like a fashion plate from one of the magazines that covered my aunt's coffee table, and girls in my class, even at the age of six, seemed quite forward. Especially my cousin Anne Dunn.

As I said, my uncle and aunt had three children. The eldest of them was named Anne for her mother, and she was in my first grade class. There was a younger boy, Charles, who was four, and another girl, Jane, who had just turned one. Anne was only six—two years younger than I was, but she already seemed much older. She was almost unnaturally sophisticated and snobbish—I think she was trying to imitate her mother, who was socially conscious, and from the first, she found me an embarrassment.

Friend, I know what You are going to say. That I shouldn't be so harsh in my judgment. That maybe I shouldn't be judgmental at all. After all, the Dunns took me in. But, please, Friend, let me say what I have to say. Then You can moralize or pass judgment on me as You wish. I'm sure I was an imposition; however, I did not order or request my existence.

My aunt put me to work, as she promised, and I did learn a lot of housewifely skills at an early age. I am sure she reasoned in her mind that she had a right to my labor, as I was an extra burden in her home, and since she was always frantically busy, she did need my help. She was on many church committees, and she also had to entertain her husband's associates from work, to help further his career. This meant semi-formal dinners and occasional parties, although not cocktail parties, as liquor was now illegal. Aunt Anne had nothing against alcoholic beverages, but she was not going to break the law, and she dutifully served tea and ice water. It took a lot of planning and cleaning up to arrange these get-togethers, and I was always asked to sweep and clan and mop, and do dishes. Anne and Charles and Jane of course were too young to help, and they were not asked to do so. During the parties I was told to watch them, and Aunt Anne would warn me that if she heard any disturbance from any of them, I would be responsible.

With little Charles and Jane it wasn't so bad. But my cousin Anne was another matter altogether.

Like I said, she was old for her age. And she wasn't shy about letting anyone know what she thought about anything.

She was in my first grade class, and the first thing she said to me was, 'I don't want you to say a word to me in school. Just because you're my cousin and live in my house doesn't mean I like you. I don't like you, and I wished you stayed where you came from. If you speak to me, I'll slap you!' I had no doubt that she would, and to be honest, I didn't want to speak to her anyway. That in itself wouldn't have been a problem, but she took it upon herself to inform our mutual classmates that I was poor and stupid, and since her father was well-known in the town, the other children wanted to stay on her good side. It was noted that I wouldn't have anything to do with Anne, and the teacher decided it was unfriendliness on my part. I tried not to mind what was hinted to me, and I tried to concentrate on learning my lessons. At least I was quick to learn, but, after all, the teacher said, I was certainly old enough to catch on.

The classwork itself was not hard, so if I had been left alone at school without Anne's interference, I might have won some respect. But I do not know. I was not respected in the Dunns' home, for all that I assisted Aunt Anne in every way possible. Aunt Anne was not a woman who could be pleased. She was forever fussing, trying to get things done, and she was always criticizing as well —'I don't know *how* we're going to manage that school bake sale' she would say, 'You can't trust Minnie Larkin to do her part helping with the layout, and I don't know why Principal Adkins asked her to do it, of all people! If I had some say about it, I'd put the right person in charge. But as usual, I'll get all the tiring work.' And—

'Did you hear what happened to Verna Jessop? I *told* you, she was up to no good! A woman like that—what was Tommy Liles thinking? There is too much white trash in this town—no wonder everyone's going to the dogs. It wasn't like that in *my* day.' As she complained, she would be vigorously scrubbing or doing some such busy work, as if to suggest, if all people would be just like *her*, the world would be a nicer, cleaner, more efficient place.

The Dunns went to church—the same kind that I went to, in the city. The building was smaller, of course, and not as lofty, but it was sharply clean and bright—just like the other. Aunt Anne was just as concerned as my mother had been about my physical presentation when we went to church, though, to tell you the truth, Aunt Anne created a far more pleasing result: she was more detail oriented, and my clothes were fresher and much more attractive than those provided by my mother. She also supervised my bathing and cleanliness procedures, and washed my curly hair in scented soap and brushed and combed the curls until they shone. I did not lack physical care when I lived with my aunt and uncle. I was given sufficient food and put into clothes that fit and wore well, and a doctor saw me from time to time. And I went to church with the family. As far as Uncle Charles and Aunt Anne were concerned, they did their duty, and no one could possibly ask them to do more.

I tried to do my duty, too. I tried to fit in.

Friend, that is probably one of the hardest things in the world to do—trying to fit in where you are definitely not wanted. Nothing ever goes right in a situation like that. Even You—dear Jesus—You were deserted by everyone when You were to die for the agitation Your Message caused—but at least You knew why. I was a child, and I did not know why. Everyone wanted to do the 'right thing,' except possibly my cousin Anne, but the 'right thing' wasn't enough. There was no compassion—no love. Just a smoldering, tired resentment. However, my mother showed signs she felt that, too. I wondered, would I be like that when I grew up?

It was not a cheerful prospect. And then it was I began to wonder if I should have been born at all, since my presence seemed to cause such anger and misery to the people who had charge of me. If I had not been there, they would have been happier, relieved. I wondered if God felt that way. Perhaps He would strike me down with some sort of illness, and take me away. Deep down, below the conscious of my thinking mind, I wondered if I was too dirty and trashed to live. But that was something I really wasn't aware of—not really.

I went to school, and to church. I studied, and learned, and did what I was told to do. When Cousin Anne or the other children shouted insults at me, I ignored them. When Aunt Anne got impatient and hasty with me, as she often did, I tried to overlook it and minimize my contact with her. On very rare occasions Uncle Charles spared me a kind word or two, such as complimenting my progress in school, but he was a very busy man and even his own children did not see that much of him.

The 1920's were a fast-paced time, full of big business, 'progress' and wild living, although the town in which I lived leaned more towards 'genteel' behavior, so the drugstore did not openly dispense anything condusive to 'fast' celebrations. Liquor was drunk on the sly, in garages and basements. Dinner parties were accompanied by water and tea and 'soft drinks,' and no one got out of hand. I did see how the young people behaved, though. During the warmer months people left all the windows open as the bungalows they lived in were usually very warm. I shared a front bedroom with Cousin Anne, and when Aunt Anne raised the windows I could see a lot of the neighborhood activity from my cot, both during the day and at night. The house next door, separated from our yard only by oak trees and a metal hurricane fence, housed two teenagers, and many parties took place there. The front porch was very large, and contained a swing, and many nights found the porch covered with noisy, gleeful young people. They smoked and talked loudly, their fresh, sleek faces glowing under the single light bulb that centered in the wooden porch ceiling. Sometimes a boy and a girl would edge off into a darker shadowy area of the porch, and began kissing. The kisses were no peck on the cheek, either—long, drawn-out kisses accompanied by giggling and unintelligeable words. Aunt Anne would have been shocked.

I did find the young girls' clothes interesting, though. At night the young women glittered and shone: sequined headbands encasing the bobbed hair and expansive foreheads, glittering short sleeveless dresses, with feathers at the shoulders, and shiny beads. Lots of beads. I never knew dresses could come in so many colors and patterns, and I also wondered how the women became so thin. Underneath the feathers and the sequins, the thick makeup and the short, tight hairstyles, there seemed to be very little of an actual woman.

The boys didn't seem to mind. They whooped and hollered; drove the painted-up girls recklessly through the shaded town streets in their roadsters, and honked at everyone in sight. It was though everybody wanted to show off, to be wild and daring, and to live in a continuous party. America was a great country, was it not? Anyone who was worth something could make a pile of money—if they did it just right. Life was supposed to be fun—why not live it, and look out for opportunities. Especially since the stock market was now going great.

That's how the people around me lived. That's how my uncle lived. That's how my Cousin Anne intended to live. Even in first grade, she was far more interested in her physical appearance and her effect on the opposite sex than she was in her lessons. Oddly enough, this did not seem to put out either her teacher or her mother—both of them were apparently proud of her precociousness, and her mother had her hair bobbed and made sure she wore the most stylish clothes to be had. Proudly she flaunted her dresses in the classroom, to the admiring classmates, both boys and girls, and when, one day, she decided to dance up on the teacher's desk, like she heard happened at club parties, the teacher was not angry at all. She laughed and said Anne Dunn was a true winner, and the world would hear of her yet.

She never said that about me. I didn't expect her to, and I was happy just to pass the tests and go to the next grade. That I did without fail, and I was in fact ahead of nearly all the students, including Anne. But that was expected of me, as I was so much older. It was pointed out that I 'did not make friends easily,' although it was never observed, or mentioned, that Cousin Anne effectively took care of that. She decided, for whatever reason, that she didn't want me to have friends, and as far as she was concerned, what she wanted, she got. The authorities seemed to think I was at fault for not being able to combat this. But I really didn't know how I could.

Anyway, I was very busy, and it was unlikely I could have spent much time with a friend. Second grade was a little easier on me— Anne and I were put in separate classes, and the teacher was new, and not well acquainted with the Dunns. Without Anne's influence, the children in the second grade class were less hostile toward me, and I was actually able to converse with a few of them. I kept this low key, not wanting to attract Cousin Anne's attention and spitefulness, but, as I said, I had little time to indulge in friendships. I worked very hard at home, and I wanted to keep up with my school work, so when the time came I would become a schoolteacher....."

Teresa lifted her head, slowly becoming aware of the cool surroundings of her quiet, homey bedroom. It was so familiar, and so comforting. Here she lived with Bill, here she rested, here she studied and graded her papers. Her old-fashioned mahogany dresser, with its large center mirror, was home to her trifles and costume jewelry, and the area around it exuded her perfume—Chanel no. 5. Bill's discarded clothing hung over one of the chenielle-covered chairs, and his belts and shoes filled the closet. From the other rooms, she could hear the boisterous conversation of her two teenagers.

Her teenagers needed her—were glad of her presence, even though they never said so, but their actions toward her showed it very plainly. Her husband needed her. So did her students, in a way. She was able to understand and accept that she was needed—that she was wanted, and her contributions were of great value to the people around her. But truly, she had taken this all for granted. It was grace and grace alone that had placed her into a loving family, with concerned parents and supportive friends. Because of her work experience she knew not everyone enjoyed such blessings. But never had it been so forcefully shown to her before.

"Rachel, why did you not come to me?" she could not help asking aloud. "I would have been your friend—I never would have turned on you. Rachel, I have seen and heard a lot. I raised two daughters to adult womanhood. I would have understood."

However, she knew in her heart that Rachel never could have trusted even her. To be fair to Rachel, if she had anything particular to say at all, she would seek out Teresa. She trusted Teresa that much. But friendship was out of the question. Rachel had not felt safe, and did not attempt to try it. How could she? Nothing in her experience enabled her to do so, and to be close was dangerous, too. But because she was not able to become close to people, she was desperately unhappy. Teresa sensed this—so had Reverend Mayfield.

In the coldness, Teresa placed the manuscript in the hatbox, and put it away for the time being. She would take it down again soon—that she knew. But now she was tired, and would turn in for the night.

Chapter 10

A FEW NIGHTS LATER TERESA DID take down the hatbox, and found the place in the manuscript where she left off. It was still February, with cold, short days, and interminable nights, and it was an evening when Bill was on evening patrol.

She found the place by the paperclip which she fastened on the page read most recently. This page began –

"Not only was I expected to help Aunt Anne and do my school lessons properly, but I was to take part in church like a proper Christian girl. To Aunt Anne, that meant going to Mass regularly, observing the holidays and Lent, and taking part in church work. I know this is not a nice reflection on Aunt Anne, but I'm not sure 'love thy neighbor' registered very strongly on her conscience; however, she *was* a fountain of good works. She took part in every church bake sale and bazaar possible, and she—in her spare time, between family duties—knitted and sewed for the poor, and for unwed mothers. She organized and gave speeches for charities, and she assisted as a volunteer for womens' benevolent groups. When I wasn't doing my homework, I helped her. She showed me how to sew and knit, and how to cook meals for bereaved families. She never thanked me for my help, nor praised me for it; but I learned many useful things for the future. I also learned from her how to save and budget money.

Church was probably the only familiar thing to me in my new life. Of course the church building was different, being much smaller and built of white-painted wooden planks, but it still had stained-glass windows and shining, polished wooden pews. The altar was bright with gold patens and brilliant candles and highly-colored cloth. The priest was a man I did not know, but the liturgy was the same, and I followed it carefully, knowing that Aunt Anne was paying close attention to my behavior in church. She intended that I should grow up to be good, and that meant decorous and properly responsive actions in public, especially in church.

Another thing was the same in this church as in the other: I was assured of my own terrible wickedness.

You—my Friend—Jesus—You suffered and died on the cross for my wickedness—my deep, evil sin. I know this is true; I know it even now, my dear Friend—but back then I did not know—You loved me so! In those stained-glassed windowed edifices, bright, shining, and sharply clean, they did not tell me that. They only told me of my deep sin and Your bitter sufferings. They told me I could not approach You directly; I must go to Your mother Mary for intercession or that I must go to a priest. I was so evil, I was told. And I knew I couldn't come before You with my broken, filth-ravaged body; I was not pure and I could never hope to be so in Your eyes. I went every week to the beautiful house of God Your Father—and my Father, too! But I never received comfort of any knowledge that I was anything other than an abominable, sinful being.

It was odd. Uncle Charles and Aunt Anne attended the same church that I did, and heard the same words—and so did my cousin Anne. But it did not seem to affect any one of them the same way that it did me, for they lived their lives as though they were not even aware they were sinners. Perhaps they felt their respectability covered all. Perhaps it did. Aunt Anne went about her business at home—I never ever saw her pray, although she did have a rosary among her jewelry. She was very, very busy, and had so much to do, and I doubt she considered herself wicked or in need of saints' intervention. She was good and did what she was supposed to do, and she made sure I followed in her footsteps. When I was old enough I began my spiritual training, as all my same-age acquaintances did, the boys learning to become acolytes. But it was all practical training and by rote. I learned again what I already knew—that I was a miserable sinner, who caused Your death, and that there things I must do, and things I must not do. I must not do mortal sin, or I would go to hell. And I must do penance, and say prayers, and do what I was told to do, or I would never be acceptable to God.

That was what I learned about You, Friend. I never met You— they did not introduce me to You. They only taught me *of* You, and taught me to fear You.

So that was how I lived my life for some years. I went to school, I went to church, and I worked for Aunt Anne whenever she needed me. I was learning everything a 'good girl' should know, and I was expected to behave and be grateful. I hoped I behaved: I'm not sure I was grateful. I was no longer still in the same class with Cousin Anne, but she was still a formidable factor in my life. She barely tolerated me, but I had to share a room with her, and that was becoming increasingly uncomfortable. Even though the 'good girl' image was imposed upon me, it was not expected of her; and she continued to dress and act in her daring way, although in such a way that it brought approval from her elders, rather than censure.

We both entered the third grade, and again in separate classes. When I saw her it was on the playground or at lunch, and she never acknowledged me. She was usually surrounded by boys, even at that early age, and she basked in the attention. Her small head already tilted in that sophisticated leer, she showed off her attractive dresses and sleek, waved brown hair. My hair would never do that. It was always curly, and could never be straightened, and besides, Aunt Anne didn't want me out there 'showing off.' I did wonder about the inconsistency but I didn't question it. After all, Cousin Anne belonged here—I didn't.

The year passed by: Calvin Coolidge—'Silent Cal'—had been our President for some time now, and the stock market was great. Everyone was making a fortune—everyone who was worth something, anyway. Roadsters plowed through the 'hard roads' in our neighborhood, the drivers honking appreciatively at the sparsely dressed girls, who hooted and hollered back. Things were much the same. Then March rolled around.

Late in that month, Uncle Charles came home, looking perturbed and worried. I was in the dining room, carefully setting the table, making sure the salt and pepper shakers were full, the gravy boat placed properly, and the napkins folded at each place. He was holding a newspaper.

'What is it, Charles?' Aunt Anne was asking. I continued to lay the table.

'It missed us—missed us by a country mile! But how can you be prepared for such a thing? There's no way to know—not even from the radio.' Aunt Anne and Uncle Charles had a huge radio in the living room—a carved affair with cloth speakers and a fancy tuning dial. I was never allowed to touch it.

'What is it?' Aunt Anne asked again.

'A real act of God,' Uncle Charles replied. 'Nothing like it ever before. Like I said, it missed us. But how could you stop such a thing--?' He, the powerful money-making businessman, felt clearly betrayed. Aunt Anne read the newspaper. After an initial gasp (I even saw her cross herself) she turned to her husband. 'Don't worry about it, Charles,' she said. 'Like you said, it missed us by a country mile. You can get together with Taylor and some of your other men and organize a Red Cross drive. We can send the money to the stricken towns and make sure they get what they need. It's not likely to happen ever again. Not one that bad, anyway.'

Little Charles, now six years old, walked into the dining room and piped up, 'What's not that bad?'

'Oh, darling, there was a bad tornado, up in Illinois. It killed a thousand people.'

'A *what*?'

'A tornado. It's a bad whirlwind, that comes out of a cloud and knocks things down and carries things away.'

'But not here?'

'Not here, darling.'

I finished with the dining room table. It was very neat and perfectly straight, just the way Aunt Anne wanted it, and all the polished silverware and crystal glass sparkled in the lamplight, set off by the pure white tablecloth. It was dark outside—evening had already set in—and I went into the kitchen to help Aunt Anne bring in the food. By then Uncle Charles told all he knew about the tornado—it had gone through three states and stayed on the ground for three-and-a-half hours, and it was a mile wide most of the time. Nothing like that had ever happened before in known history. But I was later to find out that a thousand deaths due to the storm was a greatly exaggerated figure. Still, the actual total of 695 deaths was mind-boggling enough, and most of the survivors spoke of how they were caught by surprise, the tornado was moving so fast.

We were all rather disturbed. Uncle Charles talked about little else at the dinner table, and Aunt Anne repeated to him that they should do something to help the Red Cross. I think Cousin Anne was the most scared of all, judging from her actions toward me beginning the next day at school. At least, that's the only thing I can think of, that caused her to go so completely spiteful and mean, even for her.

All the third grade classes recessed together, but Cousin Anne never deigned to notice me at all, so I could usually go about my business unmolested. This morning was rather different, for no one could talk about anything *but* the tornado. In 1925, when this happened, the Weather Bureau was not allowed to mention the word 'tornado'—especially not in weather forecasts. It was only a few years ago they were allowed to mention it now. Tornadoes did happen, and everyone knew it, but most of them came and went quickly, usually disappearing in five to ten minutes. The magnitude of the Missouri-Illinois-Indiana tornado was unheardof, and people were edgy. It was not only big, and fast, and long-lived, and dangerous—but it struck very suddenly, and the many towns in its path had had no warning.

Anne must have been shaken up. But she decided to 'project' her fears onto me—in front of all my classmates.

When we were both on the playground, I did not notice her, as was usual. But suddenly, she noticed me.

'There she is! There's the big scaredy cat!' she called out, pointing fingers at me. 'Rachel is a big scaredy cat! She's scared of the tornado!'

I was stunned to silence, the attack was so unexpected. That was probably not the best reaction, but in truth, there were not a lot of choices for me, and the ones I did have were not good ones. If I retaliated, her friends would be on me in a second, and then when the authorities found out, I would automatically be judged at fault. Doing nothing was not the best thing, but I do not know what else I could have done.

'Yeah!' she continued to taunt, for the benefit of her appreciative audience, 'when Dad told us about the tornado, Rachel shrieked and started to cry and Mom had to shake her to calm her down. Mom said she was such a baby, but what do you expect with poor kids like her? She was screaming and carrying on, and we had such a time with her!'

None of this was even remotely true. I didn't know what possessed Cousin Anne to come up with all this rigamarole, unless she was frightened herself. I shook my head, said aloud, 'That's a lie!' and turned my back on her. I walked away, listening to her taunting laugh blended with the laughter of her friends, and I was glad when the end-of-recess bell rand, and that I would go to a separate class from Anne.

However, Anne found it all very entertaining, and she wasn't going to let the matter drop. It brought her admiration and a sense of power, and nothing pleased her more than feeling she was superior to someone else. It got so bad I could not go to recess without being verbally attacked, taunted, and laughed at. Since I was so tired, anyway, from hard work both at home and at school, I finally became fed up with it. After school was over I went into the bedroom I shared with Anne, put my schoolbooks under the cot on the polished hardwood floor, and waited for her. When she flounced in a few minutes later, I said,

'From now on, you leave me alone at recess. I don't want to hear anymore about the tornado, or about me being scared of it. From now on, you leave me alone!'

'Or you'll what?' she smirked, flipping her skirts around dismissively.

That did it. I became enraged, jumped off the cot, reached over, and swatted that twitching, shameless little bottom as hard as I could. She shrieked and yelled, 'Mom! Mom! Get in here quick! Rachel's hitting on me! She's hurting me!' Aunt Anne appeared in a second and demanded to know what was going on. I did not know what to say or do. I *had* struck Anne, and was surprised I did it, but to explain why would have been impossible. Aunt Anne would never believe that Anne was bothering me during recess or that she would have done anything that deserved my hitting her. The net result was that I got into serious trouble and was banished from Anne's room: my cot was set up in a corner of the living room, and I was told to leave Anne strictly alone. I was glad to do so; I never wanted much to do with her in the first place.

It was, on balance, lucky for me that I wasn't banished from the Dunns' home altogether. I could have been, but I think Aunt Anne looked at things from a practical point of view. I was doing many things for her that she would have to pay a servant to do for her, and besides, I had learned her way of doing things, which she would have to teach all over again to someone else. I didn't have to worry about taunts on the playground, either. Cousin Anne was told to leave me strictly alone at school—not one word, no matter on what subject. So she was effectively silenced, at least in public, although I knew she whispered things to her friends about me, and there was nothing I could do about that. I knew Aunt Anne's opinion of me, too—no good could ever come of Cindy's child—what can one expect of white trash—it's no good to try to help *some* people—see what happens when you do---?

But things settled down after a while. I went silently about my business, and Cousin Anne stayed out of my way…."

"Good for you, Rachel!" Teresa was saying in her mind, "good for you! If any daughter of *mine* ever acted like your Cousin Anne, I would have swatted her myself. But these things do happen, Rachel. I know it must not have been easy for you."

It was so hard, to know what was right in a situation like that. Teresa had learned many things in her work in the slums, and one rule on the street was, "might makes right." Rachel's home with the

Dunns was not exactly a slum scenario, but as she herself wrote, she had no good choices, and she knew it. She had no business hitting Anne, but why didn't Anne do the decent thing and leave her alone? Sure, Anne probably resented her presence, but Rachel was there by her parents wishes, and she should have respected that. The high road would have been the true Christian way—Anne could have made friends with Rachel—could have been kind to her.

In any case, Rachel's statement that her utility in the Dunns' home saved her was probably a true one. The older Anne Dunn *was* getting her money's worth out of Rachel, and she knew it. Teresa recalled the day she went into Rachel's house, to collect and pack her personal items. The house was certainly spotless, and nothing was out of place. Rachel had been trained quite well. If nothing else, at least she got that from her stay with the Dunns.

Teresa moved the paper clip up, and put the papers back into the hatbox. She reflected that Rachel certainly had shown some spirit, which Teresa was never sure she had. But of course she did. She was a good woman, and lived her life bravely and well, given her circumstances. She had not been happy, though. Teresa grieved for her, now more than ever. As she put the hatbox away, she vowed she would be more sensitive to the people around her, as she went through life's daily routine.

Chapter 11

MARCH WAS NEARLY GONE. THE WINTER was slowly releasing its chill grip upon the lengthening days, and the sun peeped out more often, blessing the new buds and fresh greenery with its golden beams. The air was still cold, but it held promise, and songbirds flew in for their first claim of territory, filling the days with their melodies. Dr. Hinton and Mrs. Anderson could tell the seasons were changing simply from the sounds of the students at recess: during the cold days they were huddled against the brick walls of the school, and played subdued games; but now they began to shriek and shout and run across the fenced schoolyard. The schoolyard lawn showed changes, too; the grass took on a fresh green hue, and the purple-dotted greenery of chickweed appeared everywhere, along with clover. The sun was doing its best to warm the school grounds, and the children responded with new faith and renewed activity.

It was still cool, but the spring brightness suggested yellow daffodils and Easter egg hunts. The children, looking forward to summer vacation, found it hard to concentrate on the classwork, and Dr. Hinton did have an increase in traffic headed to his office. But he expected that—it happened that way every year, and he was an old hand at dealing with unruliness. It was fortunate, too, that it was a small town, and he knew most of the children and their families by name. The parents usually helped to enforce discipline, and because he had such a strong network to make sure the rules remained law, he was able to find time and energy to introduce school programs that made use of the children's abundant energy.

These programs included sports: softball, volleyball, and the field sports competition day. Then there were music programs—band, singing, and music theory training. The school also had a drama class, and an art class. Most of Dr. Hinton's staff were experienced, long-term teachers, who organized and led the programs year after year, with excellent results. The children could take part in the programs, which made the latter half of the school year more fun and exciting. And then there was the unofficial Easter egg hunt.

While the school did not actually sponsor it, it was organized by several teachers and parents from the school, and took place in the city park the Saturday morning before Easter Day. It was a happy time. In the best of circumstances, the sun was shining, and the park was bright with spring flowers, fresh grass, and fully-leafed deciduous trees, and the eggs were dyed with many interesting colors. Some eggs were colored plastic, with candy placed inside. A few eggs were "special" eggs—plastic eggs with paper instructions within—telling the finder to go to the main booth to pick up a special prize. The Easter egg hunt was a time for the children to play games, also, and for families to visit and catch up on gossip and family events. Kool-Aid, cookies, sandwiches, and potato chips were provided, and the children ran about in casual clothes, shouting, whooping and hiding behind the trees, while the parents and teachers sat in groups, quietly talking and watching the children play.

Teresa Anderson, one of the organizers for the Easter egg hunt of this year, saw that everything was going according to plan, and took her place at one of the wooden picnic tables beneath a huge red oak tree. The red oak, along with several trees around it, had electric outdoor lights fastened to the trunks and branches, and power lines hung all around, as the fresh leaves flapped next to them. As it was a very clear day, and sunlight filled the park, the lights were not needed, of course. Teresa watched the students at their noisy play, and she remembered last year. She had been there last year, too—and so had Rachel been. In fact, Rachel sat with her. She hadn't said much, but she sat with her. Come to think of it, Rachel had done much of the busy work at last year's picnic, and this year the sponsors did not have her help. It was very much missed. Even one of Teresa's fellow colleagues, who helped every year with the Easter egg hunt, remarked upon the lack. Rachel's help had been unobtrusive, but it had been very thorough.

Teresa sat quietly, and rested, for she had worked very hard that morning. She wore a sunhat, a casual shirt, shorts, and sandals, and felt rather underdressed, although all her coworkers and the parents were dressed the same way. As she leaned against the oak tree next to the picnic table, she heard sudden very noisy hoots and hollers from the children, and she knew something unusual was going on. She looked up to see what it was—and saw Bill, in full uniform, walking across the park lawn, while the kids oohed and aahed, looking at his uniform and his patrol car with reverence and some nervousness.

"Watch out, he's gonna arrest somebody," shouted one daring student. There was a few nervous titters, and another kid yelled, "Nah, he just wants some Easter candy!"

Laughter broke through the ranks. The children grouped around Bill as he strode across the park, and a few stared at his badge and asked some questions about his gun. He gave them straightforward answers, and when some of the students asked about jail cells, he discussed that, too. Then one bold sixth-grader said, "How come you're here, Mr. Anderson? You're not going to arrest us, are you? We're being good."

Bill laughed. "No, I'm not going to arrest anyone. I've come to see my girl."

Some of the younger students were pop-eyed. "You have a *girl*, Officer Anderson?"

"Why, sure I do," he replied. "She's right here with you all. I can see her now."

"Yeah, I know who she is," said one of the more rambunctious fifth-graders. "She's my teacher, Mrs. Anderson. She's over there at the picnic table. Hey, Mrs. Anderson!" He raised his voice. "You're in trouble! Now a policeman's coming to arrest you!"

"Oh, he did that a long time ago," observed a wiseacre parent. "He's had her under house arrest for years. Now he's making sure she isn't violating parole."

Teresa blushed a little, and welcomed her approaching husband with a smile. He looked her over, glanced at her face under the sunhat, and whispered, "Are you doing all right out here with these wild Indians? Are they behaving, or do they need a little law enforcement?" Teresa smiled again, and said everything was going just fine. All the eggs had been found, the prizes given out, and most of the food had been eaten. The children were now participating in various games all across the park lawn—some had brought balls and jump ropes and other sports accommodation, so nearly everyone was occupied. The hunt had been a success.

The Andersons walked together to Bill's patrol car, and they soon found themselves in a gathering of curious children. They wanted to look at the equipment in the car, and Bill took time to explain how it all worked. The children were impressed.

Bill was then ready to leave, to continue his rounds, and several of the children shouted, "Bye, Officer Anderson!" as the patrol car pulled away. The morning was about gone, and a few of the teachers and parents began to clear away the paper plates and cups that were strewn across the wooden tables. The Easter egg hunt was officially over, but many of the older children would stay in the park, to play softball and ride bicycles and visit with friends. The day was clear and beautiful, just right for outdoor activities, and the children were determined to take full advantage of it, especially since they would have church tomorrow and school on Monday.

Teresa loaded the supplies she had brought with her into the backseat of her red '57 Plymouth, and she started for home. Bill would be working all day, but he would be home that evening, and he would be able to attend Easter services with her the next morning, with Billy and Mandy. She cruised through the familiar town streets, shaded by now thickly-leaved trees, and she glanced at the old, well-worn houses, as she drove by. She knew most of the occupants of the houses, and taught the children of more than a few of them.

She turned onto the street where she lived, crossing the intersection that had a 4-way stop sign layout. The street was red brick, the curbs plain concrete, and a telephone pole on one of the corners acted as a streetlight pole as well—a long cantilever held a radial wave light fixture directly over the intersection. On that corner was a small house with tan bricks, striped awnings over the windows, and a silver-painted fireplug in the front yard. Next to that house was a white frame house, with wooden green shutters. Then Rachel's house—the red brick one. No one lived there, yet. Teresa occasionally saw the landlord working in the front yard, keeping everything neat and tidy, but he had not rented the place out so far. Teresa faintly wondered why. The house was as clean and well-repaired as a house could be, and even though the landlord was rather crude and oafish, Teresa knew the rate he was asking for the house was not a bit unreasonable. Rachel once mentioned what she was paying, and it was a perfectly acceptable amount. It was true Rachel had died, but she had not died *there*—she had been miles away. The house had been empty for around nine months now, which was a long time, in this particular neighborhood.

Two house more, and Teresa was home. She pulled onto the concrete-and-gravel driveway, and got out to unload the leftover goods from the hunt. She had a bag of candy and half a sack of plastic Easter eggs—Billy and Mandy would make quick work of both in a heartbeat. She had brought paper plates, cups, and napkins, and there was enough left of each to save for future parties. She folded the checked tablecloths and put them away, and put away the wicker baskets. A few more things—and everything was done. She had graded the students' papers the night before, and her shopping was caught up—she had Easter dinner planned, and her supplies ready. The house was in order, too; except for the children's bedrooms, and she declared to them firmly that the rooms were *their* problem—if the Health Department ever showed up at the doorstep, Teresa said, the kids would be answering to them—she wouldn't be. But there was nothing really for her to do now, for a few hours, anyway. Later she would be cooking dinner, but nothing demanded her immediate attention. She could have watched TV, but preferred not to. She usually didn't have time, and most of the programs seemed to her rather silly.

It had been a fun day, though. The weather had been perfect, and the children had had a tremendous amount of fun. The only thing she could have wished to have different was the presence of Rachel Evanson. She had missed her. And so had others. As quiet as she had been, she was a great help when events such as this one took place. "Now I understand why," Teresa thought to herself. "Rachel, I know your Aunt Anne used you as a servant. But she did teach you things. Things that enabled you to become a blessing for *us*—for the students and the other teachers. *We* appreciated you, even if your Aunt Anne didn't. I wished I had told you so. But surely you knew it."

If she had, she had given no indication, she was so shy. As Teresa got to know her better, she wondered whether it would have done any good to tell her, even if she were alive. She was not only shy, she was likely fearful of any contact. She had been brutally used, and then rejected, and made to feel unwelcome. It occurred to Teresa that she did not make close friends because her emotions were in fact too damaged to sustain a normal friendship.

It was a sad thought, but Teresa resolved to keep reading Rachel's words. Not today. But after Easter Sunday, when the excitement tapered off, Teresa would look. There was still much more to read, and maybe it wasn't all bad....

The church was filled to capacity, as it always was on Easter Sunday, and the pulpit was covered in white lilies, that gave off a noticeable fragrance throughout the sanctuary. The organist played the processional numbers as the members of the congregation filed in, most of them dressed in the brightest colors to be had. The men were in business suits, white dress shirts and highly-colored ties, and the women wore flowered crinoline dresses and decorated hats, and they added their best jewels and pearls for the occasion. The children were well-dressed, too, although they sported everyday manners—they ran around the church foyer and made noise, until stopped by their displeased parents. It was the most cheerful day on the Christian church calendar, but still, decorous behavior was expected, and the children knew they would be sitting through a long service.

Bill and Teresa Anderson were swept into the crowd, with Billy and Mandy in tow, all four brightly dressed, in honor of the day. The pews were not usually crowded on any given Sunday morning, but today the Andersons had to squeeze into the edge of a long, polished wood bench toward the back of the church. Mandy wore one of the new slim skirts that were made popular by Jackie Kennedy, and she didn't seem to mind being crushed against the end of the pew, but Teresa's pastel full skirt, buoyed up by starched petticoats, was practically in Bill's lap. Billy was crammed next to an elderly woman who was evidently visiting from out of town, and the smirk on his face told better than words how he felt about the situation. Teresa found herself hoping the family would survive the service. She was glad to be in church, to celebrate the resurrection, but Easter was always a crowded affair.

The service began—the congregation sang "Christ the Lord Has Risen Today" and the organ barely covered the many voices. The sun shone through the stained-glass windows, bringing out the brilliant reds, blues and yellows of the thick panes, and even though the church was full, a spirit of joyousness began to spread through the crowd, and it finally became a service of celebration and thanksgiving. The preacher, who had been the senior pastor of the church for so long that he was practically part of the furniture, was suddenly empowered with words of beauty and conviction, as he spoke of the Resurrection and its meaning for the people who sat before him, listening. Christ had arisen, allelujah! Even when spoken by the creaking, white-haired old preacher, the message was still as powerful. Christ had risen; the grave could not keep Him down. He died for the sins of all, and now He rose again. The tomb was empty. And on the Easter morning, and many Easter mornings like it, for two thousand years, the people celebrated the Resurrection, knowing, they, too, would rise again, when the Savior came to claim His own.

The vested choir sang two anthems, the Lord's Supper was given, and the prayers said. The sun was very bright now, and the organ rang out triumphantly as the congregation dispersed, covering nearly the entire church grounds as they greeted one another before going to their cars. The Andersons finally piled into the red Plymouth, and Billy was allowed to drive back, while his father sat in the back seat with Mandy. Teresa had more work to do when they reached home: she had put a ham in the oven to slow-bake, and she had to cook the vegetables as well. She had already laid out the dining room table, with a white damask tablecloth, candles, and the formal silverware, before they went to church. Now she took out the ham, which was done to a turn, put in some rolls, and finished the green beans and sweet potatoes. It was a rush job, as usual; but she was experienced and soon the table was loaded with a savory holiday feast. Her family was highly appreciative when they came in to eat.

That afternoon, when she went to her bedroom for a quick nap, Bill followed her in. She was a little surprised, for he usually watched TV on Sunday afternoon if he was not on patrol duty. But apparently he had something special to say to her. And she was surprised to hear what he had to say.

"You're doing very well, Ter," he said. "Keep it up. I know it's hard for you right now. But we do notice, and I think you're doing a splendid job. You cared about Rachel, didn't you?"

Teresa was completely taken aback, but she nodded.

"She cared about you, too," said Bill. "She really did. She didn't show it much, but—well, Ter, you're a teacher. You know how it is. You see all kinds, like I do. But Preacher was right this morning, when he said Jesus died and rose again for *all of us*. Don't worry about Rachel. Jesus loved her—and she knew it, too. I know you're sad for her loss—you can't help that—but don't worry about her."

He was now sitting on the bed beside her, and he took her in his arms. He gave her a strong, drawn-out kiss, holding her head with both hands, and then he let her go, placing her under the sheets. "You get some rest now," he said, smoothing the covers. "Tonight I'm going to be back in here—and I expect for you to be waiting for me." She smiled—even laughed a little, and Bill seemed pleased. They had been married for nearly twenty-eight years, and had four children, and still—it seemed too naughty to her to even be decent. That did make it exciting, though. She began to feel a little better.

She rested quietly, in the still bedroom on that sunny Easter afternoon, and she thought of the things she had been taught about Jesus, and about God, over the years she had been to church. With her, it had been fairly straightforward. She had been raised in the best Southern Baptist tradition, and knew all about "being saved." She had also been a strong Bible reader, so she knew about the Scriptures. She knew the significance of Easter Day.

But what of Rachel? What was her experience? And Teresa knew *she* could find out…..

Chapter 12

BILL WAS ON PATROL, AND EVENING had fallen. The days were longer and warmer, and Teresa had enjoyed the extra daylight. She had planted her annuals, and then graded her papers, as the sunset faded past the curtained windows. That done, she made sure Billy and Mandy were at home, and then she went to her closet to take down the hat box. She found the paperclip, and set it aside. She read—

"I stayed busy, and Cousin Anne ignored me. She was too occupied to worry about me, anyway, as she was already interested in the attentions of boys, even though she was only ten years old. She flirted terribly, and the boys flocked around her, even some of the sixth-grade boys who didn't usually notice younger girls. She enjoyed it all, and did just enough schoolwork to get by. I overheard her teacher say to another teacher that it really didn't matter whether she did well with her lessons, because she had found true success—social popularity. She knew how to make herself attractive to the people who mattered, and because of that, she would always be successful. At the time, I wondered if that were true—success for a woman was defined differently from success for a man, especially in those days. Besides, I was being taught something different at church. There I was told a woman must be modest, pure and holy, and her mind must not run upon relations with the opposite sex. I was confused.

I had no reason to disbelieve that Cousin Anne would have a bright future. She would marry when she was of age, and marry well: from the way things were shaping up she would have a wide choice of suitors. Her husband would be a handsome man, and he would make plenty of money: I could not see Anne married to a poor man, or to one who lacked her father's drive in the business world. As for me, marriage was unthinkable. I had reason to believe, from the hints of women who went to my church and who taught me, that eligible men preferred pure women when they sought a spouse. I did not qualify. But in my very deepest heart I was saddened: I wished I could be loved by a man when I grew up, like I knew Anne would be, but such a thing could not be thought of. In many ways, I was not good enough to hope for marriage.

I was still very young, though. And when I was not quite twelve years old, a new priest took his place at our parish church.

From the very beginning I was taught to properly reverence each priest I met, for the priest was the special servant of God, and the gateway to the Heavenly Presence. Priests were special: they were set apart. One must never question or criticize or condemn them. One must always do what a priest says. To do otherwise invited the wrath of God, especially if one was not in a state of grace. When I saw Father John for the first time, I felt he would be easy to love and obey: he was young and very handsome, with dark, smooth hair, and crystal blue eyes. His voice was gentle; almost caressing; and when he heard confession he was very kind, and pronounced absolution in the gentlest of voices. The church members began to look upon him as a true saint. He looked like one, in his pure priestly robe, his dark head shining beneath the light filtering through the stain-glassed windows. It was though an angel stood there. I find it hard, now, to describe the effect he had on people. But he seemed to be very, very much like God Himself, or at least what people hoped God would be.

I was awestruck, just as much as the rest of the church members. I soon found that I thought a lot about him, and it was important to me how he noticed me, and what he thought of me. I couldn't hope that he would like me, as no one really did, but maybe—as a man of God—he would see me differently, and not be so harsh in his judgment.

I was so happy that day, when he first took notice of me—and smiled at me—a welcoming smile!

We had exchanged no words at that time, but when I left the sanctuary that day my heart was singing with happiness, and life took on a new brightness, as though things could be bearable and perhaps even joyous. I was so light-hearted that day—and I looked forward to going back to church—where I would meet the Presence in the form of His servant, Father John. I thought maybe God was smiling upon me at last. I wanted to be His servant, too, and Father John would show me how to be that, just as Aunt Anne showed me how to clean the home and cook and serve food. And how much more pleasurable it would be! Being in the service of God would be so much sweeter, for it meant so much more, and when I went to church, I paid closer attention to the words that were said of God: especially the words said by Father John.

I could not remember a happier time in my life. For the first time it seemed someone actually cared about me, for every time I went to church Father John had a smile and a kind word for me. At last I thought someone was glad of my presence, instead of just tolerating me with veiled hostility, as the Dunns did. Someone cared about me—*me*, and the man who cared about me was a man of God. I hoped that it meant God cared about me. This man was so handsome—and so young and so kind! I said to myself that Cousin Anne could have all her admirers and playground friends at recess—*I* had something far better! I saw that Father John never particularly noticed Anne when she came to church; he appeared to prefer to notice me. I told myself it was because he could see how sinful and vainglorious she actually was, while believing me to be pure and good—though I knew I wasn't. But I would never confess what had happened to me long ago—not even to him—especially not to him. Besides, I might have forgotten it.

I confessed silly sins to him, however. Those I wanted to confess to him. I wanted to be clean and good in his eyes—and in God's eyes as well. I felt the holy beauty of love, and forgiveness, when I confessed to Father John, and heard his gentle voice granting absolution. I felt so *near* to him, and I wanted to be good for him, so he would be pleased. After all, wasn't he a representative of God? Was he not the pathway to God, the intercessor, the one who forgave sins in the Father's name? My very young, untried thoughts fixed upon Father John as the way to seek out the God of the Universe. I knew I could pray to Mary, Mother of God, and was encouraged to do so, but Father John was flesh and blood, and could actually hear me. He could also respond, and I could see him and listen to his words.

Therefore I was much happier, and for the first time, I felt love.

Aunt Anne noticed I had changed, and didn't know what to make of it, but as long as I did my chores and my homework—which I did—she didn't ask questions—she really didn't have time to be concerned with me, as she was very busy. Little Charles and Jane were both growing up, and she had to tend to their needs, and there was Uncle Charles' career to think about as well. She had her hands full, and was not interested in what was going on in my mind. My job was to lighten her heavy load without bringing in any problems or inconveniences that would disrupt the efficient functioning of her family. Hopefully I did that; I believe that I did, but I could not keep my head out of the clouds. Aunt Anne *was* glad I was taking more of an interest in attending church.

'Maybe you'll start learning to get along better with people,' she commented. I could think of no relevant reply to this statement.

I did hear at one time—I don't remember when, to be honest—that I could take any doubt, any problem, to a priest, and receive Godly counsel. I thought of that. Could I—would I dare? After all, I did have problems. The Dunns and the teachers—usually Cousin Anne's teachers—harped on the fact that I 'didn't get along with others' and maybe if I took this problem to Father John, he would help me find a way to be more agreeable. He seemed interested in me, and surely he would want to hear me. I would take his advice, whatever it was, and perhaps I would be changed for the better, and then I would have friends and people would love me. It was a dizzying thought.

One Sunday, at church, I slipped away from the Dunns, and sought out Father John. As I walked up to him, his face lit up in a welcoming smile, and I timidly asked if I could see him for a few minutes. 'Why, of course,' he said heartily, 'come into my office,' and he led the way. The office was dim, with two small stained glass windows, which were mostly red and blotted out all but the strongest sunlight. The hardwood floor was covered with a rag carpet, and most of the office was taken up by a large desk. Books were everywhere—some on the desk, some on wooden shelves tacked onto the beige-painted walls, and a few were stacked on the floor. I also saw the crucifix—this was usual—two old chairs and a small couch, and in the far corner of the room, a painting that caught my eye.

For some reason, the sight of the painting shocked me. It was not in a prominent spot on the wall, and I had to look at it twice to make sure it was there—but it was. I wondered how it got into the office, because somehow my mental picture of Father John did not coincide with a man who would place such a painting in his work area. The painting was a nude—very classically done, and artistic, with sunshine and trees and nature all around, but a full-frontal female nude, nevertheless. It surprised me, even though I had checked out art books at the school library, and knew that the Sistine Chapel and the statue of David were examples of graphic nudity—and of Biblical subjects as well. I wondered who the painting was meant to represent—Bathsheba, or Eve, maybe?

But Father John called me to attention. 'Now, what can I do for you?' he asked. I found myself blushing.

'It-it's kind of embarrassing,' I said, twisting my hands together. 'Y-you see, Father, I live with the Dunns, but I'm not really one of their children. I-I'm a niece—of Uncle Charles. Anyway, everyone seems to think I have a problem getting along with people—Aunt Anne and some of my teachers say that, and I'd like to know what I'm doing that is wrong. They won't exactly tell me—they just say I don't behave right.'

Father John looked at me quizzically, his ice-blue eyes twinkling. 'Your name is Rachel, isn't it? Okay, Rachel, this is a serious matter. Why do *you* think you don't get along with people? Is it something you say or do?'

I tried to be truthful, and I tried to think hard. 'I don't know,' I finally said, 'I don't say that much to people, and usually, I'm doing my work—schoolwork or something to help Aunt Anne. I'm usually pretty busy. I have to make good grades to graduate from high school, and helping Aunt Anne pleases God, doesn't it?'

Father John was looking at his laced fingers, and then he turned to me. 'You know,' he said, 'Mrs. Dunn told me you struck her daughter, and that's why you are not allowed to play together. That doesn't sound very friendly to me, Rachel. The Dunns took you in, you know. If you go around hitting people you aren't going to win any popularity contests. Maybe that's why you can't get along with others.'

As much as I idolized Father John, I was stung by his words. 'I don't "go around hitting people",' I exclaimed. 'Yes, I hit her that one time. Just one time. She kept making fun of me at school, and she wouldn't stop. I asked her to stop, but she was like, "why should I?" So I gave her a reason—I hit her on the backside. It didn't cripple her or anything. I didn't really want to do it. But she just wouldn't quit.'

Already, I had a sinking feeling in my heart that Father John wasn't going to be the refuge that I hoped, but I put the thought quickly out of my mind. After all, he was a priest of God, and whatever thoughts he expressed to me were given to him directly from God. If he disapproved of me, then it meant God disapproved of me, too, and wished to let me know that. I knew I had to face it, if God were angry with me. With so many people around me insisting I was remiss in my behavior, perhaps I should believe them and try to make some changes. But what change? I couldn't behave like Cousin Anne—that I knew, even though she was much admired. What was I to do?'

'I'll tell you what, Rachel,' Father John said, looking at his watch, 'I don't have a lot of time right now. But you come by and see me this week, and we'll talk about it some more. Let's say, Thursday. Come by the church office, after school. I'll see you then.' He got up and walked out of his office, and I left, too, after one final surreptious glance at the nude painting. He proceeded to mingle with the leaving parishioners, and I set off to find Uncle Charles and Aunt Anne, who were probably looking for me, so they could go home.

If I had consulted my deepest honesty, and listened to my instinct of preservation, I would have known something was wrong. But I didn't want to believe it, nor did I want to trust myself. I wanted to believe Father John truly cared about me, that he would do what was right by me, and after all, wasn't he holy, a priest? He was the mediator between me and a wrathful, angry God. Also, He smiled at me so much, and spoke with me, and recognized me in church, when so many others would rather not acknowledge my existence at all. I was so happy, believing that he had an interest in me. And I was truly excited, that I was going to get to see him—alone! on that Thursday. I could barely stand for the week to go by, I wanted to speak with him so much...."

Teresa put the paper clip in place, and set the papers into the box. She had a deep foreboding—no, this didn't sound good at all. Rachel was, not quite twelve years old? Most of Teresa's students were a year or two younger. It was an awkward age, even under the best of circumstances. And yes, priests were seen as being more than mortal—far above the people they served. Teresa had met many priests, and in her experience, most were earnest, thoughtful, serious men of God. They helped in many ways, so many ways! But—even in this capacity, the bad apples appeared.

She almost knew what she was going to read next. She knew too much about life. But she told herself not to avoid it. After all, it was another's life—not hers, and Rachel was beyond it all, now safe in her true Father's arms. Beyond it all—for some reason, the memories of last summer came back to Teresa, when she first heard that Rachel was dead. Most of the townspeople knew only that she had died on her road trip, and was sent back to town to be buried. However, Teresa herself learned from Dr. Hinton why the funeral had been a closed-casket service. When Rachel was found, she was a skeleton—still with her brown curls around her skull and her blue dress covering her bare ribs. Teresa found herself shaking a little. She put the hatbox into the closet, and looked around thankfully at her familiar room.

"Father," she said, "thank You for surrounding me with love. All my life, Father, You have done it. Thank You so much."

It was time for bed, and she had to get up to go to her teaching the next morning. As she pulled the covers over her, and turned out the light, she thought of the Lord, and clung to Him, in her heart. She was taking nothing for granted any more.

Chapter 13

TERESA WAITED A FEW DAYS BEFORE she brought down the hatbox again. The days were longer and sunnier now, and the school year was nearly over. As summer beckoned, students prepared for the final tests, and shouted loudly during recess, glad of the warm weather and the chance to play outdoor games. All the children looked forward to the carefree days of summer vacation, with swimming, bicycle riding, camping, and other activities. Often the fifth graders came up to Teresa and told her what they would be doing once school was out, and Teresa herself looked forward to being on vacation.

School was not over yet, and still the routine went on. Teresa had much to do, but she stayed organized. And one warm night, when everything was done, she took down the hatbox. It had been such a warm day she turned on the hallway attic fan, which rumbled a little at first, stirring a bit of dust, as the ceiling slats opened. The fan was off now, but the windows were still raised. A slight breeze wafted in the thin curtains, and it was somewhat cool, as the sun was setting. Teresa could hear the usual neighborhood noises through the open windows: cars went by; young people gathered in front yards, talking and laughing, and the cicadas began to sing. The streetlight at the corner had already come on, and a few of the neighbors switched on their porch lights.

Teresa listened to the sounds of the falling evening, then turned on the reading lamp in her bedroom. She took the manuscript out of the box, with unusual nervousness, and began to read---

"Thursday finally came. I was so agitated and happy, my teacher didn't know what to make of me. I confess I didn't pay as much attention to the lessons as I should have, but I was in such a state of excitement that I couldn't concentrate. I couldn't wait for school to be over so I could run to the church. The whole time my mind ran on Father John: what would he say to me? Would he tell me God loved me? Would he show me some special way to be attractive to people so that I would finally be liked? After all, everyone loved Father John, so he knew what it took to be liked. And because he was a servant of God, he would tell me. Believe it or not, I wanted so much to be cared about! But I did not know how to get the people around me to care.

Thanks to Aunt Anne, I was always neat and clean and tidy, but today I put on my prettiest dress—at least the prettiest dress I could wear without causing disapproval from Aunt Anne. She was a stickler for propriety: a few of my dresses were only for church, and not for school. I did have a 'best' school dress, though, and I put on that. I could not do much about my hair, which curled no matter how I pinned it, so I simply ran a comb through the curls and decided nothing more could be done. I was determined to look my best. I knew Father John would want to see someone pretty, and I wanted to be that someone, as much as possible.

The end-of-school bell finally rang, and I was soon out of the school building, and on the way to the church. The weather was beautiful—sunshine and blue sky and joyousness, and I covered the ground toward the church building, in great anticipation, but nervousness, too: what if something should go wrong? But I tried to tell myself God would not allow that to happen to me. He would only do what was necessary to correct my faults, and if Father John scolded me, I probably needed scolding, to make me a better person. I wanted to hope for the best.

Finally, I reached the church building. I walked into its cool, familiar, silent majesty, and made my way to Father John's office. I was there at last.

Father John was waiting, there in the office. He was expecting me. But something didn't seem quite right. His ice-blue eyes, instead of being merry and welcoming as usual, had a strange expression in them. I could not make it out. I stood frozen at the door, and then he looked up. As though he were seeing me for the first time, he said, 'Come in, come in, have a seat.'

'Where?' I asked, looking at the two chairs and the small couch.

'Anywhere that is comfortable for you,' he said, almost by rote. But to tell you the truth, I was not comfortable at all. I sat down in one of the chairs.

Then Father John did something else that was odd: he went to the office door, shut it, and locked it. He sat down in the other chair, and looked squarely at me.

'So you have trouble getting along with people, Rachel,' he said in a voice that didn't seem quite his. 'Now, why do you think that is? Don't you try to please your Aunt Anne? Your teachers?'

'Yes, I try very hard,' I couldn't help saying. 'But they don't seem very pleased, somehow.'

'Hmmmm,' said Father John. 'Maybe your body language is saying something to them that you don't mean to say, and that's why they aren't pleased with you. Did you ever think of that, Rachel? What are your thoughts toward your Aunt Anne and your teachers? Are they really pure? Do you really *want* to please them? God can detect a lie, you know. If you have displeasure in your heart toward them, then they will know it and of course they won't be pleased with you.'

'But—but—'

'But what, Rachel? I'm trying to help you. It's all in your behavior. You need to think pure, clean thoughts about the people around you, and then you will be loved and accepted.'

Maybe this was true, but I wondered how I was to think 'pure, clean thoughts' about people who obviously had less than kindly thoughts toward me, and I was confused. I was even more confused when Father John leaned toward me and said, 'You want attention, don't you, Rachel? That's why you're acting like this. You're starved for attention. That's why you want people to "like you." You really want them to pay attention to you. That's rather selfish, when you should be wanting only to serve others. When Christ was here, He didn't think of Himself. He devoted Himself to others, completely. That's what you should do, Rachel. Stop thinking of yourself, and think only of others.'

I was shocked, but I realized the judgment was final—I was the bad one. I should never expect to be liked or loved. God didn't love me either, and He sent Father John to tell me so.

Just then, Father John rose from his chair. 'I'll tell you what,' he said, 'Since you seem to want attention so bad, I'll give you some. How about a hug, Rachel? Do you want a hug?'

I figured it was better than nothing, since I never got hugs at home, and I thought maybe it would bring Father John back to me—he had gotten away from me somehow. I held out my arms, and he came forward to embrace me.

A hug would have been all right—I needed one, as all beings needed physical affection even to survive. In fact, I was starved for physical affection—just the normal hugs a mother gives her child; the pats on the back, the affirming, "I love you." I needed all of that, and never got it. But the instant Father John's arms went around me, I knew something was wrong. For one thing, his hug was crushing—not a gentle embrace designed to transmit caring, but an almost brutal grip. Then he lifted me off my feet, and hauled me to the couch. Then I knew. He clapped his hand over my mouth so I could not cry out, then threw me on my back and yanked up my pretty dress. His motions seemed practiced—he had done this before! Still with one hand over my mouth, he expertly jerked down my panties, and he was on me—this time I was looking right into my attacker's face.

'And no one would ever believe this!' was the despairing thought that went through my mind. Father John knew this, too. He was safe. Especially no one would believe me, as unpopular as I was with my acquaintances. I could not defend myself, either—Father John was twice my size and much stronger. I knew from the other experience that he would finish up and get off of me, and that was all I could hope for. He was finally done, and got up, looking at me with the most repulsive look I had ever seen. 'You are not even a virgin!' he exclaimed.

I was in shock. I know I should have gotten out of there right then, but my mind was not working and I couldn't move. Father John pulled back up my panties with the same expertise that he took them down, and as he did so he gave me a 'shame on you!' look that I could be so little concerned about my modesty. He then followed up his actions with a barrage of criticisms I didn't even know he harbored. I don't remember everything he said, but I remembered the gist of it.

'You asked for that, Rachel,' he said. 'All that silly smirking when you saw me in church—do you know how disgusting that is? Nice women don't do that—they don't try to flirt with men, and especially not with their priests! That kind of behavior is repulsive and provocative, and that's the kind of thing that's going to get you into trouble. I knew you were going to confession just to get my attention, Rachel. You got exactly what you deserved, and I don't want to hear that you've been crying about this to anyone.'

I was barely breathing, and he went on. 'Anyway, I don't want to see or hear from you again. I don't want to see you in the confessional, and I don't want you to look at me or say anything to me at church. I want you to leave me alone. From now on, you go to confession to Father Robert.' Father Robert was the elderly priest who had the run of the church before Father John arrived.

I don't know how I got out of the office, or remembered how I did. My legs carried me toward the Dunn's house, but I couldn't see or connect with anything around me—I was in shock, and knew I had nothing to fall back on. What could I do? I managed to get into the house, and sit down on my cot, so could pull myself together. I was totally disoriented, and I was not only in pain from the attack, my body felt stiff and sore as if I had been beaten. I could barely move. I wanted to cry, but couldn't—I couldn't feel a thing except for the soreness of my body, and it was in my catatonic state that Aunt Anne later found me.

'Rachel, are you sick?' she demanded. I didn't know how to answer her.

'Uh,--no,' I finally said.

'Well, if you're not, I don't have time for you to be lolling around on the cot. Charles just called me and he's going to be bringing some men from work for dinner. They are important men and I need the place to look really good tonight. So come on, Rachel, get to work. The bathroom needs scrubbing, so get the Ajax and some rags, and clean it up. Then after you're done, wash your hands thoroughly with soap, because I'll need you in the kitchen.'

It might have been a blessing, scrubbing the bathroom. I didn't have to think—I only had to scrub, and the Ajax cleanser, in its metallic green can, smelled fresh and clean and astringent—I wished I could scrub myself with it. Bits and pieces of Father John's tirade came back to me as I worked—my behavior was disgusting, it was bad, I had asked for it—I had been pushy. But if that were true, I thought, why did Father John act so nice to me at first? When I smiled, why did he smile back? He could have let me know at the very beginning that he didn't want my company. After all, I was used to that attitude.

But I did learn something that day—don't trust anyone, especially not a man. Even if he smiles—even if he beckons—don't believe in him. He'll take what he needs to satisfy his ego, then he'll hurt you and then tell you to get out of his sight. In the end, I decided that open hostility and dislike was far preferable to 'good company manners'—it was more honest and less dangerous, and at least there wasn't any nasty surprises. I shut my thoughts down and continued to scrub the bathtub; the aroma of the cleanser was my one contact with reality, and I didn't want to think anymore….."

Teresa remembered something from her Bible studies—yes, a story of King David's family in the Old Testament. It was in the second book of Samuel, Chapter 13. King David's son Absalom had a beautiful sister Tamar, and her half-brother Amnon lusted after her. Through trickery (he enlisted the aid of his cousin Jonadab, and had his father David instruct Tamar to prepare a meal for him) he got Tamar into his bedroom. Then he raped her, and when he was done, told her to get out of his sight. Teresa reflected, there was nothing new under the sun—that was from Ecclesiastes. But the sad thing was, it was not Rachel's fault—the fault lay completely with Father John.

Teresa had been a teacher for many years. What she was reading now sickened her, for she saw how Rachel's emotions were both torn and violated. Yes, she had been silly about Father John. But she had been so young, and needy. She didn't deserve that—especially at that age. Young girls—and boys, too—were awkward and unpolished at that age, and it was positively indecent to expect adult suaveness and sophistication before the child was fully grown. Mercifully, the Father John type was rare, but Teresa didn't doubt for a minute that such individuals existed. She figured there was probably a special place in hell for them, too; surely God wouldn't tolerate such a blatant misuse of His Name.

"I believe this happened, Father," she said. "I know You saw it. Please, Father, comfort Rachel. She is with You now. Please give her the touch she needs. *You* love her; You will never harm her."

Quietly, she moved the paperclip and then put the manuscript into the hatbox. She put the hatbox away and went into her living room. It was dark; the windows were still open, and a cool breeze filtered in. Teresa looked out, to the starry night beyond the windows. She seemed to feel God's presence in the stars, and she was comforted. She then closed the windows, and waited for Bill to come home.

Chapter 14

THE EVENINGS WERE GENTLE, WARM, AND beautiful, and Teresa often went into the backyard as the sunset painted the western sky with odd pinks and yellows and slender rays of the disappearing sun. Then night would fall, and if it were cloudless, she could gaze at the thousand sparkling dots of light, and even name the constellations they formed, when she could make out certain stars. The tree branches blotted away some of the heavens from Teresa's sight, but still she could enjoy the beauty, from her place on a green-webbed lawn chair near the back porch. As the school year drew to a close, she often went to watch the sunset. She cooked, and washed up, and then went out: later she would grade the papers.

One such evening Bill was on patrol, and she, Billy and Mandy sat at the small kitchen table to have dinner. She washed up afterwards, with help from both children, then went out into the darkness. When she sat on the lawn chair the back porch light flicked on, lighting up one side of the white frame garage, and the trunks of two large trees as well. Teresa turned her head, and the screen door opened. It was Mandy, curious as to where her mother had gone. When she saw her mother she came out, her face completely untroubled and young –looking. Teresa was suddenly very thankful.

"Mom, are you all right?" Mandy asked, and she too glanced at the starry sky, which seemed so calm and ever silent.

Teresa smiled. "Of course. What are you up to, Mandy? Are you about ready for your final exams?"

Mandy groaned. "Oh, don't talk about it, Mom! You always sound like a teacher. I guess I'm as ready as I'll ever be. Marcia wants to come over and study with me. Can she? Then I know I'll be ready."

"Sure she may," said Teresa. "I hope you'll spend at least part of the time studying, anyway, and not just talking about boys. Well," she gave her daughter a glance, "I know you will study, and I know you will make good grades on the tests. You always do. Now, isn't this a nice evening? The temperature is just right—not too hot or cold."

"It *is* a nice night," Mandy agreed. "I was really getting tired of all that cold weather."

She sat down in one of the lawn chairs, and pointed to somewhere beyond the tall, shadowy trees. "There's the city water tower," she said. "I can tell by that red light on top. See it, Mom? It's way over there, but it's pretty tall."

"Yes, I can see it," said Teresa.

"Anyway, Mom, its kind of hot in the house. Can I turn on the air conditioner? Just for a little bit. I won't run it too long."

"Okay," agreed Teresa. "Not for too long." Mandy went back into the house, and Teresa sat outside for a little while longer. She looked up, past the back fence and over the trees of the neighbors' yards. Mandy was right—she could see the red light that topped the water tower.

Teresa finally folded the lawn chairs, put them into the garage, and went back into the house. As she passed through the living room, the window A/C unit was noisily blowing in cold air, disturbing the window curtains and creating a contained chill. Mandy was happily stretched out on the couch, reading a book she got at the school library. Teresa grinned at her and went into the back bedroom, where her class papers waited to be graded. She sat at her desk and graded them, and when that was done, she looked at the closet where the hatbox sat. She said to herself that she would never, ever, ever let Mandy—or any of her daughters—read what she was reading. She wouldn't let Billy, for that matter.

But she would—and did—let them read the Bible. And, truthfully, the Bible had some really rough stuff recorded in its pages. Was there any real difference between family problems of today and those that were found in Genesis, 1st and 2nd Samuel, and 1st and 2nd Kings? Teresa had to be honest—not really. She took down the hatbox. She would read some more tonight, eve though she was apprehensive. Many of her questions about Rachel were being answered, but it was painful.

She read---

"After what happened I was very numb and did what I was supposed to do like a sleepwalker. I didn't want Aunt Anne to notice anything, so I kept up with my chores the best I could. But when Saturday night came, I was dreadfully sick to my stomach, and Aunt Anne came to check on me. 'You're not going to church tomorrow,' she announced, 'Not if you're as sick as that.' She supposed I would be well by Monday, and ready for school, but that was not how it happened. I stayed sick the entire Sunday, and even on Monday I could not keep anything down. Aunt Anne was in despair. 'You're going to a doctor right away,' she said. 'I hope the children don't catch what you have.'

So I was taken to the doctor, and he examined me thoroughly, but couldn't find anything wrong. Aunt Anne was worried about polio, or influenza, or something like that—something contagious that might affect one of her little darlings. The doctor reassured her, though; whatever was wrong with me, it was nothing like that. 'If I thought so,' he said pompously, 'She'd be in quarantine in no time. It's just nerves,' he added, 'some sort of hysteria. She's rather young for that, but she's not actually sick. Just give her time; she'll grow out of it.'

Aunt Anne, reassured, took me back home. She supposed it had to do with my past history, or the fact I would soon be entering my teens, and decided not to worry about it. In fact, I did stop getting sick, and settled back into my routine. I was worried about going to church, though. I would see Father John there, and I was terrified of seeing him. While I never went as far as to label his actions toward me as cruelty, I still didn't want to see him again.

The problem was solved in an unexpected way. Just as I thought I would have to endure a dreadful situation, I overhead Aunt Anne and Uncle Charles talking together in low, earnest tones.

'Are you sure, Charles?' Aunt Anne was asking. Whatever he was saying, she actually seemed to believe and accept.

'I'm fairly sure, Anne. It's unfortunate, but such things do happen. I don't want you or Anne or Charles or Jane anywhere near him. Or Rachel, either. I don't know what they were thinking. Just because we're a small parish, they guessed they could send him *here---*'

'Charles.'

Then—'Are they going to get rid of him?'

'Yes, thank God. Father Robert has already seen to that. He is so embarrassed, poor man. But he really didn't know---'

'Well, to tell you the truth, *I* never liked him,' said Aunt Anne with finalty. 'He seemed so—so overly good. And far too handsome and young. I'm glad Father Robert realized what happened before that monster got to Anne or Jane.'

'Umph,' said Uncle Charles, 'I hope he didn't get to anyone around *our* town. I'm really going to have to pay attention to what's happening in the church, as well as everywhere else. That Father John had half the parish worshipping him *instead* of God!'

'Charles! That's blasphemy!'

'No, Anne, I'm afraid not. Having that kind of a man for a priest is blasphemy. It can't happen again—not in this town. I'll see to that.'

'OOhhhhh,' Aunt Anne moaned, 'Who *can* you trust?'

'We don't have to worry about Father Robert,' Uncle Charles reminded her.

It was all true. When I next went to church, Father John was gone—for good. Old Father Robert stood in front of the church in his priestly robes, and I was glad to see him as never before in my life. He was old, half-deaf and creaky, but I knew he would never hurt me. It was such a relief. After I began to doubt, I thought maybe God cared about me after all.

Father John's abrupt departure did invite some obscene speculation. After all, it was the decade of the roaring '20's, and religion—and Christianity in particular—took quite a beating. The Scopes 'Monkey Trial' was a *cause célèbre*. Jokes were made about 'the preacher and his choir singer' who were murdered back in 1922. The steamy love letters found around their bodies seemed to be more interesting to the public than the murders themselves. Only last year Aimee Semple McPherson, the fiery lady preacher, claimed she was kidnapped, but it was whispered she was hiding out with a lover. 'You see,' it was laughingly rumored, 'preachers have sex. They *like* sex.' It was said in such a way that suggested that holy people should *never* behave in that way. Father John was sent away, but the rumors about him really didn't surprise the townspeople as much as one might expect—the 1920's was a very cynical decade.

I was relieved that he was gone. But I never really recovered from my last meeting with him. It was reassuring to know that I wasn't the only bad one—he was bad enough that Father Robert sent him away. I dared not speak of what happened to me, though. I was sure Aunt Anne would agree—even with Father John—that I brought it upon myself with my silly behavior. Even I believed that. If I had been a 'nice girl' and refrained from putting myself forward, I probably would not have become his victim.

I must have really become unusually mopey, for Aunt Anne did notice something was wrong and actually began to ask questions about it. I wished she wouldn't. I was used to taking orders from her, and doing the housework, but I did not know how to answer her questions. She was demanding and tactless, and very impatient, and I would much rather work for her than talk with her. However, she was my aunt and guardian, and I could not escape her prying.

'Rachel, you seem out of sorts,' she would say. 'What's the matter with you? Did you have another fight with Anne?'

'No.'

'Then, what is it? Is it something at school?'

'No,' I would reply, 'I'm making good grades.'

'Well, you should, since you're older than the rest of your class. Now, Rachel, you haven't been yourself for a while, and I need to know what the problem is. It's getting to be unpleasant, having you pout and not put a cheerful face on things. What is the problem? Do I need to be doing something different? If I do, you need to tell me about it.'

Honestly, I thought, she had to be kidding. She wouldn't change her ways for anybody, and I knew that she would see no reason to change, anyway. In her eyes, she was perfect and justified. I picked up my English textbook, as a way of hinting to her that I wanted to study now, to keep my grades up, and I would rather have the questions come to a halt. But Aunt Anne never received hints about anything; she only gave them.

'What is the matter, Rachel?'

'Nothing at all, Aunt Anne,' I said wearily. 'I stopped getting sick months ago. Even the doctor said I was all right. I'm just tired, I guess. You know I have some tests coming up.'

'All right, Rachel,' she replied, 'Have it your way. But from now on I expect more pleasant behavior from you, and also, I expect you to pass all your tests and make good grades. Your uncle is thinking about sending you to teachers' college so you can have the opportunity to get a good job as a teacher. I will support him in that, but you are going to have to do your part by showing me that you are worthy to become a teacher. That sulkiness on your part suggests that you are not.'

I could have done without Aunt Anne's shaming lectures, but I was relieved to hear that I *was* being considered for teachers' college. It was a dream of mine to be a teacher, and I knew I could then live independently when the time came. I brightened up a little, simply from being made hopeful by the news, and Aunt Anne looked at me and said, 'that's better." She allowed me to get back to my books, and I did that with thankfulness. It was understood that studying and homework were important, among the Dunns, and when I studied I was let alone, for the most part. It was probably the wish of the Dunns to raise someone respectably as a schoolteacher; Anne would never be one—she would likely marry instead—and young Jane didn't seem particularly interested in teaching, either.

So at least I had a viable goal in life, and that was helpful to me. The incident with Father John, painful as it was, began to fade in my memory, especially since he was apparently caught and censured—by someone at least. I knew he never would have been censured on my account, but apparently he had harmed someone who mattered, and was taken to task for it. I could breathe easier, now. I went about my business, taking care of my schoolwork, and as before, I assisted Aunt Anne, whenever and wherever I was needed. I could cook, clean, sew, and mend, and I made it my business to learn other things too—things that Uncle Charles talked about, such as balancing a checkbook and maintaining an automobile. When he had time he showed me these things—he knew, as I did, that I would be living on my own and would have to manage my own affairs. I learned about insurance coverage, making a will, saving, and paying taxes. I would not be sharing my life with anyone, and it was right I should learn about day-to-day living and what it required. After all, I would be on my own.

Meanwhile, everyone around me was partying and laughing and spending and having a good time. October 1929 came, and then…."

"And then…." thought Teresa. The Crash. The seismic shock of the economy—of all America. The party time was ripped away, to be replaced by seriousness, strict penny-counting, and in many cases, hopelessness. Teresa remembered that earth-shaking news herself. The newspapers—"Wall Street Lays an Egg." At first it was hopefully a temporary situation, but the headlines kept coming. Soon many people were out of work. It wasn't articles in the newspaper anymore—it was reality. Soup kitchens were set up, and 'Hoovervilles' appeared. Teresa's father was fortunate—he did not lose his job, nor did he play the Market, so he lost nothing that way, either. But still, as a family, Teresa and her parents had to be frugal and careful, and Teresa wore the same dresses day after day, and ate simple meals provided by her mother. They had enough to live on, but they knew not to be extravagant.

Teresa put the manuscript back in the hatbox, and as she now often did, glanced with thankfulness at her surroundings. The furniture, curtains, bedding and clothes were all fairly new, and stylish, and Teresa had a car for her personal use. She and Bill were both employed, and they could usually afford whatever they wished to have. How different from the Depression years! The Depression lasted such a long time, too—it truly stuck around until the second World War. It was such a dreadful time for many people—several of her teacher colleagues were traumatized by the decade—she could tell from the things they said and did, and from what they told their students.

Teresa put the hatbox away, and went to check on Mandy. She went into the living room, but the A/C unit was turned off, and Mandy was no longer on the couch. She heard Mandy's voice, though; a quick peek into Mandy's room showed that she was yakking on the phone with her friend, Marcia. Teresa smiled to herself. Let children be children, she thought. Fortunately, the economy was good—for now.

She smiled again, and went back into her room. And there, she opened Rachel's Bible and began to read....

Chapter 15

School was finally out. The school bell rang—the students cheered—and a happy mass exodus took place, students hooting and hollering and slamming lockers, and rushing out into the sunshiny freedom. It was true that the sunshine was often blocked by trees now fully in leaf, but the day was bright nevertheless, and the children were happy. They ran out in twos and threes and fours, and bicycles now swarmed across sidewalks and streets. Teresa and the other teachers stayed at the school for a little while longer, but soon they would leave, too. Dr. Hinton had already set up the calendar for the next school year, and he had met with his teachers to discuss any concerns. Everything was orderly as usual. Teresa collected the things she would take home with her that day, and prepared to leave.

As she glanced around her familiar classroom, looking at the desks, the blackboard, and the large windows, Dr. Hinton walked in. She was somewhat surprised, but she set her box of supplies on the teacher's desk, and greeted him. "Well, another year gone," she sighed.

"Yes, another year," agreed Dr. Hinton. "How are you holding up, Teresa?"

"I'm holding up all right," she replied. "I guess Valerie is, too." Valerie Martin was the new third grade teacher—Rachel's replacement. "She never knew Rachel, so I don't believe she was spooked the way another teacher might have been. For a brand new job she did rather well."

"I hired her brand new for a reason," said Dr. Hinton. "Mainly for what you just mentioned—she would not be 'spooked,' as you put it. But that isn't my concern right now. I'm more worried about you. Is something bothering you? You don't seem to be your usual self. I've known you long enough to know something is wrong."

Teresa frowned. "I hope it didn't show up in my teaching or the way I worked with the students."

"Oh, no," Dr. Hinton assured her. "You've done a great job all year. I've no complaints there. But you do have something weighing on you."

Teresa again looked over her classroom—her small kingdom, where she taught and disciplined and ruled thirty young childen; and then glanced full at Dr. Hinton. "It is true," she finally said, "I do have something on my mind. Rachel left, well—a diary of sorts. Not exactly a diary, but papers telling about her life. I've been reading them. It explains a lot, but trust me, Robert, it doesn't make very pleasant reading."

"Oh, dear," replied Dr. Hinton. That was all he said, but his tone implied he was not surprised.

"It's pretty bad," Teresa went on, "and I honestly don't want to talk about it."

"I was afraid of that," Dr. Hinton replied. "But there wasn't any reason I should have been concerned about the students under her care?"

"Oh, no, not at all," Teresa hastened to assure him, "the students were in good hands—with her. In fact, I think the best possible. You know I've worked beside her all these years. If anything wasn't right—I would have known. No—it was Rachel herself who had it bad. I'm just now finding out how bad. You know—she was really very strong, Robert. She overcame a lot and took her place in the world. It isn't everyone who can do that—not like she did. She was an odd sort, but she became a useful, decent member of society. No one can ask any more."

Dr. Hinton gave her a strange look. "Teresa, do you really think you should be reading her papers? You seem to be bothered by it."

Teresa ran her hand over the box of supplies on her desk. She finally said, "No, I am not sure I should be reading her papers. But they came my way, and I did decide to read them. Since I made that decision, I'm going to go ahead and go through with it. In a way, it does help to know. I've worked with her all these years, and now I'm getting to know her even better than I did before. Some of it is very painful. But I haven't read it all, and I am hoping to come across something that lets me know she did have some happiness in her life. I guess that's why I keep reading—I hope for that. So far, it has been rather rough, I'm afraid."

Dr. Hinton looked at her and smiled. "Okay, Teresa, carry on," he said. "But I want to see you in the fall, bright and cheerful, as you always are. You help this school run as well as it does. Don't let this get you down. I need you, your fellow teachers need you, and especially the students need you. You are one of the best teachers I have here, if not the best. Now—class dismissed. See you next fall. Tell Bill hi for me, and I'll make sure none of these imps we are training will make trouble for him in the years to come."

Teresa laughed and picked up her supplies. Leaving the room, she closed the heavy door, and then started down the locker-lined hallway. The janitor was already making the rounds, the overhead hall lights were dimmed, and Teresa's footsteps echoed in the hall. She reached the metal double doors and exited into the bright, sunny day. The breeze rustled the fresh maple leaves as Teresa walked to her Plymouth. The air was pleasantly soft and warm, and beyond the thick canopy of heavily-leaved branches, the sky was sharply blue.

Teresa set the box in the backseat, then got behind the steering wheel. It finally became clear—she was on vacation! She would have time to do things she wanted to do; she could go swimming, or to a movie—or even sleep late now and then. She understood how the children felt about the last day of school. Even though she enjoyed her job and the routine was comforting, she still looked forward to vacation, where more of her time was her own, and since the summer days were warm and sunshiny, they lifted her spirits and helped her to see the more hopeful side of life.

She drove through the tree-shaded neighborhood, passing the park grounds, which now was populated by students on bicycles and students walking in groups. Some of the students recognized her and waved to her, and she waved back. As she drove on she heard the happy shouts of children at play, and she thought of how happy the world could be. Then, out of the blue, she thought of Rachel—and her heart suddenly froze. Outside, it was beautiful, with the fullness of springtime—flowers and blossoming trees, blue skies and soft white clouds, and birds singing. But just outside of town, in a quiet, secluded cemetery, shaded with trees and covered with fresh grass—what was left of Rachel rotted within a tomb. The headstone was finally in place, with her name on it and her dates, and that was all. She would not see anymore beautiful summers, after a year of teaching her students.

"But could she see the beauty?" Teresa wondered aloud. Her life was so lonely and painful. There was so much rejection, and it occurred to Teresa that Rachel may well have welcomed her death, whatever caused it.

Teresa knew she would have to keep reading. Surely—surely there was more to it than what she read so far. As she pulled into the driveway of her home, she thought of the hatbox. It still had many pages left. Rachel was a church member and a schoolteacher—there must be some explanation or comment on the direction her life took, for it was a useful one, even though it appeared not to be a happy one.

Teresa parked and took her supplies from the Plymouth, and entered her house. Billy and Mandy were not home yet, and she did not have to worry about preparing dinner for a while. She went into her bedroom, set the supply box down by her desk, and went to the closet. She brought down the hatbox, and found where the paperclip had been placed---

"October 1929 came, and then so did the Depression....

So much is written about the Depression these days. It is still fresh in the memory of many people today, and they say so much about they did without, as the money was so tight, but I think the main problem was lack of optimism for the future—the optimism that characterized the '20's. The stock market crash was like a slap in the face—it was so sudden and unexpected to many, and it dashed so many hopes that people were afraid to look ahead.

Most people lived day-to-day, without the party atmosphere that existed before the crash. And, of course, many people lost jobs, and banks failed. Uncle Charles, fortunately for us, was not really affected by what was going on; he was a careful and knowledgeable businessman, and he did not take unnecessary risks—he never had. But still, he couldn't avoid unpleasantness. Many of his friends failed in business or otherwise fell upon hard times, and a lot of them looked to him to help them out—and of course he could not do it. He could not help everyone. So even though he kept his home and his standard of living, he lost many acquaintances, and we no longer had dinner parties as often as we did before. Aunt Anne became even fussier as the dreadful months passed. She worried incessantly and began to place strict economy on everyday living: food, clothes, and expenses had to be carefully watched and budgeted.

Part of her economy consisted of cutting out unnecessary friends and acquaintances—if any neighbor suffered a job loss or was otherwise likely to be needy, then she dropped the said neighbor from her social list. Her daughter Anne followed suit—I was no longer the only girl at school she did not 'speak' to, and, in a way, that helped me. Some of her ex-friends decided to get to know me, and, indeed, misfortune seemed to be a great leveler. Many of my schoolmates learned what it was to do without; to be dependent on someone else, and to not always have stylish dresses or ready spending money. I was not so out of place anymore. And Cousin Anne's snobbishness was beginning to grate on a few people, as times and values began to change, and access to money was no longer assured.

Aunt Anne saw herself as practical, not mean-spirited. After all, she gave to charities, and she made sure Uncle Charles assisted with the establishment of soup kitchens and work programs. The poor needed to be cared for, but she didn't have time or energy for 'the poor' in the flesh, and certainly not in her living room or at her dining table. I think it scared her a little, to see her former friends in old clothes, living in worn out houses, eating makeshift meals, wondering how they would ever make ends meet. She did not want that obvious failure to extend to her; she saw failure and financial trouble almost as a contagious disease, and she didn't want to be around people who had it.

My life really didn't change at all. It wasn't any better, but then it wasn't any worse. The Depression called for making do—resewing old dresses, planning and cooking inexpensive meals, and making every penny count—but I was already trained to do those things. Much more so than Cousin Anne. She was often angry about wearing the same dresses day after day, and she complained about the food—she saw no reason why we should eat like 'country people.' But Aunt Anne was too busy, or worried, to scold her. I think, for the first time, that Aunt Anne was actually grateful for my presence. Even the friends she did keep on her roster had to give up their maids and cooks—they couldn't afford them anymore. But she didn't have to give up me; I was her 'duty' and I performed many of the functions that would normally be given to a maid or cook.

Time passed, but not much improved. Some of the downtown shops were now vacant, and men stood on the street corners selling apples or newspapers. Some men did not sell anything, but loitered in vacant warehouses, picking through piles of trash during the day while sleeping on newspapers at night. It became legal to drink alcohol again, but who could really afford to? It became hard enough to buy coffee or tea, let alone anything else, and drinking would be an expensive habit. Occasionally, at a very special dinner, or during the holidays, Uncle Charles would bring out a bottle of wine. But it wasn't often, and, as I said, we hardly had dinner parties any more.

Aunt Anne was always looking for a way to cut corners. One night I heard her arguing with Uncle Charles.

'Absolutely not, Anne!' Uncle Charles was saying. 'We took her on, and we did not take on her brothers, so we are going to do the right thing by her. My mind is made up, Anne, so don't even waste your breath on the subject. It's bad enough Sammy was killed up in

New York City.' Sammy was my older brother. 'He was killed, and we did nothing about it. But Rachel *is* going to teachers' college, and that's final. Don't argue.'

'Well, we didn't have to take her in in the first place,' said Aunt Anne, 'she was never our responsibility.'

'That is true,' replied Uncle Charles. 'However, she has relieved you of a lot of housework. Don't think I haven't noticed. Sure, she should help you out, but she does it willingly and well. I think she will make an excellent teacher. She is good at her studies, and seems to like young children.'

'Except Anne,' Aunt Anne pointed out. At that, Uncle Charles hurrumphed.

'I'm going to have to have a discussion with you about Anne,' he finally said.

I was about eighteen when I overheard this conversation, and Anne was about sixteen. She was running true to form, even with the chill of the Depression years, for nothing could dampen her wish to be socially superior. Although she hid it by being very insincerely polite to the general public, she was very calculating, and she dated only 'rich boys.' I knew why Uncle Charles was upset. She had her eye on a much older boy—a man, rather—Jeff Milner, who was the son of the richest family in town, and whose father was the current mayor. It was well known that Jeff was very nearly engaged to a lovely young woman close to his age, named Letitia Fairchild. The engagement wasn't formal yet, but the town had no doubt it would be announced soon, and everyone considered it a suitable and desirable match.

'Why, what's bothering you about Anne?' Aunt Anne wanted to know. 'I should think Rachel would be the one to have indecent morals, living the way she did. You know what girls like her—'

'Anne, stop it this minute!' cut in Uncle Charles. "Rachel hasn't done anything wrong. And I don't want any scandalous talk about her. I would like to see her become a teacher. As for Anne, what's bothering me about her is Jeffrey Milner. Oh, don't pull that innocent act on me. I see more than you think I do. Anne's too young for him—she's not even out of school. And Letitia Fairchild is the right woman to be his wife. She is accomplished, and well-trained, and her character is excellent.'

'I suppose you're saying your own child does not have an excellent character,' said Aunt Anne unpleasantly.

'I'm saying she is too young for Jeff Milner.'

I was old enough to understand why Anne was pursuing Jeff: he had money, and social prestige, and she wanted both. I doubted seriously that she actually loved him. I did know she was sneaking off with him while I studied my lessons; what surprised me was why Jeff paid her any attention. I had met Miss Fairchild and thought she was a lovely woman; even though she was rich and very pretty, she never put on airs, even with me. She was worth four Anne Dunns—at least to me, and why Jeff would take such a chance as to lose her was beyond me.

I had entered twelfth grade in 1934. Most everyone was used to the Depression by then; nobody liked it but everyone did the best they could. Uncle Charles and I selected the college I would go to, and he set aside the funds. My grades were excellent, and I stayed out of trouble, so that was all set. I was very grateful to Uncle Charles far what he had done, and I didn't want to let him down. I would be the best teacher possible, and I hoped to stay independent for the rest of my life. I was glad I was going far away from town to go to college.

Soon after these plans were made, I heard the only actually screams I heard in the Dunn house—from Aunt Anne.

'How could he!!?? How could she!!?? What are we going to do??' She was truly in hysterics. I had never seen her like that before.

'I told you, Anne, I told you, I *told* you!!' exploded Uncle Charles. 'Why didn't you listen? It's a mother's place to keep tabs on her daughter. Well, do what you want. I will tell you one thing, though—I'm not paying any butcher to do any foul play.'

'Well, she can't have it unmarried.'

'She can stay with relatives, like all girls who end up like that do.'

'And then what?'

'I don't know. Maybe the Milners will want to adopt an orphan child.'

'Charles, you're impossible,' moaned Aunt Anne.

Well, I thought to myself, Cousin Anne always got what she wanted, no matter what, and I didn't see this situation being any different. After all, she was desperate. In the Depression, rich young men were hard to come by. It was bad luck for Letitia Fairchild, but after all, Cousin Anne had to have whatever she desired…."

"Well, well, well," Teresa was actually chuckling a little. She had heard that same old story many times, but she was guiltily amused at the shock Anne Dunn must have felt when her "perfect" daughter turned up pregnant at the age of seventeen. It always seemed to be that way—the daughters of proper, highly critical mothers, even indulgent ones like Anne Dunn, often ended up "in trouble." Rachel, for one, suspected young Anne was trying to "trap" the rich Jeff Milner, and she was probably right. Some women needed to be rich and highly regarded, no matter what the price. Teresa wondered, with interest, what would happen to young Anne.

That would have to wait for another day. Teresa heard her own daughter, Mandy, come through the front door. She, like all of the rest of the kids, was glad school was out. "Mom?" she called. "Can you take me to the store? I want to get some Coke and some other stuff so Marcia and I can bake cookies tomorrow. Can we? And we'd like to have a party here soon, if it's okay with you, and Dad's home to help."

Teresa didn't kiss her daughter—it would have surprised her too much. But she gladly went out again into the bright sunshine, as her daughter climbed into the red Plymouth. Together, they rode to the supermarket, chatting all the way.…

Chapter 16

It was a cheerful summer, with prosperity, the space program, and rock'n'roll. Elvis Presley wowed the girls with his gyrations, and all over the country, people watched the Ed Sullivan show, hoping to see new thrills. Cars no longer had tail fins, but they had as much chrome as ever, and even more horsepower. Teenagers went swimming—and surfing, if they were lucky enough to live near a coast—and crazy new songs blasted from transistor radios as the scantily clad young people played water games and ran about. In the soft, warm evenings, many silver-chromed and highly painted automobiles could be seen at the malt shops and drive-in hamburger stands, and later on, as the night enfolded the lively world, the drive-in movies were filled to capacity. One could watch three-hour-long sophisticated romantic comedies, or creepy science fiction flicks, but usually the young couples didn't care—the drive in movie gave them a chance to be alone together—in the starry darkness.

Although Teresa didn't really go out very much, she intended to enjoy the summer to the full, and she did it. Sometimes she and Bill held evening backyard barbeques, and had some of the neighbors over to share the fun. Billy and Mandy held parties with school friends, and on these nights the hi-fi would be playing almost continuously. Teresa had to smile at the music, or what passed for music. The friends brought their own personal supplies of records, so that Teresa got a fair sampling of what was popular—'Do You Love Me' 'Earth Angel' 'Duke of Earl' and of course, Elvis Presley.

The boys all seemed to have grease in their hair, and the girls seemed ironed and trussed and tightened into dresses or stretch pants. But they appeared to be having fun, and with Bill around, they were on their best behavior. It wouldn't do to get too wild at a police officer's home.

Teresa knew she was getting up in years, but teaching kept her young. Every year the styles changed, and the music, and even the speech among the students. Since she had so much contact with the students, she was usually knowledgeable about the going trend, and of course Billy and Mandy could tell her what was going on. So could Bill—when it came to that—but she wasn't as happy about the events Bill came across from time to time. Still, she had reason to hope things would go well. America was a strong country—the space program held everyone's interest—and medical science was making great advances. Psychology was in full swing, and everyone hoped to create perfect, well-adjusted families in the future. Teresa wasn't sure about that, but she smiled at the optimism.

A handsome young man resided at the White House with his pretty wife and two charming young children. A famous astronaut circled the earth just the year before, and the only real worry was "those Communists in Russia." Of course, people were concerned about the nuclear bomb, and what "those Communists" might do with it. But most people tried to ignore the threat, and enjoy the positive direction America was taking. America was the richest country in the world. And didn't it also have the best government?

It was a good summer. It seemed to have such a glow, before the tragedies and the storms ahead.

Teresa had her routine: she cooked meals, cleaned the home, and kept tabs on Billy and Mandy. The days were very warm, so she often turned on the attic fan and raised the windows. But some days were so hot that this wasn't enough, and she had to close the windows and run the A/C unit. She was glad so many old trees shaded the house. It was nice to go out into the backyard and listen to the birds' cheery melodies, and on most of the days it was bearable to sit in the shade. She went outside often, to relax, and then she returned to the house to complete a few odd tasks she had otherwise been to busy to do. And she remembered Rachel.

It was nearly a year since Rachel had died. But Teresa still took down the hatbox, and read the papers she had left behind. What had college been like for Rachel? And what happened to Anne?

One warm, balmy evening, Teresa took down the hatbox. The windows were all raised, and night was falling, and the cicadas were in full chorus in the darkness beyond the window screens. Occasionally the curtains blew inward, but it was a quiet night. Teresa wondered when it would rain next, but apparently that was not yet in nature's plans. She sat in a living room chair beside one of the windows, and took out the manuscript. She removed the paper clip and began reading:

"I graduated from high school with honors, and finalized my plans for entering teacher's college the next fall, where I would be moving. It was so far away that I would be staying in a dorm, and I welcomed the change. I was a little apprehensive, as I had no idea with whom I would be sharing a dorm room, but I comforted myself with the thought that she couldn't be much worse than Cousin Anne. This should have been a momentous time for me, as I would be leaving, probably (and hopefully) for good, but, as usually appeared to be the case, Cousin Anne was stealing the show. My packing, list-making, letter-mailing, and college details were overshadowed by her upcoming marriage to Jeffrey Milner. Apparently my uncle, whose social and financial situation was almost equal to that of the Milners, was able to negotiate some sort of agreement with Jeff's father, and the marriage would take place. The Fairchilds, naturally, were not happy about it, and I don't think the Milners were, either, but Anne's condition would not permit delay.

Aunt Anne wanted to have a quiet marriage, preferably in the Justice of the Peace's office, and I think that was Uncle Charles' wish also. But Anne wouldn't have it that way. She wanted everyone to know what a great match she had made, and she wanted white veils, bridesmaids, a tall decorated cake, and a reception worthy of the House of Milner. It never occurred to her that anyone would object to that, or that anyone would object to her marriage to the richest boy in town. She had had everyone's approval all her life. And, since she wanted things done her way, and she expected it without question, it was done for her. She had her big church wedding, her reception, a fancy trousseau, and a honeymoon in the Caribbean to finish everything off. I was at the wedding, but I had not been selected to do anything—I was not asked to be a bridesmaid, or even a server at the reception. I was not seated with the family during the ceremony, but I did notice none of the Fairchilds were there at all.

I watched Anne as she proudly walked down the church aisle on Jeff Milner's arm; she was swathed in satin, lace and pearls, with a coronet set on her brownish waved hair. A white veil streamed to her shoulders. Her bridal dress was very pretty, but I was not so sure *she* was pretty. She was quite young, but her face already had the same sharpness that characterized Aunt Anne's, and truly, she contrasted unfavorably to the older and more mature Letitia Fairchild. I idly wondered how Jeff Milner *really* felt about his new bride. I didn't waste any pity on him, as he created his own problems; Anne might have pursued him, but he had the option to be true and faithful to Letitia. I didn't think the marriage would be particularly happy, but as long as Jeff paid the bills he would probably keep his wife satisfied and content.

Thus Anne was out of the house first. I would leave next, and the time was soon to arrive. My luggage was ready; my train tickets and necessary papers were in my purse. Uncle Charles would see me off at the train station. Aunt Anne *really* didn't think it was quite needful to see me off, and she didn't go herself, but she couldn't persuade Uncle Charles to stay home.

I left the house the same way I came to it: in a taxi. But I could tell that many years had passed since the last drive so long ago; the car was a much more recent model, and it had a totally different shape. It was rounded, while the taxi I rode in back in the '20's was rather squarish. The driver was different, too, but still snide. Uncle Charles directed him to the train station, and he said, 'Righto, Mac. I'll help you guys elope. I won't say a word.' Uncle Charles apparently didn't find it worth while to notice him; he did not reply. Once we were in the back seat, Uncle Charles turned to me.

'Rachel, I want to say a few things to you before you leave. First of all, I'm proud of you. I know it wasn't easy for you, and I'm sorry I wasn't in any position to make things better for you. But you did well, and I hope you continue to do well. I know you will. You do what you have to do, without complaining, and you accomplish things. That's what you need to keep on doing, and don't worry about the money. I will see that you get your education.' He frowned. 'You—you are not much like Cindy, not really. I always worried about her, from the time we were kids. She could never straighten out her life—and then she married that drunk…'

'Well, it wasn't easy for you. But I know strength when I see it. Just hang on until you get it right—don't give up. Well, here we are. Do you have all your papers? Good.'

I was almost in tears, and that surprised me. I didn't expect to miss any of the Dunns; they gave me a home and I was grateful, but I had never become attached to them. My uncle carried my luggage to the depot, and I walked quietly beside him. The train was pulling up, and I realized this was it: I would be totally on my own. My uncle stayed with me until the whistle sounded; I nodded to him, and then he left. I sat by the window, and took one last look at the town that had been my place of residence for so many years. I could not think of anyone whom I missed: not even my uncle, really. I had formed no close attachments to anyone in town—not my teachers, not my classmates, not anyone. I didn't know if I was afraid—because of Father John—or because I had not been generally accepted.

The train began to move, and soon the town was no longer in my vision. I heard the loud whistle blast, and then the countryside swooped past, as the train went faster and faster. I was in the coach, and most of the people with me were very silent. One man did comment that we were lucky to be able to ride coach, because most people nowadays could not afford to. The guys he knew mainly rode in boxcars, when they needed to get from one place to another.

I watched the panorama taking place outside of my window, and it was depressing. Many of the farmhouses were vacant, with nearly all the paint peeled off and dust and dirt covering the grounds. The fields were not healthy, nor did they have growth: barren stalks were broken across the dry dirt, and I saw no water whatsoever. The sun seemed brassy and merciless, too. It was almost as if it never rained. In fact, that was true: the country was experiencing what would be later known as the Dust Bowl; it would be one of the hallmarks of the Depresssion.

The train was a local and pulled into several small towns, and I saw how the Depression affected them as well. I sensed a general malaise in each of these towns—everybody and everything seemed worn out—even the gas stations. The buildings around each railroad station appeared to be empty: paint was fading off the brick walls; the glass windows had splintery cracks, and dried grass poked through crevices in both the sidewalks and the hard roads in town. The billboards had no advertisements, or faded ones left over from the Roaring '20's. Tired old men leaned against the vacant shops, and I didn't see any children at all.

I carefully remembered the town's name where I was to get off, and finally it was called. I glanced out the window, as the train began to slow down. I was relieved, for this town seemed more prosperous than the others. The train station was built with fancy stone siding, and healthy trees shaded the area. As I got off the train, evening began to fall, and the station lights shone very bright. So did the streetlamps. I secured a taxi and named my destination: everything was worked out beforehand, so I made it to the campus grounds in time to get to my dorm before lights out. I heard dorm mothers were strict about such things.

I was very tired, so I was glad to be shown my room. I was introduced to my roommate, a girl named Mary Jones. I smiled at her briefly, and went about my business. I unpacked carefully, put everything in its exact place, as Aunt Anne taught me, and then I fell asleep......

I awoke suddenly, and for a moment I could not remember where I was. Sunlight streamed through a double-sliding window, which was flanked by flowery yellow calico curtains. The bed I was in was plain, but clean and reasonably comfortable. It was much better than the cot I was used to.

Then I remembered. I was at college now. I would go to breakfast, and register for my classes, and find out where I would go to get my books.

I greeted Mary, who was waking up; got dressed, and went about my business. I was almost mechanical about it: nothing went wrong, and I finished the morning out with nearly all my tasks done. I had lunch, and then went back to the dorm. After all, my things were there, and I was new to the area.

My room was on the second floor. Mary was not there—she evidently had things that needed her attention. I went in and sat down on my bed, and looked around. The dorm was probably built in the 1910's, but the rooms were freshly painted, and the hardwood floors had woven black and white rag rugs. The bathrooms—one between two rooms—had fairly modern fixtures, small hexagonal white tiles on the floor, and large round mirrors over the sinks. The atmosphere was that of an old-fashioned but well-kept home, and I heard the cheery treble voices of girls laughing in the hallway as they went in and out of the building. Well, I thought, it was a place for teachers in the making. I pushed up the lower part of the six-paned window, as the room was rather warm, and as the breeze floated through the screen and into the room, I glanced out to see what kind of view I had of the outdoors.

It was the second floor, so the view was more extensive than it would have been otherwise. The dorm—and the college—must have been built on the edge of town, for I saw the grounds—a mowed, fresh green area, and beyond that, open fields. The blue sky and sunshine were nearly unobstructed by anything—even trees, and I figured the breeze blew so well into the room because nothing hindered it. And there was such quietness—such peacefulness. I could rest now, not having to worry about Aunt Anne's constant demands. Hopefully, too, I would not have much contact with men—Uncle Charles had basically been a good man—but I was now of the opinion that men were not only opportunistic but also vicious and dangerous. I wanted to limit my contact with them, until I met one I could trust.

I lay down on the bed, and allowed the wind to blow. It did, whistling sometimes, and other times quietly swishing, and the calico curtains furled gently against my painted dresser. It was a quietness I had never known. I would not have to clean up everything—just my personal space; I would not be responsible for anyone else. I would not have to cook my meals—they were provided for me. All I would have to do is go to class, study, and do my homework. I heard college work was very hard and intense and I would be required to take it seriously. But I could do that.

And so it proved. The college courses were difficult, but I kept up with them, and made excellent grades. Mary was not a troublesome roommate: we never talked, but we never fought either, and we each went about our business. I learned who the dorm mothers were, but I never really got to know them. Since I stayed out of trouble, and didn't date or hang around with men, I mostly stayed out of the spotlight. I tried to treat everyone around me as pleasantly as possible, but I shied away from friendships I saw the other girls having. I didn't understand closeness or such friendships, and besides, I didn't want to provoke any adverse emotions—my own or anyone else's.

That was my first year of college. I made good grades, and I took a summer job at one of the local bookstores. I knew times were hard, so I counted myself lucky to get the job. I didn't want to go back to the Dunns', but I received word from Uncle Charles that he was pleased with my progress. I noticed he said nothing about Aunt Anne, or Cousin Anne for that matter, other than to mention that the latter had a little boy now….."

Teresa replaced the paperclip on that particular page, and put the manuscript back in the hatbox. She became aware that she, too, was sitting by an open window, and the warm breeze filtered in. Billy and Mandy were out with friends—in fact, they had taken the Plymouth—and she heard the car pulling into the driveway. Good, she thought. It must be late now, but my children are safe. As if to confirm this, she heard the cardoor slam, and Billy shouting, "Oh, come on, Mandy, I wasn't trying to be mean or anything. I just didn't think Joe was the right guy to play that position. He dropped so many balls in the past I began to think he had holes drilled in his hands."

"Well, Ted didn't do much better, that I could see," retorted Mandy. "He seemed to be in the wrong place whenever a fly ball flew his way!"

"Yaaaah. See? This is what I get for taking my sister to a ball with me. And all you really want to do is gang up with the other girls and yak all the time. All during the game, in fact!"

The front door burst open, and both children found their mother sitting in the living room. She smiled at them, and asked, "Did you guys enjoy the ball game?"

Billy snorted, Mandy laughed, and the tension was gone. The children departed to their separate rooms, and Teresa replaced the lid on the hatbox. She rose and went to her bedroom to put the box away, and as she put it away she thought of her own college years. She had almost been Rachel's contemporary: she was less than three years older than Rachel had been. But in many ways, she was much older than Rachel. She had not been afraid to make friends, to date, to marry—she thought to herself: she was fortunate. She was not lonely.

Bill would be home soon, so she went to the kitchen, and assembled some chicken salad sandwiches that she knew he liked. It was a pleasant night, and she was happy. Tomorrow, she thought, she would read some more, and see how Rachel did on her own.

Chapter 17

Teresa did take the hatbox down the next evening, as the various members of her family had other events going on that night. She began to read---

"I did find it interesting that Cousin Anne was a mother now. I wondered what she thought of being one, or how she felt about her son. She should be grateful to him, I thought, because his existence brought about the marriage she wanted. But I knew she liked having a good time, and I knew from experience that a small child meant full-time responsibility. I had spent many hours caring for little Charles and Jane as they grew up, and I knew children needed attention, and a lot of it.

Well, Anne could probably afford a nanny if Jeff was as rich as everyone said he was. She could argue, like her mother would, that hiring household help would put a paycheck in someone's pocket, which for these hard times, would be beneficial. Anyway, I just couldn't see Cousin Anne changing diapers. Such work was simply beneath her.

College started up again in the fall, and I was still in the same dorm room. I had a new roommate, though; Mary had moved to another room.

It was explained to me very simply, and it made sense. Mary's cousin Emily had entered teacher's college as a freshman, and she wanted to room with Mary. That was perfectly understandable and reasonable, but I did hear, unofficially, that Mary did not find me a satisfactory roommate. Apparently she considered me 'stuck up' and 'snooty,' and she wanted someone with whom she could converse. I hadn't meant to come across that way, but Mary made no real indication that she desired conversation or friendship with me, and I learned not to put myself forward.

I tried not to think about it: I needed to move on. I had studying to do and grades to make, and I hoped my new roommate would not take offense at my busyness or shyness.

In fact, I approached her rather nervously, as we were introduced. But she was not like Mary Jones at all. She welcomed me at once, with no reservations. Her name was Nancy Lindeman. She had clear, untroubled, beautiful gray eyes—that was the first thing I noticed about her. Somewhere I heard someone saying that the look in one's eyes was a window to one's heart, and in Nancy's case that was certainly true. She was free of snobbishness, and appeared even then to have the capacity to see the good in anyone, anytime. She was not one to judge harshly, or hastily; she liked to know the truth before she decided about someone. I wondered where she got her gentleness. I was afraid of it, remembering Father John, but I told myself not to be ridiculous. She would hardly physically attack me, and what ulterior motive would she have? I made up my mind to not be afraid of her, and I would make an effort to talk with her—if she wanted to.

She had a lot of friends and an adoring family; I soon found that out. Her mother and father had come with her to settle her into her dorm room, and they were there when I came into the room that evening. She introduced me right away. The parents seemed like caring, approachable, and friendly people, even though they were obviously well off financially. Mrs. Lindeman commented on my hair—'So cute and curly' she said, and even the brief attention I received from her was much more memorable to me than years of Aunt Anne's admonitions.

I was rather sad, wondering when Nancy would find out how truly bad I was, and turn against me, but wonder of wonders, that never happened—she was truly gentle. She respected the fact I was shy, and that I needed to study, but she made time for me.

Sometimes she invited me along with her friends for a burger or an evening out. I had the money, thanks to Uncle Charles, but I was nervous, because the evenings out included being with men. She had men friends, and a lot of them at that, but I soon learned she was discerning. I also learned that one of the men who escorted her about was actually her brother Lawrence, who was also in college. He had a car, and he often helped her out when she needed it, and gave rides to her friends.

At first I didn't say much to Nancy; I couldn't. But her benign presence in my room everyday began to have an effect on me; I was less uptight and more willing to talk. She did not ever force me to talk, like my Aunt Anne did, but she encouraged me when I did speak, and asked a few gentle questions. We had a few college classes together, and one day she remarked to me after we each got our graded test papers, 'Rachel, I cannot keep up with you. You retain knowledge like no one I ever saw. Could you help me with my algebra? I like the way you explain things—it clears them up for me, while the professors act like they would rather confuse me, instead. You will make an excellent teacher.'

I did explain things to her, and thus I began tutoring, for she had friends who needed help with their studies as well. Most of the girls would rather go out, having parties and dates with the boys, but when they found, like Nancy said, that I could help them with the schoolwork, they sometimes held study sessions in my dorm room. I decided early on that each girl, after I had given an explanation of the homework at hand, must work a problem of her own without my help. If she absolutely couldn't understand that time, I would help her to the solution, then assign a similar problem to do—again without my help. I had done this often with little Charles and Jane, and their grades improved quite a bit, so I tried it with Nancy. That seemed to yield good results, too, so that's how I helped her friends. They were very grateful, too, for some of them looked forward to being scolded mightily by parents for flunking classes, or even college.

My experience at college became happier, then; I was able to give something, and I was appreciated for it.

I learned more about Nancy: among the many beautiful things she kept on her side of the dorm room was a handsome Bible, placed on a white doily on her dresser next to her shimmering jewel box. It wasn't there for show, either; Nancy took it down nearly every evening no matter how busy she was, and studied from it. On Sunday mornings she was always gone—her brother came by to get her, to take her to church. I didn't know which one she went to, but it was evidently not the one in which I had been raised; she didn't have a rosary, or any icons or pictures of the Holy Mary, and she never spoke of a priest. I heard her pray, too, and it always seemed directed to the Father Himself. I wondered at her nerve, but after all, she seemed good—God wouldn't reject *her*.

I wondered about it. And as spring of that year came on, and the days became longer and brighter, I began to think of Lent and Easter, which was soon upon us.

One night, after lights out, I lay in my bed and listened to Nancy's whispered prayers. The calico curtain was closed, but I could hear the March winds blowing against the window panes. Nancy finished her prayers and climbed into bed. I lay still for a few minutes, and then said, 'Nancy?'

'Yes, Rachel?'

'Aren't you afraid to do that? I mean pray directly to God, just like you do?'

'Why, no,' replied Nancy gently, 'of course not. I couldn't be afraid. I know God loves me.'

'Yes,' I said, rather sadly, 'I'm sure He does. Everyone loves you, Nancy. You're so good.'

'Why, Rachel,' she laughed a little, 'I'm not good. I'm no better than you or anyone else, trust me. But I know God loves me. And Rachel—He loves you, too. Don't think for a minute He does not. He sent His Son to die for you, as well as me, and everyone we know.'

I was silent for awhile, and she asked me quietly what church I had been brought up in. I told her, and she sighed. Then she said, 'Do you still go? Do you wish to? If you do, I know there is such a church within walking distance of the college. I could find out for you if you like.'

'No,' I finally said. 'No, I don't want to go. I haven't been, and I don't want to. I—I feel so wicked all the time. I don't even want to talk about it any more. I—I haven't been to confession , or taken communion—or anything. I don't see what good it does. If God hates me so much that I have to forever be confessing and atoning and begging the priests and Mary to intercede with me, then I'd rather go straight to hell and be done with it! It doesn't seem to make any difference! I'm always bad! And God will never care about me!'

It was quiet for awhile, and then I said, 'Nancy, you aren't mad at me for saying that, are you?'

'Of course not, Rachel,' Nancy replied. 'I'm not mad at you at all; why would I be? But I am sad to think you believe God doesn't love you.'

'How could He? I'm not good or—or anything.'

'None of us are,' Nancy said. 'Not a one of us. But that doesn't stop God from loving us. We are separated from Him by sin, but He even fixed that—He sent us His Son Jesus to die for us, and cover our sins. And more than that, Rachel—Jesus became a human being such as we are, so that He could experience first hand the pain—and the happiness, too—of being a human being on this fallen earth. Jesus was very forthright and stern, but He loved very much, and He still does. He loves you, Rachel. Let me show you some places in the Bible where He talks of that. He came just for us. He wouldn't have if He hadn't loved humanity—including you.'

'But why do I always have to keep thinking about my sin?'

'Rachel—you don't. That's why Jesus died, to pay the penalty for you. So you can be forgiven, and you can move on, past the sins. You must look forward—toward Him.'

'But don't I have to atone for them, like the priest says?'

'No, Rachel.'

I had trouble comprehending that. My church had a system—so much sin, so much expiation. Prayers on the rosary beads, money to the church, fasting, mortifying the flesh.....I could die suddenly, and where would I be? If I were not in the state of grace......

"Rachel,' said Nancy, 'You know what was meant. Your sins are forgiven in Christ. But you must not deliberately and willfully commit them. For example—suppose you got angry and hurt someone with a very cutting remark, and it caused her much pain. You know it would please God to go to that person, tell her you are sorry your remarks caused such pain, and that you would try never to do it again. That's the kind of atonement God would want to hear, not the repetitions of rote prayers when they really mean nothing to you. But still, you are forgiven when you place your faith—and life—in Jesus. You have to understand Him as Someone to love—not to fear unreasonably.'

'But—but—'

'But what, Rachel?'

I lay flat against the small pillow, looking up at the ceiling, which because of the darkness now appeared to be colorless, and at the outline of the light fixture, a nondescript glass bowl with three set screws. My chest felt tight, and I could not venture another word. I couldn't talk about it. I of course would never venture to describe some of the details of my life, even if I could consciously remember them, but my main question now was, 'if God loved me so much, why did He let it happen? Why didn't He protect me? Where had my father been—my mother? Why had I been stuck so many years with my malicious cousin? I didn't understand. From my training, I supposed such things were sent by God to punish a bad kid like me, but what had I done? Was my thinking evil or bad, or had I done something awful I didn't know about? Why was God mad at me?'

'Rachel,' Nancy finally said, 'if you would like to, you could go with me and Lawrence to our church. We'd be glad to have you. It's not really the same kind of church you grew up in, but I think you will find some familiar things there, such as the liturgy. The pastor there is a fine man—he went to school with my father, so we had known his family for quite a while. He cares about people, and he knows the Bible, and—maybe, you'd like to go with us.'

I thought about it….would I? After all, Nancy would be there, and probably some of my other classmates as well, and the church would be full of women. When I still lived with my uncle and aunt, I went to church because they required it, but as soon as I went to college, and moved away, I stopped going. Priestly robes frightened me—I kept thinking of Father John. His saintly face, suddenly dissolving into a vicious sneer, haunted my dreams and woke me with a cold sweat, and I resolved anew never to set foot in a church building. Besides, my body wasn't pure. I had been sexually violated, and had no business being in God's Holy House.

But God loved me, Nancy said. Maybe He would *want* me to be there. Maybe He sent Nancy—to ask? I learned not to fear Nancy. Sometimes I even laughed around her and she laughed with me, and I went places with her, and got back safely, with no horrible memories. I could go to church with her, too. I would be riding with her brother, who was as sincere a young man as I had ever come across yet. He was very slightly like a younger version of my uncle, and his manners and behavior were decent and courteous at all times. Perhaps I could take the chance. I said aloud, 'Nancy, I'll go.'

'Good,' said Nancy briskly. 'Services start at nine-thirty, so Lawrence will be waiting for me at ten after nine. Afterwards we'll go somewhere for lunch, and then we'll come back here, because I've got to catch up on those fifty problems Professor Gorham assigned us. He's such a Tartar, and I can't hand onto everything I hear in class the way you do. I wish I had your brains.'

Thus it was settled. I would go with Nancy and Lawrence that Sunday. I was very nervous and apprehensive, not knowing precisely the condition of my soul, and even wondering whether I would be struck by lightening on the spot. I was never told the story of Paul of Tarsus; he was, in a sense, struck by lightening and blinded, but that was done to get his attention, convert him, and began to fit him for God's service; it was not to destroy him. But the churches I went to never explained such things; the service was mainly by rote and the priest read and interpreted the Bible.

I was frightened, but I wouldn't dare confide in Nancy, or anyone. It was too risky for my reputation, and I knew at my age that sexual assault carried its own stigma: 'You asked for it. You had no business going there. You shouldn't have been wearing those kinds of clothes.' Even nowadays psychiatrists, ministers, and reputable women had a hard time understanding sexual assault as an out-and-out act of violence. I found out later that young women were not the only victims. It happened to men, to boys, to nuns, to older 'respectable' women, and it very often happened in homes, prisons—and churches. It happened in Bible times—and was recorded. And I was scared to go into a church building.

I couldn't tell Nancy anything about it, though. And so I went with her to church....

Teresa replaced the paperclip onto the yellowed page, and put the manuscript into the hatbox. She tried to remember—yes, Rachel had died a Lutheran. Teresa knew the church—Reverend Roger Mayfield was the pastor—and Rachel had been active in the church. One of the other Lutheran teachers at Teresa's school had told her that Rachel Evanson had the most beautiful soprano voice—

"I wish I could sound even half as good," she said. So Rachel had been in the music program. At any rate, she stopped being scared of going to church at some point, and maybe when she had a better understanding about God and Whom He truly was, she was able to go. Teresa was glad to know that, at least as far as church identification went, Rachel's story appeared to have a happy ending.

"Wherever you are, Nancy Lindeman," said Teresa aloud, "Thank you very much."

She put the hatbox in the closet, and left the bedroom. She would read more tomorrow evening, when she was done with her work.

Chapter 18

As she planned, Teresa finished her work, and took down the hatbox. She found the page with the paper clip, and she began to read—

"Lawrence picked us up at ten after nine that Sunday morning, as planned, and I put on my best dress out of respect for both the new church I would be attending, and the Lindemans. Nancy sat in the back seat with me, while Lawrence's girl friend Connie sat in from with him. In no time he pulled into the parking lot of a beautiful stone church with the usual stained-glass windows, but this church was practically covered by many tall, ancient shade trees, and a bird feeder was placed in the branches of one of them. Nancy, Connie, Lawrence and I all followed the gathering congregation to the church steps, where the minister stood in his white robes and colored stole. I nearly panicked, but forced myself up the steps and into the cool, dim building. The organ was already trilling out an opening Bach number, and I sat down in the pew indicated by Nancy, clutching the church program I was given by an usher.

The opening song was sung, and I decided to test out my singing voice. I never sang in church when I was living with my aunt and uncle, and I did not recognize the hymn printed before me now. But I could read music. It was one of the things Uncle Charles insisted I learn, and Aunt Anne grudgingly gave me music lessons. I didn't use the music very much back in my old home, but I remembered most of the lessons.

The song was 'Beautiful Savior.' I had never heard if before, although I now know it to be a well-known hymn among Protestant churches. The organist played out the melody, and then I noticed carefully the words. I began to sing, shakily at first, but when I thought about the words and what they meant, I forgot to be nervous. My voice sailed high above the other voices, miraculously on pitch, and clear as a bell. Nancy looked surprised but pleased. I was just surprised.

Then the service proceeded. Nancy was right: we had the liturgy, the bible readings, and the Psalms. Some of it was familiar to me. But the atmosphere was different. I couldn't think of why, not at the time.

The pastor, whose name was Paul Altenburg, stood before the congregation, and delivered his sermon. I was really surprised then. He talked about Jesus, but Jesus as a personal Savior. An accessible Savior. He quoted often from the New Testament, and he encouraged us to open our Bibles and follow along with him as he read the verses. He made Jesus the focus of his sermon. He never mentioned saints, or Mother Mary, or anything like that. We prayed in the name of Jesus only, and at communion (in which I did not take part) everyone received both the bread and the wine. Pastor Altenburg blessed the Elements, but everyone partook of them.

I felt rather disoriented when I finally left the church building, after services were over, but Nancy was soon exclaiming, 'Rachel, you can sing! Where on earth did you get a voice like that?' I could honestly ask myself the same question—I never heard my mother sing, and as for my father—a drunk? He could have never been a good singer. But I could sing, and did. I hoped the Lord heard my voice, singing words of praise to Him, and I hoped He would not reject me outright. At least I wasn't struck down in the church sanctuary.

Instead, I was walking back to the roadster with Nancy, Connie, and Lawrence, and we all piled in, to go out for lunch. It was a beautiful day. It was bright—not a cloud in the sky—and the town was well-shaded by trees which were now in full leaf, and everyone around seemed happy and cheerful. The horror of the Depression was beginning to lose its hold on the country, and people were looking forward to a better future. It wasn't the wild enjoyment of the '20's, but a more mature hope, born of discipline and reevaluation of ideals, brought on by necessity, but maybe of greater value.

It was the spring of 1937. As we rode back from lunch I sat in the backseat of the roadster with Nancy, and heard the conversation between Lawrence and Connie, as we rode through the quiet, well-shaded and well-manicured neighborhood, toward the college campus. The conversation sounded serious, not quite what I expected between a boy and girl friend.

'I told Dad it would definitely not be a good idea to go to Europe, even for a short visit,' Lawrence was saying. 'Certainly not to Germany, but that of course was out of the question as far as Dad was concerned. He does *not* like what is happening over there, and I don't blame him. That Hitler's a total basket case—I don't know what they were thinking, letting him get in charge. Italy's a mess, too, and France and England both better be careful. The Abdication Crisis didn't help anything, although, honestly, I think Bertie will be a better King than his brother.'

Connie looked worried. 'What does it all mean?' she asked. 'They won't go to war, will they?'

Lawrence shook his head, guiding the roadster around a flowered median, 'It's too soon to tell. I hope not. But I have a hunch Germany is going to go crazy, trying to show how powerful she is—she took quite a beating in the Great War, and she hasn't forgiven nor forgotten. The Germans now hope Hitler will lead them into greatness, and he likes military shows. I don't know—it seems like a powder keg over there. It usually is, but now it seems worse than usual.'

'Maybe, if they do go to war, they'll keep it in Europe,' said Connie hopefully. 'They can beat the Germans, can't they? They've done it before.'

Lawrence laughed shortly. 'Oh, yeah,' he said. 'The War to end all wars. "Drop it, Kaiser Bill!" Well, it was a nice thought, but I'm afraid it was too good to be true. And don't forget—we have another fun factor—Russia and her Bolsheviks. Not nice, if they team up with Germany. But I think Hitler is aiming for Czechoslovakia, then Poland, and that won't put him on Russia's happy list.'

'Oh, Lawrence,' grimaced Nancy, whacking him from behind the seat, 'You sound just like Professor Burnham—Rachel and I have him for history. I am sure if we wanted a history lecture, we'd—'

'Okay, Nancy, okay,' cut in Lawrence.

'—Besides, you're boring Connie to death.'

'I know,' Lawrence conceded, 'and what's more, I hope I'm wrong. But things are looking rather scary over there. Never mind. Here's the college, and here's your dorm. Rachel, make sure Nancy studies and does her homework like she's suppose to do. I'm glad you came with us, and I hope you come again. Bye, Sis. Behave yourself.'

Nancy and I got out, and watched Lawrence and Connie drive away. The day was still very bright, and the warm breeze brought forth the fragrance of newly blossoming flowers, some from the campus gardens. Nancy glanced at the large brick dorm building, with its many windows, and then turned to me. 'I really don't want to go indoors just yet,' she said, 'I'm going to get my books and bring them outside.' I nodded and went with her, entering the dorm entrance, then up the echoing stairwell to the second floor, with its long, waxed-linoleum-and-painted-plaster hall. The hallway was dim, as it was lit by silver-ringed hanging ceiling fixtures positioned at wide intervals. Each end of the hallway did have a long window, but that did not dispel much of the dimness. Nancy opened the door to our room, and began going through her books.

'This one, this one. And I need to take some extra scratch sheets with me. Rachel, I'm going down to the courtyard to study. Will you come with me? I might need your help, and besides, I like to have you with me. I'm not keeping you from anything, am I?'

'Oh, no, of course not,' I replied. I reflected, silently, that it would be a good idea to study with her, as the subject she was concerned with was one I was also taking. The professor in question had a reputation of being one of the worst in the college, and he was often nicknamed Professor Gorgon, instead of his actual name,

Professor Gorham. I understood Nancy's concerns completely, and I pulled my own books out as well.

The courtyard was an ideal place to study. The benches and tables were white concrete, and they were placed in the center of the campus grounds, near the flower gardens. When Nancy and I took our place at one concrete table, several students were already there, books open, while some students sat on the lush grass, propped up against the tree trunks, to study. Nancy opened her textbook, and we began to tackle the problems. None of them were easy, but between us, we made a lot of headway. Soon we were halfway through, and it was yet mid-afternoon.

'I almost understand this!' exclaimed Nancy, very pleased. 'Let's try another problem.'

'Problem is right!' I groaned, exhausted from thinking so hard. 'I hope my brain doesn't crack open.'

Nancy laughed, evidently pleased that I had lost some of my wariness, and indeed I had. We tackled the next problems, which, as usual, got harder and more complicated as we went on. It was several hours before we were finally finished, and the sun was definitely dipping toward the west. The evening was bringing on its own special hallmarks: the streetlamps came on, the students began pairing off for dates and other amusements, and their talk and laughter could be heard across campus, and the breeze became cooler. Nancy sighed, and closed her textbook.

'Done!' she shouted aloud. 'Take that, Professor Gorgon!'

I laughed. The sun had nearly set, and the western half of the sky was luminous brownish-orange, while that above us was deep blue, with the stars beginning to appear. The lights of several of the dorm rooms were now on, shining through curtained windows, and the outdoor lights attached to the dorm roof came on as well. Laughter and conversation came from every direction, and automobiles passed by the campus grounds with great regularity. 'I guess, if we want dinner, we better get to the main building,' I said. 'It's about that time.' Nancy agreed, and we scurried across the lush campus lawn toward the noisy Students' Hall. We had our dinner, and Nancy stayed at the Hall, chatting with friends she knew. I was getting tired, though, so I waved goodbye to her and started toward the dorm.

It was not really that late, but I was exhausted. Perhaps it was helping Nancy with her lessons, or it was because I got up early to go to church. But surely that wasn't the case, because I got up early for morning classes all the time. However, I dropped onto my bed and was soon fast asleep. Nancy didn't come in until much later; apparently she chose not to disturb me, but spent most of the evening in the dorm living area.

I wished I had Nancy's energy, and spirit for living. But—I didn't.

It was Thursday of that week that I was awake enough to speak with Nancy again. She was turning in for the night—I was already in bed—and had finished her prayers. She had already read her Bible, and it was back on its place on the doily. As soon as she pulled the covers over her slim, long body, I said, 'Nancy?'

'Yes, Rachel?'

'Could—could you show me those passages in the Bible about God loving me? I mean—when you have the time. I—I still can't believe it. I thought God hated people, really, with all that stuff in the Old Testament about floods and fire and brimstone and everything. Your preacher didn't seem to talk like that, but I don't know *what* to believe. Doesn't God send bad things to people to punish them for being wicked?'

Nancy sat up slightly in her bed across the room. 'To answer your last question, no,' she said. 'Things happen to us simply because we live in a fallen, sinful world. But that doesn't mean God doesn't love us, or that He doesn't care. In fact, Rachel, my personal thought is, if God didn't care so much, He never would have gotten angry— He would have been indifferent and would have done nothing at all. But, be as that may, He did care, and He does. He sent His Son to die for us. And not only that, He sent the Holy Ghost, to call for us and to give us wisdom.'

'The Holy Ghost?'

'Of course. Wasn't the Holy Ghost mentioned at the church you attended?'

'Well, yes, in the Apostle's Creed and at my confirmation lessons, but I never really figured out what they were talking about. They said "The Holy Ghost" and it sounded sort of creepy to me. Like medieval catacombs and saints and all that sort of thing—like superstition and Halloween.'

'Oh, Rachel!' Nancy reproved. 'It's not supposed to be creepy at all. It's suppose to be comforting. That is Whom the Holy Ghost is meant to be—a Comforter and Counselor.'

I raised my head, gave my pillow a punch, and turned over. 'Well, they never explained it to me like that. If that were true, why would I need to beg for intercession, and pray to saints? Oh, and—what about good works? Doesn't it say somewhere that a branch that doesn't bear fruit is going to be cut off and thrown into the fire? That sounds pretty angry to me.'

Nancy sighed. 'It does say that, in John Chapter 15. But you must read all the verses, from verse 1 to verse 17, and then you will have a far better understanding of what was meant. *Jesus* is the vine, *we* are the branches. Jesus said in verse 5 that if a person remained in Him, and He in that person, *then* the person would bear much fruit—apart from Jesus he could do nothing. So there has to be that close relationship with Jesus before you can bear the fruit. And if you look at verse 9, you will find Jesus saying "I love you."'

Now I was really awake. 'Nancy, you'll have to show me that, tomorrow,' I said. We couldn't look just then. If we turned on the bedroom light, the dorm mother on duty would be knocking on the door in no time, wanting to know what was wrong, since it was officially 'lights out.' But I was really curious now. I always believed in the existence of God, but I looked upon Him as a stern, angry taskmaster, ready to throw me in hell at the slightest provocation, and the terror I experienced at the hands of one of His priests confirmed that terror. What I experienced then was to be a foretaste of the evils to come, when my unworthy soul suffered damnation.

Oh, Friend, how little I knew You!

I had been hurt—I had been violated.

And so had You. Nails driven into the palms of Your Hands, and into Your feet. A spear tearing into Your side....

You knew pain.

But at the time, I did not know that, Friend. Nancy asked if I wanted to go to church with her again. I said yes...."

Teresa put the paperclip on that page, and returned the manuscript to the hatbox. After putting the hatbox away, she took Rachel's Bible and read John Chapter 15, in its entirety. Having been raised Baptist, she had never studied Luther's catechism or heard the Apostle's Creed. But she had been encouraged to read and search the scriptures, and she had been instructed to "go, and tell the world."

She, too, had been introduced to the Third Person in the Trinity, now more commonly known as "the Holy Spirit." That sounded less "creepy" as Rachel had put it, but whatever the name, Teresa knew the Presence was very real.

So what was next? Teresa knew some of the answers: Rachel would graduate from Teachers' college, and Hitler would invade Poland. But somewhere, somehow, in all the chaos, Rachel would meet God. Not as a dangerous enemy, but as a loving Father. When would that be? Teresa closed the Bible after she read John 15, and began to pray.

Teresa intended that she should read the entire manuscript before the school year began. She still had time. The summer was at its height, and was so very warm....

Chapter 19

AUGUST WAS APPROACHING, AND SO WAS a new school year. The days had become so hot that even with huge shade trees, the house had become unbearably warm and the A/C unit had to be run. Bill and Teresa recently had a second A/C unit put in their bedroom window, and the children were given box fans for their bedrooms, with strict orders not to be careless with them. Even at night it was hot, and during the day Billy and Mandy were rarely at home. They usually went off to the municipal swimming pool several blocks from their home, which was near the park. Teresa knew they would meet their friends there, but it was also a good chance to cool off.

One day Teresa had finished cleaning house, while Billy and Mandy were gone, and she noticed the light outside was beginning to dim. The A/C unit was running, but she shut it off, and listened carefully. Sure enough, she heard a far-off rumble of thunder. Instantly, she was in gear. Billy and Mandy had gone swimming, and they had walked—and they would have to walk back—beneath a lot of tall trees! Teresa ran to her bedroom, grabbed her carkeys, and raced to the Plymouth. She was quickly on her way to the swimming pool. Not a block away from the park, she spotted Billy and Mandy, looking like a forlorn pair of bedraggled birds. Overhead, a huge dark thunderhead was unfolding.

"Get in!" she shouted, flinging the passenger door open. Billy and Mandy got in, enfolded in huge beach towels.

"Gaw, Mom, you're so worried!" protested Billy.

"And why wouldn't I be?" demanded Teresa. "One good thunderbolt—through one of those trees—would turn both of you into crispy critters. Or haven't you studied electricity? Do you know the meaning of the word 'conductor?' "

"You mean like the guy who leads the orchestra?" said Mandy, grinning. She then ducked under her beach towel.

"No, Miss Mandy, I mean like you," replied Teresa. "Get under the wrong tree out there, and you'll find out. Especially as wet as you are."

"Oh, Mom, we got sense," protested Billy. "As soon as we saw the cloud coming, we got out of the pool. Well, of course they made everyone get out, but Mandy and I were out first. Anyway, thanks for getting us. Those trees were rather scary."

The thunder rumbled, and sprinkles of water appeared on the windshield. Teresa turned on the wipers, and her headlights as well, and she pulled into the driveway as a flash of light illuminated the thunderhead. Another crackle of thunder, and Teresa practically chased her offspring into the house. "Stay away from the windows!" she ordered. "Mandy, you probably better not talk on the phone. The storm seems pretty close. It isn't safe."

"What'll I do, then?" Mandy moaned.

"Well, for starters, you can put on some dry clothes. Then you can find a good book to read—you've got a bookcase full of them. Why don't you read that book your Aunt Tess got you, about the adventure stories for girls?"

"All right, Mom. Go on now. I'm going to put some dry clothes on."

Teresa smiled and went to the living room. The storm was in earnest now, and powerful raindrops struck against the windows and rat-tatted on the roof. The thunder banged again, and lightening flashed unnatural light that contrasted eerily to the dipping, purplish clouds. It was really dark outside, except for the flashes of light, and the raindrops were so heavy that Teresa began to suspect the rain turned to hail. She turned on the small transistor radio for the latest weather report.

"—summer showers, severe thunderstorms locally, hail in isolated areas—"

Teresa clicked off the radio, and listened to the thunder rattle the entire house. The storm was severe, and there would probably be a backyard full of hailstones before long, but she glanced at the clouds and decided nothing worse would happen. The clouds were not ragged and lowering, and nothing in them was visibly rotating. It was just a summer storm, with noise, lightening, rain, hail and some wind. She turned on the lamps in the living room, as it was so dark.

Billy came into the living room, to get some of his father's field and fishing magazines, to read in his bedroom while the storm raged. Mandy apparently found the adventure book for girls and was stretched out on her bed, reading it. Teresa decided to go into her room as well. She switched on the front porch light for Bill, as he would be home that evening. Then she went into her bedroom and went to her closet, taking down the hatbox.

As she lifted the lid, she glanced out the bedroom window. Outside, the wind and rain conspired to whip about the tree branches, as thick as they were. The one mimosa tree was stripped of all its puffy pink blossoms, and the wind tore at the clothesline, trying to tangle the wires with the tree limbs. Rain slapped against the window panes, and then a loud crack of thunder, directly overheard, nearly deafened Teresa. She lifted the manuscript from the hatbox, and found the paperclip. Using the small table lamp by her bed as illumination, she began to read---

"I began going to church regularly with Nancy, and I was readily accepted as one of the students who accompanied the Lindemans every Sunday morning. I avoided Pastor Altenburg, which was not aimed at him personally: I just didn't trust anyone in a white robe, and I avoided male church leaders on principle. If I had a question, I asked Nancy. The church had an adult Bible class also, and I attended that with the Lindemans. The class was very helpful, and I felt safe with Nancy, Connie and Lawrence. There was something down-to-earth about the way this church approached Christianity. In fact, it seemed almost a living thing in the lives of my three friends, and to many of the others in the congregation also. They took the Bible instruction seriously, and they tried to live it as well.

I was interested, but I was scared, too. Friend, it is hard to describe the kind of conflicts that were raging in my mind at this time, when I was trying to go to God. I felt almost like I was under attack, from something unseen and unknown, but very malignant. My emotions started to roil and turn toward evil, as though my past wanted to reach across to strangle me. I began finding myself wanting to do evil things—I would look at one young man in my class, and then another, and start having fantasies which I knew were sinful and wrong. I would never do it—and risk my teaching career—but I had an almost irresistible urge to do so. I couldn't understand what was wrong with me; I knew I should never have dealings with a man. Then I had inexplicable inner episodes of rage against Cousin Anne, who had been such an unpleasant part of my life, although I quite reasonably never expected to see her again. What was the matter with me?

Of course I didn't say anything, to Nancy or anyone. Just having the thoughts I did was enough to have me labeled with several of the many foul words used to describe "loose" women, and that would not be good for an aspiring schoolteacher. I did apply those words to myself, however. I didn't know why I wanted to do such nasty things, and the only explanation was that I was a secret _____. I kept this to myself; feeling like a hypocrite, I continued to go to church with the Lindemans.

At least I was not expected to go to confession. The church I now attended saw confession of sins as a helpful part of a Christian's life, but there was no confessing to priests as such. It was between me and God. And I could only imagine how God felt about me at this point. I heard that committing sins in one's heart was as bad as actually doing them openly. I felt hopeless, and I wondered if I should stop going to church altogether.

I must have changed somehow. Nancy seemed concerned about me, although she asked no questions. Somehow she knew I was struggling. But I could say nothing to her about what was wrong. I had to go through it alone.

I managed to keep up with my classes. But I became more tired and more easily exhausted.

The school year had ended: I passed all the examinations, and spent the summer in the college town, as I had the summer before. Uncle Charles sent me a letter which didn't say very much; he was happy with my progress, and hoped I would continue to do well. He said nothing of Cousin Anne, although he did mention that Aunt Anne found housekeeping irksome and tiring: she was getting old. There was a veiled hint that she missed my help. It was no matter, though; I did not plan to return, even for a visit, and I had my job at the bookstore.

I did not go to church during the summer, but when the fall of that year came about and school went back into session, I happily welcomed Nancy, whom I truly missed. She was happy to see me, too. She had not changed in the least, and she did not have some out-of-town cousin who suddenly wanted to share a dorm room with her. We had our same room on the second floor, and she had all her beautiful things placed on her bureau, including her Bible. I was glad that had not changed.

I began to attend church again, with her reassuring presence, and Pastor Altenburg actually came up to me and said he had missed seeing me. I didn't see how that could have possibly mattered to him, but apparently it did. I still hung back from him—I knew he wasn't Father John—but he was still male and in a position of authority. I didn't think he would hurt me, but if for some weird and out-of-the-way reason he chose to do so, then I would have a hard time defending myself. In fact, I doubted my ability to do so.

It was hard to describe the conflict that arose within me that third college year, and what frightened me was the strength of my feelings—the outrage, the anger, the sense of helplessness. What brought it on? Outwardly, I never seemed to have it so good. I had a real friend, I was doing excellent college work, I went to church, and I went on many outings with college acquaintances. My uncle made sure I had plenty of money. I went to the college football games with Nancy and her friends, and I became part of the Glee Club. I went through all the motions, and said what I was expected to say, in

each situation. But I could feel a volcano building within me, raging
with burning lava, and at nights I began to dream of soldiers and of
Father John. In these dreams I was stripped naked, and hung from
a pole while all my acquaintances taunted me and laughed. I would
try to strike back at the taunters, and then some respectable patriarch
would come up, slap me and tell me, 'Your behavior is inappropriate.'
Then Father John would laugh and shake hands with the patriarch,
and the soldiers would roar with approval.

I always awoke from the dreams terrified and in a sweat, and I
was physically paralyzed as well. It took me several minutes just to
dare to move. I tried to remember that I had classes to attend, and
that I was reasonably safe on campus. The dorm mothers were mainly
middle-aged, fussy, nosy and sharp-tongued, but they seemed to be
just as suspicious of men as I was. As long as I 'didn't ask for it' they
would protect me.

By November I was really exhausted, as the third year classes
were very difficult, and I had a hard time keeping up with them,
study group or no study group. I began turning down invitations to
go out, and I could barely make it to classes. I saw Nancy glance at
me worriedly from time to time, although she said nothing to me. I
continued to go to church with her, but in my heart all I wanted to
do was argue with God. 'Why didn't You help me? Why didn't You
protect me? You are one big lie, with Your pretenses of perfection and
goodness. You love *me?* Not a chance! All You want to do is make
life miserable for me, and punish me when I am bad, or when You
think I'm bad. Who are You to think I'm bad, huh? Look at Yourself,
You big powerful meanie!'

One day I was sweaty and shaky and ill, and could not go to
class. The dorm mother, Mrs. Ryde, came to check on me, and
took my temperature. It was close to normal, but I was sick at my
stomach, and she brought in a heating pad. Nancy had not yet left
for class, and she said, 'I'll stay with her, Mrs. Ryde. I'll let you know
if I need anything.'

Mrs. Ryde nodded and left, and Nancy opened the calico
curtains. It was November, and very dull and windy outside, but

some light filtered in. Nancy drew her small chair, which she brought from home, beside my bed, and sat down.

'Rachel, can you tell me what is wrong?' she asked.

I shook my head. I became aware of a terrible lump forming in my throat, threatening to choke me, and I was fiercely afraid of losing control. I thought I would be sick again, but I was not. I turned away from Nancy.

'I really don't want to ask too many questions, Rachel, but I can tell whatever it is has been affecting your life. And Rachel, you're too wonderful a person to let anything, no matter how terrible, beat you down so that you cannot live. You have so much to offer, Rachel. I don't know who hurt you, and I'm not going to ask. But please understand that you have value—in this world, in this college, and in God's sight. Please, Rachel, believe me. You are truly of value. It doesn't matter what has happened in the past, or what anyone said to you before.'

Then sorrow and pain overwhelmed me, and I could no longer hold it in. Tears streamed from my eyes, totally against my will, and soon became a flood that threatened to rip apart my chest. Nancy reached down and quietly took me into her arms, and while holding me took some tissues from her dresser. I was engulfed in sobs, and she lay her hand gently on the back of my head, stroking my curls. 'Rachel, it's okay, let it out,' she said. 'It will help you to get better. It is your way of speaking to God of your hurt and pain, and He can hear you and understand. Don't be afraid. Whatever it is, don't be afraid.' I *was* afraid—I didn't know how she knew that—and even though her touch comforted me, I still feared violation. But I stopped trying to restrain the tears; I cried very bitterly, and when I was done, Nancy put me back into my bed, and pulled the covers over me.

'Get some rest, now, Rachel,' she said. 'I'm going to get some lunch, and I'll bring you back some hot tea. I think you'll be ready to go back to class tomorrow. And—if you want to talk about anything, or if you need some special prayer, let me know. You don't have to do this alone. I'll help in any way I can.'

She left, and I lay my tear-stained face on the thin pillow. I was sore all over, but I felt somewhat less stressed, and began to believe I could take on the world again. But what of God? Could I take Him on? I believed I hated Him, for allowing awful things to happen to me. Couldn't He have stopped it? And since He didn't, Who was He to demand good behavior of me?

An odd thing happened, though. I raged and hated, but my heart began to turn to Him, and I whispered my first prayer to Him. I didn't ask for forgiveness at that time—I was not ready to do that, as the unfairness and pain still rankled with me—but I reached out in prayer, as though clinging for some kind of hope. I had heard Pastor Altenburg's sermons and learned a lot about God that I had not been told before, but I knew faith was important, and that I didn't have. I had no peace within my soul. However, the tears I had shed drained out a lot of the burning anger that threatened to drive me into untentable conduct. As the afternoon drew to a close I ceased to be nauseated as well, and I agreed with Nancy that I would be able to go to class the next day.

I kept down the tea she brought me, and I did go to the Students' Hall for dinner, although I didn't take much. I finished my homework, and when the 'lights out' announcement came, Nancy and I said our prayers together before we retired. I sensed that I had some ground beneath my feet again.

The nightmares didn't stop entirely, and I still had rage in my heart. But it was more bearable. I continued to attend the Lindemans' church, and I began to pray on my own, this time with conviction. I was plenty mad at God, but I wanted to make contact, too; and Nancy showed me places in the Bible where 'The Spirit and the bride say, "Come!" And let him who hears say, "Come!" (Rev 21:17).'

I was angry with God, but I think then I began to love Him, too. And things changed for me, although not outwardly, but in another way.….."

The storm was winding down. It was still dark outside, but the rain no longer drummed against the windows, and the thunder did not rumble as loud or as insistently. Teresa moved the paperclip to the new page, put the manuscript in the hatbox, and put the hatbox away. Then she left the bedroom.

She went to the front porch, to see what the storm had done: hailstones littered the front lawn, and a few broken branches were scattered about. The tree trunks were positively black with sopping wetness. The rain gutters were still pouring water near the foundation of concrete, and the driveway shale was now very gritty and covered with muddy leaves. The Plymouth wasn't damaged, though. The rain freshened the red paint, and the white paint on the sides of the car and under the taillights shone, as the rain had washed the dirt away. Teresa was thankful none of the windows were broken, or the headlights or taillights, either.

It was late in the afternoon, and Bill would soon be home. The air was still very damp, and the clouds still hung over the area. It was humid. Teresa went back into the house, and raised some windows. She didn't think she would need the attic fan just yet, for the breeze was still cool enough to be bearable.

She would read some more tomorrow. She went into the kitchen, to start dinner....

Chapter 20

THE NEXT DAY WAS HOT AND humid, as Teresa knew it would be. She had planned to do the laundry, but supposed it wouldn't hurt to wait a day, when the outdoors had a chance to dry out. Even though the sun was out, the ground was still muddy. It would dry before long, and Teresa doubted it would rain again for quite a while. She had lived many summers in ___ton, and rainfall was not that common in July and August.

Bill was on patrol, and Billy and Mandy were back at the swimming pool. The house was silent as well as hot, and Teresa considered watching television. But she decided against it. She went into the bedroom and turned on the A/C unit, and went to the closet to get the hatbox. She had left off where Rachel had begun to seek answers and direction, and it seemed that she found leading at last. It may have bothered Rachel that Mary Jones didn't like her and wanted a new roommate, but in view of later events, the change turned out to be a blessing. The Lord knew Rachel needed Nancy, and that Nancy probably needed Rachel, too. Teresa believed in the Lord's involvement in individual lives, especially when He wanted His will to be accomplished. She took the manuscript from the hatbox, to continue reading. She was very interested now, and she read—

"It was odd that I received spiritual instruction at the same time, and in the same place, that I received my teaching education, and that I was free to decide on both—I was not compelled to go to church as I had been when living with my aunt and uncle. I didn't even tell Uncle Charles *where* I was going to church—I simply said, when the subject came up, that I was going to church with my roommate, whose brother had a car. My uncle didn't ask any questions; he probably assumed I would continue in the faith in which I was brought up, and anyway, I don't think it mattered to him that much. He never made actual family worship a part of his family's life; I think he assumed Sunday morning church, confession, and Aunt Anne's charity projects took care of the 'religious' part of life. He was more concerned about financial security, and making sure the family had a respectable place in the town's social structure.

But going to church with Nancy, and observing the actions of the congregation and the church leaders, I began to experience God as a real, concerned entity, and not as an abstract idea or a threatening, unapproachable judge. It was that experience that drew me to church again and again, even though the pastor's white robe frightened me, and I became slightly ill every time I crossed the foyer and looked into the dim, perfectly kept sanctuary. It helped when I sang the hymns, for somehow, when my voice rose above that of the other members and blended with organ, I was not silenced by the solemn stained-glass windows and polished wood pews and carpeted floors. I was heard—maybe God heard me. I listened intently to the preaching, and to the prayers that were said. I looked at the empty cross in front of the church, and at the altar with the communion rails and embroidered kneelers, and I wondered if I would ever trust God enough to go up there, and receive communion, as Nancy and Lawrence did.

I thought about talking with Pastor Altenburg—and I would make sure Nancy was there with me—but I continued to think about it only, and I did not actually do it. Father John still had a terrorizing hold over me, and I could not reach out. But I wanted to come to a decision eventually. I prayed with Nancy and asked her questions, and one day she bought me a Bible.

I learned about 'Grace alone.' I learned that the death on the cross completed my salvation, and I didn't have to do anything extra to atone for my sins. I learned that God truly loved me and wanted me to come to Him, and leave the life of sin behind. I also found I couldn't remain neutral. Either I believed in, and accepted Christ—or I didn't. I decided I hadn't accepted Him yet, as I really didn't know Who He was. Now I did know—and I had a Bible and a church body to help me with that knowledge. I was asked to become close to a living God—and I was terrified to be close to anyone, any time, for any reason at all. I feared pain and violation—even in a church.

Finally, I asked Nancy about 'joining the church.' She was pleased to hear that I asked, but she said I must see Pastor Altenburg.

I was completely distraught at the idea. But slowly—I don't know how to describe this—I noticed a glowing in my soul—faint at first, but growing as I continued to study and pray. I seemed to understand the Scriptures as I never had before, and something awoke within me. I wondered if it was the presence of the Holy Ghost. I didn't really want to go near Pastor Altenburg, but I had to do something now, and he would not be any worse than any other. After all, I knew no harm in him.

I think Nancy knew I would not move forward on my own. One Sunday she very firmly marched me up to the pastor, and said, 'Rachel would like to join our church. Could you explain about the classes for adults, and when you might have them?'

Pastor Altenburg gave me a beautiful, heavenly smile, and I cringed and stepped back behind Nancy. It was very rude, but I almost couldn't help myself. But the pastor did not take offense, and he said, 'I'm glad you came to me just when you did. I was going to make the announcement next Sunday that I will be leading an adult Confirmation class because so many of the college students asked about joining the church. I believe God is truly working in this congregation, and it is good to see that. So many young people, with their lives and families ahead of them. It would be such a blessing, to bring God's love and protection into those lives—I am planning to begin the classes three weeks from today, and will hold them in the evenings. Rachel, may I count on you to attend the classes?'

I hesitated, and whispered, 'I'm not sure. I don't have a way over—'

Nancy cut in, 'Oh, Rachel, don't be silly! You know Lawrence and I will come, and bring you with us. I had confirmation when I was young, but it never hurts to go back and hear everything again. I would like to go to the classes. Please, Rachel, won't you come with me?'

I nodded. Pastor Altenburg smiled again and said, 'Good. That's settled. And—Mrs. Altenburg will be with us, too. We look forward to a full class.'

Lawrence and Connie sought us out at that point, and we left the church building and walked out into the windy day. I climbed into Lawrence's roadster, still shaking a little; Pastor Altenburg was wearing his white robe, and even though he was close to fifty years old, he was still handsome and very personable. I did not trust that. It was not based on anything reasonable: I had been attending the church close to a year now, and Pastor Altenburg always behaved in an exemplary way to me, to Nancy, to everyone in his pastorate. He was involved in a more or less open battle with one of his senior elders, and everyone knew it, but they worked side by side anyway, and that should have been reassuring to me. It showed the pastor was not perfect, and he wasn't a phony, either. But—white robes frightened me. So did dim, silent, sharply clean and shining church buildings, if I were completely honest with myself. Could I go into the church, and worship God, without fear of violation? I wanted to worship, but I was afraid—afraid that I would be attacked in God's holy House.

I had lunch with the Lindemans, and then went back to my dorm room. I had no homework to complete that Sunday, and I told Nancy I was going to take a nap. She smiled, told me to have a good rest, and left the dorm with some friends. I lay down and pulled the thin woven blanket over my shoulders, and stared at the ceiling. My mind was busy with many thoughts, and I couldn't sleep. I was tired, and I wanted to be alone. So much was happening at once.

I could go to the classes and join the church. I could study the Bible, hear the sermons, and take part in some of the programs the church sponsored. But was it safe? Would I be safe? I still could not rid my mind of the thought that if God really loved me, He would have protected me from physical harm, especially when I was a child. But He hadn't done that, and how could I trust Him? How could I worship Him with all my heart, when I was hurt by one of His own priests, while He turned the other way, and did nothing.

…..My God, my God, why have You forsaken me?

Friend—those were Your words. You were the Son of God—of Whom He was well pleased. Yet—did You, too, feel abandoned, when You hung from the cross? The nails were driven into Your hands, into Your feet; You felt and heard the hatred of the crowd watching You die, and gloating as You did so. Maybe it did seem to You that God, Your very own loving Father, turned His back on You while You were in great pain. Then—Friend—would You understand what was taking place in my heart? Why I was so terrified? I wanted to be near You—I wanted Your love. But if I ever became vulnerable and willing to receive Your closeness, then I knew I would be hurt— the people I knew came close to me only to take advantage of my 'weakness' to inflict pain. I could not risk it. I could not trust.

I continued to stare at the ceiling of my dorm room, and I listened to the hush that usually pervaded the dorm building on a Sunday afternoon. Most of the girls were taking part in some sort of activity, or going on excursions with male friends, and even the girls who stayed in the dorm went into the living area, where they listened to the large mahogany-cased radio, or entertained dates on the sofas. All the girls seemed so happy—so young. Many of them were confident; joyful, even—I envied that, and knew that joy could never be mine.

I would have to make the most of my life as it was, and not wish for something that could not be. But I would try to avail myself of anything within reach. And being a part of the Lord's church was in my reach…..

The classes began, and Lawrence, Nancy and Connie all attended them with me. Pastor Altenburg was right: the class was large, and it was a very friendly, welcoming group, such as I had never encountered in a church before. The pastor seemed very anxious that we understand what we were participating in; he did not want it to be a rote lesson, to be learned and tested on, and then forgotten.

I had never met a pastor so concerned about 'going and making disciples' as this one seemed to be. He was probably one of the most practical men I ever met, but conversely, one of the most spiritually sound, too. His knowledge of the Bible was almost unreal. As a budding schoolteacher, I could see the signs of a man who studied and mastered his subject thoroughly, as though it were a part of him. He could teach, too—he both taught us and put us to work, so that we would do our own searching and studying.

He wanted to get to know each of us individually, and he spoke with us one on one, although I wouldn't talk to him without Nancy present. However, he sensed my discomfort, and for a wonder, made allowances for me. He was gentle, and tried not to startle me. I did have occasion to visit his office in the church building—and it was a reassuringly proper and rather disheveled office, with no disturbing artwork or anything that wouldn't be found in a thousand other pastors' offices. It was all Bibles, study books, 'God is Love' banners, crosses, and a respectful, beautiful picture of Jesus with children surrounding Him. Pastor Altenburg also had pictures of his wife and children in various places, and embroidered knick-knacks that suggested elderly female relatives. He was obviously a decent man, but still, I would never seek him out—or any other male leader.

It was in these circumstances that I completed the classes, and joined a Lutheran church. I went to the communion rail for the first time, fully prepared, and knowing the seriousness and the significance of what I was about to do. And I meant it. I wanted it to be that way. But I despaired of ever truly understanding God's love the way a little child did—trustingly. I told the Lord, 'I don't know if I can love You the way You want me to. But I'll come to You the way that I am—frightened, damaged, impure, and a little angry. I can't do anything else. But here I am, Lord.'

So I knelt at the altar rail, and received the Body and Blood of Christ. Friend—I learned Who You were, and Who You are—my friend. I could talk with You and share things with You—for You knew pain, and shame, and what it was to be rejected. I could not share this with anyone else—not even Nancy. Even good people are limited in what they can understand and accept. But not You—

Friend. You know about it all. And I received Your Body and Your Blood—the most intimate sharing I can think of—and there was no pain. There was understanding—and love, and for the first time I felt truly accepted.

That's how I began my life with the new church. And though I was still in much pain, I began to have some hope..."

Teresa moved the paperclip to that page, and placed the manuscript into the hatbox. She was beginning to be aware of something she had not thought of before—Rachel, for all her problems, had a deep sense of nearness to God that could have only been brought about by suffering and pain. Teresa almost envied her. Teresa herself had been a Christian all her life, but it was something she took—well, not for granted, exactly, but she never had any real refining process in her life which would severely test her faith. She had been happy for the most part—she had the normal sorrows and trials that most people experienced at one time or another, but nothing that would break her or cause her to doubt her faith. She would have never wanted Rachel's pain, but she thought, because of that pain, Rachel knew the Lord in a special way. Teresa considered this as she put the hatbox away, and she took Rachel's Bible to read, as she wanted to look at the Gospels again.

The A/C unit hummed and blew cold air into the room, and Teresa looked out the bedroom window, still holding Rachel's Bible. Outside it was sunny and bright, and, Teresa suspected, still very hot. A couple of birds flew by the window, cheeping and fighting, and the strong flapping wings struck the panes. Then Teresa heard the slam of the front door, and the voices of Billy and Mandy, as they argued about something inconsequential. Teresa couldn't hear the words, but she could tell by their voices that it wasn't serious. She finished reading the final chapter of the Book of John, then put the Bible on her dresser. Then she got up and switched off the A/C unit, and left the bedroom.

Tomorrow she would wash clothes. Looking outside, she could see everything was very nearly dried up, and the next day would probably be a sunny day, too. At least her life was a smooth one, all things considered. And for that, she was now very thankful...

Chapter 21

THE SUMMER WORE ON, AND WOULD soon be drawing to a close. Teresa knew the time was moving toward a new school year, with new students and new fashions, but the same routine as well. She also knew the hot, sometimes humid days would hand on for much longer than anyone would wish—often the school was in full session before the first cooling off. Even so, the color of the sunshine seemed to change, to a softer, more golden hue, instead of the white rays of Midsummer, and that meant September would soon arrive. Teresa already had her lesson plans set up: she had reviewed the textbooks she would be using, and she had so much teaching experience that the new year, to her, would be just one more year.

It would be the second school year without Rachel. The grave was now covered over with fresh, green grass—the stone had shifted slightly, and had an appearance of settled eternity. The school doors would open, and hum with life and activity, but Rachel's place was now with the other townspeople whose "voices were silenced." Teresa had been to the grave one or twice, to plant flowers—she had done so on Rachel's birthday, July 9th. Even though it was very hot, the cemetery was shaded by tall, ancient pecan, oak and maple trees, and the effect was that of peace and rest. As it should be. Teresa reflected that Rachel's life had its troubled and painful moments, and surely she rested well now. And, as the Apostles' creed stated, "I believe in the resurrection of the body, and the life everlasting. Amen."

As Teresa read through the manuscript, she found a few things pack in between pages she had not noticed before. She had Rachel's Bible, of course, and according to the date on the flyleaf, it must have been the one given to her by Nancy when she attended college that third year. It only made sense, although no mention of Nancy, or any relative, was recorded on the thin, gold-edged pages. Teresa also had Rachel's Small Catechism. When she first sorted Rachel's books, giving the textbooks to the school and the other books to the town library, she found it and set it aside. Since she was not a Lutheran, she didn't understand much about it, but she knew Rachel used it for study, probably in her adult membership classes. Teresa kept it in her bookcase, for possible future reference.

But as Teresa moved the paperclip further and further into the manuscript, she began to find small envelopes, as yellowed as the pages, pushed in between. Teresa pulled them out, and stacked them, as she came to them. Most were from Nancy, as Teresa expected. The first of those had the return address as "Nancy Lindeman" for three or four years, and then, as the came about and the letters were postmarked '1942' and thereafter, Nancy's name was Nancy Taylor. And, after 1944, the letters from Nancy abruptly stopped. Rachel had never, in Teresa's memory, mentioned anyone named Nancy— or anyone by any name at all, to be honest—but it was clear Nancy meant a lot to her. She had kept Nancy's letters, and the Bible, too. It did not seem to be a case of a falling out.

Teresa also found about five letters that bore the name "Mr. Charles A. Dunn." They were probably the only ones Rachel received from her uncle, as he was a businessman who had many cares and little leisure time to write, judging from Rachel's description of him, but Rachel *did* keep them, and apparently, she valued them. Teresa ran her hands through the last pages of the manuscript, to see if any other letters rested between the yellowed leaves. But there were none. Just the letters from Nancy and from Charles Dunn. She found nothing from "Aunt Anne," and certainly nothing from Cousin Anne. Teresa set the letters back into the box, for future reference, and she turned to the paperclipped page, to begin reading—

"I entered my senior year of college with much more hope and energy, although I never shook off the uneasiness that seemed to follow me when I met new people, especially men. I knew I would have to meet people, as I would have to go into the world to make my living, and I developed a certain amount of social ability to make that entry into the world possible. After all, I had joined a church and attended Sunday School class, and the people there allowed me to associate with them, without the continuous, veiled, but seething hostility I had experienced in my aunt and uncle's town. I made it a point to speak with the young children at the church, to find out what they liked, what their needs were, and what level of intellectual development they had attained. I did this as I knew such information and experience would help me to understand my future students. It would be my job to be with children, interacting with them and educating them, and by observing the children, I could best decide what methods to use to teach them, together with what I learned at college.

My last year in college was happy, but very, very busy. The courses were as difficult as they could be, and I did not agree with everything I heard the professors say, although it went without saying that I did not challenge anything. Also, I was made uncomfortable by one of the maiden female professors, who took her female students on a special 'ladies only' outing, and proceeded to lecture about 'purity' and 'chasteness.' She said, with much hemming and hawing and hard-to-understand euphemisms, that a woman was not worthy to be a teacher unless she was completely sexually pure. A woman who sinned with her body, she said, opened herself to evil influences and risked harming the innocence and decency of the children in her charge. I said nothing at the time, and tried to betray no distress; but that night I became violently sick, and for several days I could eat very little. I tried to avoid Nancy at that time, for her concern for me frightened me, and I wanted to hide the overwhelming pain.

No one would have suspected me of 'sexual impurity' in any case. There were many college boys who wanted to 'date' me, but it was unthinkable---I was frightened on two accounts. One, of course, was being assaulted, which I had reason to know was a real possibility. The other was my own urges—for some reason, I wanted to throw aside all inhibitions and 'commit fornication'---almost as an act of defiance, but also because I felt it was expected of me and I was 'suppose to.' As a Christian woman, and a novice teacher, I could not, and I was confused about my feelings. Fortunately, my known shyness protected my reputation from certain speculations, and, after all, it was a teachers' college, and old maid schoolteachers were not an unknown phenomenon.

I did envy my female friends, however, as they had such relaxed, happy relationships with the men, and sometimes I wished I had a male friend of my own, whom I could trust, who would see me as a human being and not as a functioning object to be bullied, or-- or---

I had read the Gospels. I knew Jesus was such a man—he treated women with respect *without fail*—and with patience and sensitivity. And He was the Son of God......

I still attended church, with Nancy and Lawrence and Connie, that final college year. 'I'm going to miss you, and Lawrence too, next year,' Nancy sighed. She was a year behind me and her brother, as she was now a junior. 'I'll miss you, too, Nancy,' I replied, and I meant it. I knew that, in the years to come, I would do what I had to do. But Nancy's encouragement had helped me a lot, and I was sad at the thought that we would have to go our separate ways, although I knew we would keep in touch.

The year drew to a close. I already had a job lined up, in another town, and I would be living in a tiny duplex near the elementary school where I would make my teaching debut. I had first to go through the graduation exercises, wearing the cap and gown, and I would receive my certificate and step toward my new life.

Was I fearful? Not really. I was not allowed the luxury of fear— or choice, for that matter.

Graduation Night was a warm one—outside the night was clear, sultry, and full of stars, and the campus was decorated with ribbons, banners, and an air of celebration and excitement. In my dorm room, which was now familiar and homely—and which I would soon leave—I put on my shining robe and stiff mortarboard, while

Nancy combed my unruly brown curls. The door to the room was open, and I could hear excited voices in the hallway, as groups of girls went toward the stairwells, to leave the dorm. For the first time in my life, I felt a pang of regret. The college was a happy place, full of hope and expectancy, and I was at home there as I had never been in my life. I looked out of the curtained window of my dorm—it was one of the last times I would do so—into the starry night. A slight breeze blew in from the darkness, billowing the curtains, and I heard the song of cicadas and the croaking of frogs.

Nancy smiled at me. 'Okay, Teacher!' Are you ready?' I nodded, and together we left the room and traversed the hall to the stairwell. We were followed by several noisy girls from the other rooms, and then we were on the campus grounds, joined by many girls in caps and gowns, as we made our way to the Student Auditorium. The auditorium was well lit, with banners, ribbons and posters everywhere, and the crowd was tremendous. Nearly all the professors were there, not to mention the families of the graduating students, and mayhem abounded. It was happy mayhem, though, and I hugged Nancy and then fell in with my class, which congregated behind the stage area in preparation for the actual ceremony.

That passed all too quickly. I heard the names called; I heard my name called; I walked beneath the blinding spotlights in my cap and gown, and received my diploma. I had graduated with honors, and walked with the honors group. It was done—I was now an 'educated woman' with a bachelor's degree. I was certified to teach, and would soon be earning my own living.

I was not expecting any of the Dunns to be at the graduation ceremony, but as I mingled with the post-ceremony crowd, I heard my name called again.

Not only was Uncle Charles present, but so was Aunt Anne!

I can't say that I rushed forward to greet them with ecstasy, but I did smile and go up to them, my tassel still hanging over my curls. Uncle Charles was clearly proud of me, and even Aunt Anne managed to direct a sentence or two of commendation to me, showing approval of the honors I received. We walked together rather awkwardly to the punch table, and each of us had a paper cup of punch and a piece of cake with white frosting on a Styrofoam plate. All around us people cheered and laughed and talked, and for once, I really felt like I was a part of things—that I had a place in the world.

Aunt Anne took a sip of her punch and said, rather irrelevantly, 'Charley will be in his sophomore year in college this fall. I hope he can complete his education before the war comes this way.' I was a little surprised, because even though everyone talked of war, it really wasn't a reality just yet. Aunt Anne spoke as if it were an assured thing. I wondered where she got her information.

'How is Jane?' I asked.

'She is dating Thomas Barrett, who lives next door to the Milners,' Aunt Anne replied. 'She's young yet, but I think it will be a match. John Barrett is the Milners' lawyer, you know. Tom will probably become a partner in his father's law firm, and he should do well, by all accounts.'

I didn't ask about Cousin Anne, but Uncle Charles mentioned her. Aunt Anne frowned. 'Charles—' she began.

I was still silent, but Uncle Charles filled in the rest of the family information. 'Anne and her little boy are staying with us right now,' he said. 'She and Jeff have some things to work out.' I didn't register any surprise, because I didn't feel any surprise—I knew that marriage was off to a rocky start. But Aunt Anne was clearly agitated, and she wanted to keep up the fiction that nothing really bad was happening, and the problem would be solved soon. Uncle Charles was right—Aunt Anne was getting older, and she was worn out. Her pace was still brisk, but her face had many lines, and her eyes were tired. It was possible her grandson was using up her strength.

Before any more could be said on the subject, Nancy came up to me, greeting me happily, her robed brother and her family in tow. I was happy to introduce the Lindemans to my aunt and uncle. They were of similar social and financial backgrounds, but the Lindemans were far superior in kindliness and social graces. Uncle Charles seemed especially pleased to meet them. He had an instant rapport with Mr. Lindemen—a fellow businessman like himself—and Mrs.

Lindeman and Nancy impressed him with their friendliness and good will toward me. It seemed to please Uncle Charles that I had succeeded in making friends—and with such a family. I sensed that I was rising in his good opinion.

The visit was actually very short—my uncle and aunt were to leave on the eleven o'clock train, and they soon told me goodbye, and left the celebration. I doubted I would ever see either of them again. They had done their duty—they had launched me into the world, with sufficient knowledge and education, and I was grateful. But I had no further claim on them. I really wasn't attached to them, so it didn't much matter, although Uncle Charles and I had a better understanding. I still would not miss them.

The graduation party continued noisily and happily far into the night. Finally, dead tired, I strode across the crisp lawn of the campus, with Nancy, as the darkness pressed all around me. The clear night was filled with stars. We quietly entered the dorm and climbed up the steps in the stairwell, and went to our room. We were both tired, and as soon as I shed my robe and mortarboard, I collapsed on my bed.

'Night, Nancy,' I said wearily.

'Night, Teacher,' Nancy replied, and she, too, dropped into her bed.

I slept like a log that night. And never, ever in my life, did I feel such a sense of worldly accomplishment….."

Teresa smiled as she replaced the paperclip on the manuscript. She remembered when she, too, graduated from college—it was a sense of accomplishment that was very real. She could only imagine how important it must have been for Rachel, who, up to that time, seemed unable to achieve anything that gave her an actual, respected place with her peers and associates. Also, Rachel now knew she could make her own living, independent from those who were 'forced' to tolerate her. She could make her own life, and use her knowledge and talents as a teacher—which she subsequently did.

Teresa and Rachel had become teachers in the same year at Dr. Hinton's elementary school in _____ton---the year 1941-1942. It was during World War II, and around the time the United States had entered the war. Teresa had not taught consecutively throughout the twenty years as Rachel had—some years she was out, as she had Billy and Mandy, but she soon returned. But she remembered that first year well—Rachel was shy and sweet and so young—with her mop of brown curls and her big brown eyes. She had already taught school for two years, and transferred in from another town. Dr. Hinton though her a likely candidate, and had hired her to replace a male teacher who decided to enlist. He was quite pleased with his decision, as Teresa remembered, and he did his best to keep her teaching in his school.

It was so long ago, though Teresa. The war was a tense, dreadful time. In the end, Germany and Hitler were beaten and the atrocities in Europe were exposed and stopped—but during the war, there was no guarantee this would happen. Teresa, with everyone else, rejoiced at the Normandy invasion, and followed closely the battles fought by the Americans and British, and was thankful when the Axis was defeated at last!

Teresa set the manuscript in the hatbox, and put it away in her closet. Perhaps, when she read on, Rachel would say something about the war—or about Nancy—or about her new school. But she hoped the most painful part of the reading would be over. She was now reaching the part of Rachel's life when she actually knew her. Surely things had changed for her, by then......

Chapter 22

THE SCHOOL YEAR BEGAN, AND TERESA slipped into her routine of teaching, grading papers, household chores and family time. The sky already had that hint of golden blue, that suggested colder weather ahead, and after all the hot days of the summer preceding, Teresa was rather looking forward to it. It was still very warm, however. Teresa drove to school with the windows rolled down; she used more hairspray to keep her curls in place, and the sticky smell of hairspray pervaded the Plymouth.

Getting to know a new roomful of students—learning and remembering the names—was always the first weeks' challenge for a schoolteacher, and for awhile, Teresa was busy with that. But her memory for names was good, and time and habit helped her, too—she soon was acquainted with her students. Her colleagues were the same ones: no new teachers were hired or needed, and most of the faculty had worked together for many years. The school term promised to be like all others.

It was the fall of 1963. America had reached a plateau of success as a country—or so it seemed.

America was a prosperous country. It had been strongly instrumental in winning World War II and bringing it to a close. The post war boom placed emphasis on both families and materialism: families were trained how to coexist together, while thriving businesses supplied the goods to make family life easy and pleasant: homes, cars, kitchen conveniences, ready made clothes, televisions.

Men were to make the living in the business world; wives were to stay home and minister to the needs of husbands and children, such as home-cooked meals and clean clothes. Boy children were to become educated so they could take on lucrative jobs; girls were to learn their place—housekeeping and pleasing a man. And if anyone had any trouble adjusting to his or her role in this prosperous, strong America, then a psychiatrist or some such professional could be called in to "fix" the person's mind so he or she could learn to perform as society asked—and be happy about it. Above all, the surface of America's society must stay smooth—otherwise she would cease to be a strong country.

Teresa smiled a little ruefully as she saw how the social mindset evolved in her community. She knew, from her knowledge of history, that no country ever settled into a groove of conformity while retaining greatness. And she was nervous about the future—things were optimistic now, but she felt it would not last, and there were already storm signs of restlessness. It would not be a new thing—America had weathered many storms in its short history as an independent country—but it would be a time of conflict for many people, and complacency would soon be destroyed.

She thought of Rachel—Rachel, who had been victimized, but had no recourse—because if she had complained aloud, she would have been censured and labeled, and probably blamed for what had happened to her. However progressive society was, it had no place or opportunity to see that she got justice. Rachel knew this; her words proved it, and she lived her life in silent torment. And now that she was dead, no one would ever know—Teresa would not have known, had she not found the manuscript. But Teresa knew, from her work in the slums, and in other situations, that many of these untold stories lurked beneath the smooth functioning of the social world. What would be the final result?

She did not know. She continued with her job—teaching children. And she continued to read the manuscript.

She pulled it out in early September, and read—

"I taught school for two years in a very small town that had few children, but that was probably the best way to begin—I could give each one of the students the most attention necessary to assist in their studies, and I could get to know the students as well. No one child is like another, and some learn easily, and some do not. Sometimes, by finding out what was of interest to a child, I could try another approach to teaching, and get better results in the long run. I'm sure I made many mistakes, but I hoped they were not bad ones—I always wanted to do the best for the children in my care, and I hoped I had never hurt any of them. I did not want to do that—I had been there, and I never wanted any child to ever go through what I had.

It seemed I was doing all right. After two years, I got a message from a Dr. Robert Hinton, the principal of an elementary school in _____ton, who was losing a valuable third grade teacher and needed a competent replacement—fast. I would receive a larger salary, and also, I could rent a small but decent home near the school for a reasonable price. That was important, for housing in wartime was hard to find at any price. I went to _____ton, and found everything very satisfactory. Dr. Hinton was a no-nonsense military type of man, who had the respect of both the teachers and the students, and he was very astute at hiring the kind of teachers he wanted. The same year he hired me, he also found a wonderful teacher to take a fifth grade class—Teresa Anderson, who was a treasure much as Nancy had been. Teresa was everything one could possibly be: she was well-educated, with a master's degree and several years teaching experience; she was married, with two sweet little girls, and most of all, she was a caring, Christian woman. She helped me to adjust, the same way Nancy had. We sometimes talked about lesson plans and compared notes—she had taught in 'inner-city' schools before and she had learned a lot about children. I felt I had at last found my home.

I heard from Nancy quite often during my first two years of teaching, and she was happy that I had secured a job right away and was doing well. 'But,' she wrote, 'I knew you would. You were always able to make things clear to me. I missed you, that last year of college.' She did graduate—and fell in love. I never had a chance to meet her husband, but she sent me a picture of him—he was quite a handsome man, and had a strong, kindly smile. His name was Henry Taylor, and he and Nancy married the summer after my first year in ____ton. He was in uniform by the time of their marriage: America had entered the war and he enlisted. I wanted to go to the wedding, but unfortunately, wartime was a rather unusual situation and things could not be done as they normally were. I had no way to travel to Nancy's hometown, and in any case they were married quickly at a JP's office: war rationing usually made a normal wedding hard to plan.

I taught at the elementary school at ____ton during the war years, and received more letters from Nancy. She and Henry were very happy, but she was understandably nervous when he was deployed. But she was brave. She was thankful when he came home on leave, and wrote him faithfully while she waited for him. For a time fortune seemed to smile on the young couple; Henry saw action on the front but received only minor wounds, and late in 1943, Nancy discovered with delight that she was to have a child. I was happy for her, and even though I was busy with my students, I kept up correspond-ance with her—I knew my letters were important to an anxious war bride.

Then, just as spring was ending in 1944, God in His wisdom did one of those things I could not comprehend, stirring up new doubts within me, although I knew He saw things differently from my perspective, and He must have had His reasons. Around the time I was expecting to hear about the birth of Nancy's child, with all the happiness and excitement of the occasion, I received a letter from her brother Lawrence instead. As I took the letter from the old coppery mailbox outside my front door, I already had a feeling of dread and foreboding, and for the first time, I could truly understand the fears of all the mothers, sisters and sweethearts who lived around me. I knew something had happened to someone dear to me. I went to my bedroom and tore open the envelope. I read:

'Dear Rachel: this is a terrible letter for me to have to write, and I don't know what I am writing, so please forgive my faulty grammar and language. I am writing to you because I know Nancy would want me to do so. To tell you quickly—she passed away two days ago at _____ Hospital. The baby, a little girl, was stillborn. I didn't know this could still happen—I thought medical science could take care of such things. Henry is still at the front—he doesn't know—he may never know. I've heard big invasion plans are in place. Please, Rachel, know that Nancy loved you. This may be the last time you hear from me. I hope we win this war, but what a cost it will be!'

Of course, I didn't write back asking for details, but in my secret heart I wondered if the war kept Nancy from getting the proper care in the hospital, although I should have known that women died that way in peacetime as well. But Nancy—she would have been such a loving mother. Why, Lord, why?

Then the invasion came. Henry and Lawrence were both casualties. Both had believed in what they were doing: our country had to be defended and the vicious dictatorships across the Atlantic had to be brought down. Just how vicious they were came to light soon after the war was concluded: people had been taken to camps, gassed, baked in ovens, and starved. Not just soldiers—but civilians, who were not a threat to the armies. I knew that Henry and Lawrence would consider their lives well given. But—it was hard. I would never see my friends again—the ones who led me to You, Friend. You took them to Yourself.

After that, I went back to routine—and buried myself. It was likely I could have made a friend of Teresa Anderson, for she was a caring woman and well educated, too. But I didn't dare. I now knew, as I never had before, that making friends was risky. I valued Nancy, and Lawrence, too, and now they were both gone. I didn't want to lose anyone else.

As far as blood ties were concerned, I had not lost anyone. Occasionally I heard from Uncle Charles. Anne was back with Jeff, he said, who came safely through the war. Uncle Charles didn't actually say it in so many words, but I had the impression that Jeff's father had some pull with the War Department, and Jeff was able to secure a safe position until the war was over. He went on to find a lucrative job in his father's business, and he and Anne moved into a large home, complete with servants and a nanny. It was probably a relief for Aunt Anne, who was slowly losing her stamina. Uncle

Charles told me in his letter that she had seen several doctors but so far hadn't found any help—she apologized for not writing herself—but she was so tired. I wondered if she had not simply worn herself out—she had always been so edgy and fussy and concerned about minute details and having everything just right—and she never seemed to relax or take pleasure in anything. She had never had any real joy, not even in her own family. It appeared she would finally have to take some rest at last, but actually enjoying it or benefiting from it—that was another matter.

Uncle Charles submitted a few more facts concerning his family in the letter: Cousin Charles was home and looking for a well-paying job to match his education; Cousin Jane was to marry the lawyer's son Aunt Anne had mentioned earlier. Everyone was well-placed, and that included me. We survived, and we would move on. The post-war years in America placed a great emphasis on education and teaching—I think because of the growing fear of Communism, and the powers-that-be reasoned that Americans, with proper training and knowledge, would never fall to the menace of socialist thinking. So teachers were looked upon with great favor, and it was our duty to impress upon the young minds the love of country, patriotism, and freedom—freedom to work as one chose to work, and to get ahead in life as far as was possible. I really was not a fanatic about the idealism—I was hired to teach, and that's what I did. I did everything in my power to help the children learn what they were required to learn, and if they took that and made something of their lives later on—more power to them! But I did not trouble their minds with such scary things as H-bombs, Red Scares and Joe McCarthy. What is more, they never asked.

I would have many happy years teaching at the elementary school at _____ton. As quiet as the town was, and as ordinary as most of the citizens were, it had to be the happiest time of my life….."

Teresa smiled as she moved the paperclip to the next page. She was even a little happy. So Rachel really did like her—Teresa—it had been so hard to tell! Rachel had always been sweet, but distant, and never confiding. Teresa honestly hadn't known whether Rachel liked her or not, although all indications were that she had. But

Teresa read the written words of commendation with a new found happiness, and she was thankful she had always been kind to Rachel. Many of the teachers had indicated they found Rachel a little stiff and unapproachable—and Teresa knew even Dr. Hinton was at times unsure how to converse with her—but Teresa was able to sense that Rachel had never meant harm to anyone. She kept that in mind as she taught alongside Rachel during the school years, and now she read that Rachel realized her value—it was humbling in a way, for she now found out how troubled Rachel had been.

"Thank You, Lord," she said, "Thank You for guiding my actions, for allowing me to be understanding, even when I did not understand. And help me, Lord, to keep on with that understanding, as I see my thoughts and actions do affect those You have placed in my life and in my circle. Please keep me from hurtful actions that could harm such a soul, even though I do not know it. In Your Son's Name I pray—Amen."

Chapter 23

Outside rain poured copiously against the windows, and thudded loudly on the roof, when Teresa next took down the hatbox. The fall weather was setting in, and the days with sharply-blue skies and golden sunlight were giving way to overcast, leaden-looking clouds, with weepy rain. It was not yet really cool, and Teresa cracked the windows slightly, where she could see clearly the raindrops clinging to the window screens. Both Billy and Mandy were home, watching the television in the living room, and Teresa didn't have any homework papers to grade, as that day was a "free" day. Bill was out on patrol, and Teresa had completed her grocery shopping after school. She mixed together a meatloaf and put it in the oven; she took note of the time and then went into her bedroom.

She took down the hatbox, and noticed she was getting toward the end of the manuscript. There were still quite a few pages left, and she wondered how much real peace Rachel had found. As the day outside was dim with rain, Teresa turned on her reading lamp, and she also set the timer on her clock-radio. That way she would remember to take out the meatloaf and fix the vegetables. She sat down on her bed as the rain splashed against the roof and windows; it was getting darker, but she ceased to notice that as she began to read---

"I truly grieved at the loss of Nancy, and I even cried about it, when I was alone, but I tried to think of what she would want me to do, were she alive. I knew the answer to that—she would want me to continue to live in my faith, and I tried to think of God as my loving Father, and not as a wrathful entity who removed Nancy and Lawrence from my life. I knew I should seek a church home. It took me over five years to do so, believe it or not, and by then the war was well over. I finally settled on a Lutheran church, as my most pleasant association with church-going took place in a Lutheran church, and besides, I believed Lutherans to be the closest in actually interpreting the Bible correctly. I was relieved to be done with rosaries, penance, and private confessionals.

The Lutheran church I settled on had a brand-new pastor and his pretty young wife—Roger and Selena Mayfield. While I didn't trust men—and especially not preachers—I felt more secure knowing that Lutheran pastors were basically required to be married. Besides, married preachers usually understood about family problems, having plenty of their own, and so far I had a good opinion of pastors' wives. Mrs. Altenburg in my college town was a sociable, outgoing type who did a lot for her husband's church. Selena Mayfield was much younger, but she had a sunny personality and time would give her the experience she needed. It was difficult being a pastor's wife, and I admired such women. I decided this Lutheran church had possibilities, and went there.

Thus my external means of worship was established. And that was very important—Christians, I knew, were not to forsake the assembly of Christ's body, and surely, who could learn fully about God and His Will for us, unless we worship with those also called to Him? I was glad to have a church home, and I felt safe there—Roger Mayfield, as young as he was, proved to be an honest and faithful man of his office, and he grew into leadership as he matured. The other members of the church were apparently serious their faith, by and large, and wanted to do the right thing. They accepted my presence but did not overwhelm me with demands, and after a year I joined the choir. The director seemed pleased with my voice: he began to use me for an occasional solo.

My life was thus quiet and orderly. It was the way I felt most comfortable. I coexisted peacefully with people at church and at the school, and taught my students with little interference or trouble.

It wasn't that I was equally peaceful within my heart; in fact, I was not. But I needed the serenity. I knew my life had pain in it—pain I could scarcely deal with. The regularity of my life was like an anesthetic: I did not really feel my pain—I did not feel anything, for there was no earthly reason to do so. I was not attached to anyone in my heart, and no one needed my love, in any case. But even as detached as I knew myself to be, I knew the situation was not a normal one. I saw everyone around me in families and even at the school, have a closeness that I almost never experienced and did not trust nor understand.

O, Friend, I knew it was not what You meant for me. I knew You meant for me to love, as You have loved. You suffered very great pain because You loved. But—forgive me. It was hard to risk, even for You—I was walled off, and could not break through. I cannot even use the excuse that You wouldn't understand such pain as mine. You did experience it on earth—and far worse. Yet You broke through it all—rose from the dead—and said, 'I love you—take and eat, this is my body… Drink from it, all of you. This is my blood of the covenant, which is poured out for many for the forgiveness of sins….' And I knew Your prayer—Your prayer of John 17:20-26….. You spoke to Your Heavenly Father…..*about us*….

Oh, Friend, I could not break through….

Oh, Lord, I knew how much You loved me. I learned that when I went with Nancy and Lawrence to a church body that was truly Yours. I learned what it was to be loved—I learned that You loved me, even though I was filthy and broken and unfit for decent people. But, Father, I wronged You—You loved me so much, and yet I could not break through my pain and pass it on. Why not, Father? You did.

In my soul I knew Your existence, and from Your Word in the Bible, I learned of Your true feelings for me. My heart responded to You, and I was comforted and made stronger. But I knew what You wanted of me, Father. You wanted me to reach out to others—with my heart—and become loving and vulnerable as You were on earth. And Father—I could not!

I knew You made every effort. You placed me with Teresa Anderson, with Dr. Hinton, with the Mayfields, with many children. Any one of them would have been glad to befriend me. I think Teresa would have loved me, as I would have loved her. But I was frightened, Father—in so much pain. I feared if I opened up again, I would be violated, hated—even destroyed. I remembered the contempt in Father John's eyes. I remembered the brutality of the soldier. I remembered the tired, wearying disgust my Aunt Anne felt for me—not hot, brutal hatred, but a chronic disapproval and lack of understanding that withered my soul and caused me to question my right to exist.

I could not rise above it, Father, although I knew You wished me to. And—for the most part, unacknowledged even to myself, I was very, very angry at the injustice. I tried not to think about it, and would not allow it to affect my external life. I had plenty to keep me busy, after all; I had my students to teach, and I gave most of my energy to that. I took my teaching seriously, and was determined to give it my best. Then, too, I was renting a pleasant house, for not very much by rent standards, and it was up to me to keep the house clean and well kept. Although I was filthy and violated, I was determined my surroundings should not be. After all, my Aunt Anne taught me how to keep things up, and I could make sure the house had no trace of dirt. I kept my clothes and sheets spotless, and I felt cleaner that way. I bathed myself every day, as well—even though some experts said women should be careful what they did during certain times of the month. Even though hot water was supposed to be harmful, I applied it anyway—and finished off with lilac fragrance. I could not stand my filthiness.

Outwardly my life was organized very well. I was thankful for that. But inwardly—it was awful.

Sometimes I dreamt of Nancy. Other times I dreamt of Father John and the soldier. I was occasionally sick for no reason, and now and then I awoke crying. If it was a school morning I shut that off in a hurry, and placed my mind in 'teacher' mode. But if I awoke so on a Saturday, I would let it go. I knew no one would see or hear me, and the tears eased my pain. Once or twice I wept for hours, and the violence of my emotions shocked me. I knew it was not right or considered respectable behavior. But no one was around to be bothered by it—that was the advantage of being alone, and not always having to worry about the importunities of others.

I remembered Father John's accusations—that I wanted attention, that my behavior was not appropriate for my age or gender—and I did not step forward, but associated with others as minimally as possible, drawing no attention to myself.

However, at church I was called upon to break the rules I imposed upon myself. The choir director at church decided he wanted me to be a soloist during the church service, and he wanted me to sing, 'Fairest Lord Jesus.' And then—Father—then my voice could openly express my love for You. I could praise You, then, and not be condemned. I was surprised how strong and powerful my voice became ,and I saw the tears in the eyes of other church members, even Reverend Mayfield's. I knew then my singing was not wrong, not a bid for attention, but a offering in praise of You, my Friend.

I thank You, Lord, I could at least express my joy in that way.

Time went on. I saved my money, and some time in the early 50's, I purchased a second-hand Henry J—the original owner needed the money, and he hadn't used the car very much anyway. It turned out to be a reliable and serviceable car, and I was able to go places, especially during the summer, when school was out and I had time on my hands. Since I had no family members to look after, I could set my own schedule and go about as I pleased, and I decided not to worry about the bogeymen that elderly women whispered about during my teenaged years—anything from summer polio scares to frightening service station restrooms. I had been assaulted already, and I decided I would not fear anyone who could kill the body, but rather fear one who could kill the soul. The world was made by God to be enjoyed, and I enjoyed my solitary vacations—delights such as the Grand Canyon, Yellowstone Park, and even Big Ben National Park.

I always got back in time for the next school year, and nothing untoward ever befell me.

1957 came, and so did a letter from Uncle Charles. Aunt Anne
had died in the town hospital, possibly from a kidney ailment,
although the doctors were not really sure what was wrong with her,
and had trouble prescribing treatment. Uncle Charles sounded tired
and worn out himself, and from the tone of his letter I suspected he
was ill himself. He was upset over Aunt Anne's death, and again,
Cousin Anne was a trial to him. Jeff Milner was apparently straying
in his marriage, and he and Cousin Anne fought fiercely, especially
when she caught him in an infidelity, as she inevitably did. Uncle
Charles never knew when she would suddenly show up on the
doorstep with her two boys, demanding to be taken in for the night,
only to return to Jeff a few days later. Uncle Charles suspected she
was headed toward divorce. She couldn't make herself the center of
Jeff's world, no matter how much she tried, and she was even more
brittle and irritable than she used to be. I wondered how much of
this was upsetting to Aunt Anne.

Cousin Charles and Jane were in better situations: Charles
settled down with his job and married a nice girl he had known in
high school, and Jane's marriage was not fraught with drama the
way Anne's was. In truth, Cousin Charles and Cousin Jane were not
awful the way Cousin Anne was. They were both indifferent to me;
but they did not show open hostility; it wasn't worth their energy.

Since I had the Henry J, I could have visited Uncle Charles,
and in retrospect, I wish I had. I should have known he would have
liked that. But I was too unsure of my own worthiness. It was a sin
of omission, for which I had no excuse---"

The clock radio sounded its alarm, and Teresa put down the
manuscript. She placed the paperclip on the page, and closed the
hatbox. From the kitchen, the meatloaf was sending out the savory
odor of near doneness, and Teresa had the vegetables to steam. She
put the hatbox into the closet, and went into the kitchen. Outside
the sky had become much darker, and rain still pelted against the
windows. Teresa opened the kitchen door, to let some of the cool
breeze in, and she could hear the rain thudding against the eaves and
metal rain gutters. The gravel driveway was soaked, and the large
trees, swayed by the breeze, dropped sodden dark leaves. The breeze

felt cool and heavenly, however, as it flowed through the screen door into the hot kitchen.

"Mandy," Teresa called out as the vegetables steamed, "come set the table."

Mandy's voice called back over the television in the living room, "Ah, Mom, it's Billy's turn this time."

Billy, also in the living room, said something inaudible, but Teresa went to the adjoining door between the kitchen and the dining room. "No, sweetie, it's your turn," she said. "Billy set it yesterday, and he's going to help me with the dishes tonight. Of course, if you'd rather wash dishes---"

"Oh, no, no," said Mandy. She was soon in the dining room, opening the drawers to the large china cabinet. The dining room was almost formal, under a chandelier with very bright lights, and the table was covered with a shining white tablecloth Teresa kept washed and bleached. The table was easy to set, with all the clean dishes nearby, and Mandy soon had it set for three people. Teresa brought in the meatloaf, vegetables, and some rolls.

The children really didn't have much to say, probably because they spent the afternoon watching television, and also because it was so damp outside that they couldn't go anywhere. Mandy briefly mentioned that one of her teachers, Mrs. Jackson, went into one of her anti-Communist tirades when one of the boys in the class was seen making a two-fingered "peace" sign to another boy. Teresa had to smile about that, but she still remembered the Joe McCarthy era, and she wondered when her neighbors and friends would stop being paranoid about the subject. She didn't really believe the Communists had that much power—or support—in America.

After supper she and Billy washed the dishes, and then she was free to think her own thoughts again. She was able to think about what she had just read. First of all—Rachel would have loved her. She had mattered to Rachel. Teresa was happy to know that, because even though all the signs pointed that way, she was never really sure Rachel cared. But here was proof, as before. Teresa thanked the Lord that at last she knew to a certainty. She was glad—again—that she had always treated Rachel with kindness. Because she had been kind, she was sure that it made Rachel's life a little easier.

The rain quietly pelted down, and outside it was completely dark. Teresa sighed, and reached for her book of lesson plans for the next day. It was time for routine.

Chapter 24

It was mid-November when Teresa finally reached the concluding pages of the manuscript. When, later on, she looked back upon the events of that month, she found it interesting that she finished reading Rachel's story barely a week before the United States would suffer a shock of seismic proportions. However one may feel about the leaders of one's country, it was still a tragedy to have one's president cut down so sharply and ruthlessly, with no warning. It cast a cloud over a country that had been so optimistically and cheerfully proud, and ushered in a new era of unrest and anxiety, that had not shown so strongly before.

That November, for Teresa, had progressed as expected. She carried out her lesson plans, handed out the tests, and then graded and handed them out again. She prepared her home for Thanksgiving, as was usual, and telephoned her married daughters, to find out when they would arrive with their respective families. She had the shopping to do, but this year Mandy helped. Mandy helped Teresa plan what dishes would appear on the Thanksgiving table, and she also kept in touch with her two sisters on the phone, finding out what they planned to bring and reporting to Teresa afterward. It was a great help to Teresa, who couldn't be near the telephone at all times.

Even though she was busy, Teresa remembered what she read about Rachel. It was sad, but it seemed Rachel never returned to her aunt and uncle's home for any holiday festivities, nor did it seem that she was wanted. In her final years, Aunt Anne appeared to be sick and exhausted, and Rachel certainly had the capacity to plan and cook the meals—after all, hadn't Aunt Anne trained Rachel herself? But Teresa acknowledged it might have been awkward. Cousin Anne would have been at the family get-togethers, and she had a way of making her displeasure known. She didn't want Rachel there, and apparently the family bowed to her wishes, as they always had. Uncle Charles had been too detached—and Aunt Anne too tired—to have it any other way.

Teresa had read that Aunt Anne had died, and Uncle Charles had been slowing down. It seemed to be not long ago. Teresa knew only a few pages were left to be read—and these remaining pages were on much fresher paper, not yellowed like the most of the earlier pages in the manuscript.

The night she read the last few pages was a quiet one—a lull in her usual routine, when Bill was out and not expected until morning. The day being short, it was dark when supper was finished and the dishes were washed, and Billy and Mandy had gone out with their friends, leaving Teresa alone. The house was unusually still, except for the ticking of the living room clock and the occasional crackle of the lit floor furnace. The wind moaned and rustled the dry leaves outdoors, and the window panes were cold to the touch. Teresa went to her bedroom, clicking on the overhead fixture, and went to the closet for the hatbox. She lift out the final pages and read---

"It was the middle of the year 1958 that my Uncle Charles died. Like I said, I could have visited him, but I held back. After all, I was only his niece, not his daughter, and I did have the impression my mother had given him problems of one kind or another, although he had not specifically said anything. I knew both of my brothers were dead, under circumstances which were not to be scrutinized closely, and to Uncle Charles it was probably a blessing that I had not married or had children. Thus his sister's line would not be perpetuated, and once I had passed on, the situation would be closed for all time.

The story was not closed on his family, though. One year after Uncle Charles died, Jeff Milner finally left Anne, and took up with another woman. I never even learned the woman's full name, but I did hear that Jeff filed for and received a divorce, cutting off Anne with a modest alimony and child support. He then married his new flame, and decamped to another town, becoming in the process a social 'big shot,' for he knew how to work the status game. I did not learn any of this from the Dunn family. When I attended Uncle Charles' funeral, I met a neighbor of my uncle and aunt's who knew *of* me, and decided to keep in touch, at least for a while. I did give my address, phone number and the phone number of Pastor Mayfield and his wife to each of my three cousins—in case something should happen to me. None of them accepted the information very graciously, but they took it; and I kept Cousin Anne's information, too.

I thus decided I had done all that was expected, and I purchased a small life insurance policy to cover my burial expenses. I entrusted this jointly to Pastor Mayfield and Dr. Hinton, which was a highly unusual procedure, but I couldn't think of anything better, as I couldn't trust the Dunn cousins. Fortunately, both men saw my point, and I believed them to be trustworthy. That being taken care of, I went on with my life.

I was an 'old maid schoolteacher' –this I knew. But at least it was respectable, and better than some of things I could have been called. By the time Uncle Charles died I was in my mid-forties, and nothing was likely to change in my life. In a way, I was sad about it, but after all, what else was there to do? I would never have a family of my own.

It was around 1960 that I noticed some odd symptoms—my chest got tight, and I couldn't breathe very well—and my left arm hurt rather fiercely. But I didn't give it much consideration; I was still fairly young, and I knew heart attacks happened to stressed-out businessmen. I was just a schoolteacher—who had nothing to be stressed about. Heart attacks happened to businessmen who had many money worries and the stress of living in the 'real world.' I lived in a world of small children and the grown people who taught them, and that was not a significant world. Certainly, I had no reason to be sick from it, and I did not think my symptoms meant anything.

I was restless, though. I could not understand why, but two separate sets of thoughts came to me and began to trouble me: one, that I had missed out on many good things in life that other people enjoyed, and two, I noticed a well of deep anger and rage taking hold of a corner of my heart. Why, I couldn't decide. I wondered if the devil was trying to take hold of me, and snatch me from the cradling arms of my Father. But what could I do? I couldn't speak with anyone. I couldn't afford a psychiatrist--and I didn't trust the breed in any case-- and I dared not seek out Reverend Mayfield, though I probably should have. I still feared white robes, and it seemed I would never, ever, get over it. I still had the dreams, too, and when I awoke from them, sometimes I had trouble breathing. I decided I needed to try to reach out to people—maybe that was it. Maybe if I tried to make friends....I remembered how some of my teachers used to scold me for 'not getting along well with others.'

And, after all, Nancy had been my friend......

Dear Nancy. I loved her so. Friend, she was Your representative to me—she let me know that You loved me. In a way, I now understand why You took her—she was ready to go to You—to her final home in Heaven. Lawrence—he was ready to go, too, and he came in defense of our country. But, Lord, I became so lonely without them. And—in the business world—you don't make close friends like Nancy and Lawrence—you meet acquaintances. That is one reason I did not befriend the other teachers, besides my fear. But I still went to church. I could perhaps become closer to people there, but......

I was well respected in the choir, and greeted the other choir members, but I could not talk to them. I could only sing with them. I was called upon often to take a soprano solo, and gladly did so, but why could I not speak as well as sing?

I wanted to change that. Lord, please help me. Friend, please help me. Can You not bind the wounds that broke my body, and ultimately, Father, broke my soul? I know, Father, that when my heart is broken, You can best come to me and touch the pain, to heal it, but Father, how can I trust enough to allow that healing? It was that I had yet to learn, and I knew I had to do my part in learning it.

Lord, what would You have me do?

I decided it would be best to begin reaching out in connection with the church. My home congregation was used to me and my reserve, so I didn't want to frighten anyone by becoming suddenly open and friendly with out any reason. I would have to change my surroundings and try again, this time out of town. And now—June 1962—I would have my chance.

That's what I am going to do now. That's why I am about to leave town for the summer.

I hope it works out. I know of a church, out of state, where the Lutheran women will have a large missionary meeting. Several of the members of my church spoke of it, although no one I knew of was going—we did have our own women's missionary groups. But I was going on vacation in any case, so this sounded interesting and a chance to start over again—and, just maybe—begin to make real friends. Maybe, just maybe...

...I will meet another Nancy......

As I am writing this, my left arm is hurting, almost unbearably. But at least I am right-handed, so I can write reasonably well. This has been going on for some time now, and I'm not going to let it spoil my vacation. I'm really looking forward to the meeting, and I have packed and have notified the landlord. I will rest, since school is now out, and be ready to go this Monday.

Afterward, maybe, I will see my doctor. I do get short of breath quite often, and then I have a slight grip in my chest. I feel nauseated then.

I will try not to think about it. I will try to think of You, dear Friend....

Be with me, Lord...."

The manuscript ended. Teresa lifted the paperclip, and laid it aside. She put the last few pages with the rest of the manuscript, and then she put it on the bed while she went to find her sewing basket. She searched through the jumble of thread spools, cloth pieces, and needle cases, until she brought up a pinkish velvet ribbon, which was long and thin. She bound the manuscript with the ribbon, and placed it into the hatbox, possibly for the last time. She did not know if she would ever look at the manuscript again. But she would keep it as a priceless treasure, and she was thankful she got to know Rachel at last. She wished she had known her, living, though.

".....I will meet another Nancy..."

Perhaps Rachel had rejoined Nancy. Maybe Nancy met her, as she passed from this world and had gone to the other, and they went happily together. Teresa would have liked to think so. Circumstantial evidence suggested that Rachel had had a heart attack out on the road near ___shire, and the account of her symptoms made the guess almost a certainty. For a moment, Teresa was angry with Rachel. Why didn't she see a doctor *before* she went on the trip? Then she wouldn't have missed out on so much.

"Believe it or not, Rachel," Teresa said aloud, "We valued you. You should have valued yourself that much. After all, you belonged to Christ. He valued you, too."

Teresa closed the lid to the hatbox, and it was very nearly like closing the lid over Rachel's body—again. She sighed, and went to the closet to put the hatbox away. That done, she glanced around her familiar bedroom, sharply lit by the overhead light fixture. The venetian blinds, framed by delicate curtains, were insistently pale, but seemed to draw attention to the cold, dark night outside. Teresa glanced at the window which held the A/C unit, and she shivered— that would not be needed for quite a while. She turned, and after a final glance, left the room, switching off the overhead light on her way out. As she touched the switch she felt a nip of static electricity; it strangely fitted with her mood, but she was not happy about it.

She passed through the hallway and into the living room. Outside, the nippy wind blew; the living room clock chimed, and she heard the floor furnace crackle. Life went on, as it always did. And now Rachel's picture was complete.

Chapter 25

Dᴇᴄᴇᴍʙᴇʀ ᴡᴀѕ ᴜᴘᴏɴ _____ᴛᴏɴ; ᴛʜᴇ ᴄʜɪʟʟ but bright and sparkling Christmas season. Even though the celebrations were muted as the nation had recently suffered a great shock, the townspeople did their best to create a sense of normal routine. The usual decorations were up around the town square, and heavily bundled shoppers went from store to store, toting packages and greeting one another as they passed by. Large automobiles swished through the slushy streets, and the garish gold and silver tinsel glittered during the rare times the sun appeared. The days were short, and when night came, the holiday lights blazed with festive glory.

School was out for the semester, the Christmas play over and the lessons wrapped up and complete. Teresa had done most of her shopping and the gifts were now covered in colorful paper and ribbons. The tree was put up and the gifts now hugged the base. The living room was neat and inviting, and Teresa had also cleaned the kitchen carefully, polishing silverware and washing the cloth napkins, and made sure the dishes were in place in the cupboards. She would need to have everything handy for all the fancy cooking that would be expected, and Bill's parents were coming to visit that Christmas, so Teresa had another reason why she wanted things to be just right. It was not that she was nervous—she wasn't—but still, being inspected by one's in-laws had a different meaning than being "just family" such as when her married daughters came.

The routine was going well, however, and most people were in shock from the assassination, and they were not quite as observant as usual. In fact, the Christmas celebrations, no matter how they were conducted, were very welcome. Many people wanted to feel that the world still had beauty—even if it wasn't safe. Christmas was a familiar, age old traditional holiday, and families came together in thankfulness. It was especially true of Christian families—no matter what happened, Christ the Savior was born.

The Anderson house was in reasonably good order, and the senior Andersons had not arrived yet, when Teresa decided to drive by the cemetery on the outskirts of town. It was still daylight, although it was a very bluish-gray and dismal daylight, and the streets, although not particularly dangerous to drive on, were full of dirty sludge. Teresa got into her Plymouth—still in good shape, after six years—and backed out of the graveled driveway, crunching the chilled and damp stones. It was so dull outside that the greenish-yellow glow of her lighted instrument panel was far more noticeable than was usual in the daytime. Teresa passed through downtown, taking note of all the decorations—tinsel around lampposts, stretched overhead across Main Street, Christmas lights outlining the store roofs—and a gaudy large Christmas tree in the middle of the town's park. Even though evening had not fallen, all the lights were on. Teresa could barely see the traffic lights; fortunately, few people were out driving, and she made sure her headlamps and tail lamps were switched on.

Finally she arrived at her destination—and it was a truly lonely area. The winter had made the cemetery a sad place—the shade trees were bare, with blackened branches, and no flowers bloomed. The grass was sparse and yellowed, and covered partially by frost. The stone markers seemed very, very cold, and Teresa shivered as she got out of the Plymouth.

She had with her a poinsettia wreath, to place near Rachel's gravestone. The bright red and evergreen stood out as a contrast against the grays and pale whites of the stones. Teresa found the grave and knelt down, fastening the fresh wreath to the now weathered marker. As she did so Teresa realized something: Rachel trusted two men—she trusted not one, but two men—at last.

Nor was her trust misplaced; the two men—Reverend Mayfield and Dr. Hinton—did right by her. She trusted them to bury her properly, and they did. Her gravestone was as nice as any in the cemetery, and the spelling of her name and her birthdate were correct. Her death date had to be guessed at, but it was determined as close as possible and recorded. After her funeral expenses were paid, the very little remainder of her insurance money bought a picture for the front hallway of the elementary school. It brightened that part of the hallway, and Rachel's name was posted beneath it, with her dates. Teresa thought it was sweet and fitting.

"You see, Rachel, not *all* men are bad," Teresa said aloud. "I hope you saw what your boss and your pastor did for you. Dr. Hinton made sure you were remembered at the school, and Reverend Mayfield directed the gathering of your personal belongings. In fact—he directed the most important of them to me. And I am glad he did. But, Rachel, I wish you had lived. God would have wanted you to live fully. I wish you had."

She stood by Rachel's grave for a little while longer, even though it was bone-chillingly cold. The cemetery seemed almost swept by the frosty wind; the poinsettia wreath stood out sharply among the gravestones, and in the rickety graveled parking lot, Teresa's red Plymouth was a very powerful contrast of color, especially with the chrome trimmings. The day was fading fast; soon the crimson of a small sunset would appear at the west end of the blanket of grayish-white clouds, and then darkness would come. Teresa knew it was time to go back home.

"Good night, Rachel, sleep well," she said. "I hope you like the poinsettia wreath. I wanted you to have something for Christmas."

She got into the Plymouth, glad to be out of the chilly wind. She turned the key and heard the familiar metallic sound of the ignition, and soon she was on her way home.

Teresa had passed by the Lutheran church many, many times, but she had never but once been inside of the building. Most of her family and friends were Baptists, and when she went to weddings, funerals, and other get-togethers, they usually took place at a Baptist church. The one time she had been in the Lutheran church was for Rachel's funeral. It was not very much different, except for the liturgy, but it seemed much quieter and more subdued. She spoke very briefly with Reverend Mayfield at the time, but now that she had read the manuscript, she wanted to speak with him again. Not that she intended to say much about it. But she could perhaps reassure him on some points.

She apologized to Reverend Mayfield when she called him, saying she knew it was Christmastime, and a busy time for him and his wife. But she had read the manuscript, and could she see him for a short time? He readily assented, and named a time for her to come.

For the second time, she stepped into the quiet, well-kept building. She remembered Rachel's words, about her childhood church—"I was glad to go to His beautiful house, with the candles and the red carpets, and the shining gold patens. The stained glass windows were so high, and so glorious!....." These words could be justly applied to this church also, and in the stillness Reverend Mayfield quietly met her at the front pew of the sanctuary. As they sat down the organist appeared and began his practice—very subdued, and Teresa wondered at the beauty of his musical selections.

Reverend Mayfield was somewhat nervous. "What did you learn?" he asked.

"A lot," said Teresa, "and much of it best not spoken of. But—" she gently tapped the pastor's shoulder—"I do want to assure you she was happy at this church—as happy as it was possible for her to be."

"I thank the Lord, very deeply, for that," whispered Reverend Mayfield. He seemed troubled.

"The other thing," Teresa went on, "is about the coroner's report. You did hear about that?"

Reverend Mayfield nodded. "Yes, from ___shire. The coroner wasn't sure. He thought it was possibly a fainting spell or an attack of some kind, and she went off the road."

"Yes," said Teresa. "Now, from what I read from her most recent papers, I can fairly confirm that. She mentioned a painful left arm, pressure in her chest, and shortness of breath. All this, just before she left on her trip."

Reverend Mayfield looked up, and straight at Teresa. "And she didn't go see a doctor, did she?"

"No, apparently not. She-she was rather wary of doctors, I think. It—well, she had her reasons. Anyway, she is now in the hands of the Great Physician. He would make everything right for her."

Reverend Mayfield sighed very deeply. Then he said, haltingly, "Tell me—please—was there anything I should have known, anything I should have done? How much pain was she in? I never could understand—I prayed and prayed about it. Every member of this church is a member of my flock, you know. I am responsible for the spiritual well-being of every soul under my care. If I were remiss in anything---"

"No, no, no," Teresa gently broke in. "You didn't make it any worse, and that was the main thing. Yes, she was bruised and broken, but she saw this church as a safe place to be—and that was the important thing. Please believe me when I tell you that it would do no good, at this point, to tell you what had happened to her. But I want you to know she found healing here, and had she lived longer, she might have allowed herself to love and be loved. There was nothing you could have done differently. And like I said—she was happy in this church."

Reverend Mayfield nodded. "Thank you for letting me know," he said, and turned away. But Teresa saw the tears in his eyes. She rose from the pew, and again, lightly touched his shoulder.

She spoke the next words almost without knowing that she did so. "Reverend Mayfield, you know the Lord placed Rachel in your care, knowing it would be best for her. He knew the kind of man you were, and are, and knew that, whatever pain she was in—and believe me, it was very deep—she was safe with you. The Lord entrusted to you a very great responsibility, and I can tell you—from what I read—that you were worthy of the trust. Please believe that. Her death was an accident, and from the fact that she failed to see a doctor—nothing more. She was happiest just before she died. This church was a good place for her."

The pastor nodded again, and Teresa got ready to leave. She knew Reverend Mayfield wanted to attend her to the door, as was proper and polite, but she saw he was barely in the condition to do so. She said to him, "it's okay, Reverend. I will see myself out. And— go ahead and cry. Jesus wept, you know, for His friend Lazarus, even though He knew He would raise him from the dead. Goodbye for now. Thank you for caring the way you did, for my friend Rachel."

She then left the beautiful church, knowing that, at least in this sanctuary, Rachel found God's love.....

Christmas Eve was very bright within the Anderson house— sparkling with color and alive with cheery voices. The Christmas tree shone with many-hued lights and ornaments and hanging tinsel. Throughout the kitchen and living room and dining room, candles gave warmth and light, and women's voices came from the kitchen as pies, cookies, and other assorted goodies were placed on the table with tempting drinks. In the living room, men discussed cars and sports, and children ran through the hallway to grab a few cookies before hiding in the back bedrooms, where the toys could be found. The home was quite full, and full of eager anticipation.

It was another happy Christmas Eve, and Teresa looked forward to many more. She was rather exhausted, but everything was going according to schedule. Her daughters were helpful, and at this point, one of them told her to lie down for awhile, she'd take care of things.....

Teresa knew she would. And, as she went into the bedroom, before she lay down, she looked into the closet, where the hatbox sat upon the high shelf.

"Good night, Rachel. Someday I will see you face to face. Until then....."

"The Spirit and the Bride say, 'Come! And let him who hears say, 'Come!.....'"